Adventures at

Rick's Place

a novel

inspired by true events

Terry J. Kotas

Artwork by Travis Johnston

Black Rose Writing

www.blackrosewriting.com

ISBN: 978-0-9821012-4-7

PUBLISHED BY BLACK ROSE WRITING

www.blackrosewriting.com

Printed in the United States of America

To Heidi & Carly,
who have filled my life with love and adventure.

In memory of
Terry Alan Bingham of S/V Secret O'Life

**Terry was the epitome of the solo sailor
and a heck of a nice guy**

Author's Notes:

After sailing over 20,000 miles, reality and fiction sometimes start to blur around the edges. *Rick's Place* is a "semi-true" story in that most of the events are real, but took place at different times. Locations were sometimes changed to make the story more linear, characters are often composites, taking a name from someone and a trait or two from someone else. Of course, names have been changed to protect the innocent and insane. And yes, we did travel thousands of miles with a cat that used the toilet.

CHAPTER 1

In The Beginning

"The Road to Success is always under construction..."

-Unknown

It was a dark and stormy night. I mean, really, it was. The wind, building steadily all afternoon, was approaching 50 miles per hour. The gentle Hawaiian trade winds that I had become accustomed to these past few months in the islands had turned into something much more ominous.

The Coast Guard had just made sure the last people had been evacuated from their anchored boats as night began to fall. So far, four boats had crashed ashore due to the huge hurricane-generated swell. I was sitting on a rock near the shoreline because the wind was blowing too damn hard to stand up. Plus, by keeping my lanky frame closer to the ground I was less of a target for the flying palm fronds and other debris sailing through the air.

I watched in helpless disbelief, as *Rick's Place,* the thirty foot sailboat I called my home, disappeared again behind a deep swell. Wiping my long, curly brown hair out of my eyes, I looked around to see how the driving rain mixed with the churning and tossing water had transformed the palm lined beach into a dark green blur. I had taken shelter near one of the many condo buildings that stood along the road near the boat ramp where I had come to shore a short time ago. Those buildings had changed, too, as the once colorful flower laden balconies were stripped of their flora by the relentless wind and now stood bleak and stark.

As I sat, I tried to think what bit of cosmic timing put me in this spot. A spot that looked like the opening for Gilligan's Island (You know, somewhere after "The weather started getting rough......") except there was no Marianne or Ginger.

I guess I should start this story at the beginning.

My name is Rick. My mom named me Rick after Humphrey Bogart's character in the movie *Casablanca.* Good old

Mom was in love with Bogie, and better Rick than Humphrey I always thought. Mom, not unlike her matinée idol, was a tough old bird. She grew up as the oldest of six children raised in the rugged Canadian Rockies. She didn't enjoy running water, or indoor toilets or electricity until she moved to the U.S. when she came to live with relatives in Tacoma, Washington.

When Mom was 23 she became a U.S. citizen and also met my father. They had an adventurous first few years of marriage traveling around the country on a motorcycle. Just as they settled down to start what they anticipated to be a large family, Mom tragically became a widow just three weeks after she learned that she was pregnant with her first child, me.

I remember growing up that Mom would often have to work two jobs, a teacher's aid by day and a nurse's aid by night, to support us. She still, however, always stayed in touch with what I was up to. When I would get out of line it would bring an instant response either verbally or on some occasions with a whack from my ping pong paddle which she kept handy at all times. Her slightly plump, 5'2" body could pack quite a wallop! Mom never did remarry, and looking back it was probably because it was a full time job keeping me on the straight and narrow.

Like my namesake, and my parents, I've always had a flair for adventure. When I was young, my friends and I would build toy boats and sail them across the pond in our backyard in Gig Harbor, a small fishing village on Puget Sound, about thirty miles south of Seattle. We would make believe we were pirates going to distant ports plundering and pillaging. We were a rough and tumble crew, just like most kids and the band aids that covered our bodies were seen as badges of courage. We wore them proudly.

My little group of minions included Steve, Randy and Donnie and we dubbed ourselves the Adventures Club.

Steve, Randy and I had grown up in the same area. Our street consisted of simple wood frame houses, circa 1950's, with a smattering of vacant lots. Your typical blue collar neighborhood. The three of us went to the same grade school. Donnie, on the other hand, moved in later and went to a different school somewhere across town. We were kids. I don't think I ever asked

Donnie what school he went to. All that was important was that he was a member of our club. Every morning at 7:30 when we were heading out the door to walk to school, a short yellow school bus would pull up in front of Donnie's house and he'd happily get aboard and go off to who knows where. We knew that the other school and the short bus were usually reserved for "special kids" and we didn't ever really understand why Donnie was in that category because he seemed to fit right in with our group. But in the back of my mind, I thought it might have something to do with his spontaneous outbursts of obscenities which we all found hilarious. It wasn't until I was much older that I learned of Turrets Syndrome and finally understood what made Donnie "special".

By the age of 14, my adventurous spirit combined with my interest in mechanics nearly had me headed for the Junior Graybar Motel. It was never anything malicious on my part that got me in trouble. It was more a matter of my pushing the envelope a bit too far. One example of this is what happened to me while trying to fund my many misadventures. I used to deliver the Sunday Seattle Post Intelligencer newspaper. Since it was the Sunday paper, it was three times as large as the normal weekday paper. It quickly occurred to me that in order not to get permanent back strain I would have to get some help in delivering said paper. So I turned to the only help I could find for the 3:00 a.m. delivery: a 57 Chevrolet. This beautiful piece of machinery was in perfect condition. A two door model, it was baby blue, with the coolest fins on the back and sporting large chrome bumpers. The interior was still in show-room condition and retained that "new car smell". It even had plastic seat covers as part of its original equipment.

In fact, the only problem was the Chevy wasn't mine. It belonged to Fred and Esther Jones, an elderly couple who lived a few blocks from my house. Fred and Esther were well known throughout the neighborhood because of their daily walks together. I could never understand at the time why they would walk when they had that great car sitting there. It was during one of those thoughts that I decided to "borrow" the car to deliver my newspapers.

Since I didn't have a driver's license, I couldn't very well ask permission to borrow the car, but borrow it is what I did. I would push the car away from the house, hotwire it, and take it to a gas station and fill it up with gas. I would then collect my papers and go on my delivery. I always had the car back faithfully by 5:00 a.m. without anyone knowing it had been liberated...or so I thought. This went on for several months until finally one Sunday morning I opened the car door and there was a note on the steering wheel. The note explained that although the car was parked in the exact same spot, the owner knew someone had used the Chevy because the fuel tank always had more gas and was cleaner than it had been when he had parked it. Since I had to give up "borrowing" the car, I gave up the paper route as well.

Several years later, after I'd graduated from high school, I was sitting in a doctor's office waiting to have my strained back looked at (a Sunday paper injury that happened before I started using the car). As I waited, I ran across an article in a Reader's Digest about the new sport of hang gliding. The concept intrigued me from an adventurous standpoint. Being a do-it-yourself kind of guy, before the month was out, I had gathered up all the parts necessary to build my own hang glider. Some parts, such as the aluminum tubing and the stainless steel wire were easy to find locally, but other things like turnbuckles and the sail cloth had to be ordered from catalogs. After cutting, drilling and sewing (with Mom's help on the sewing part) my very own flying machine was ready to go and I took my first flight on my 21st birthday. I'm not really sure why Mom helped. Maybe she was just tired of swinging the ping pong paddle at me and figured this would break my neck and prevent me from getting into any more trouble.

Of course, in the beginning, I would fly off small sloping hills and I thought I had discovered the greatest sport in the world. With a gentle breeze, the wing had no problem lifting my slender body off the earth and I would be thrilled soaring above the ground. Plus, it turned out that hang gliding was quite an attention getter and spectators would gather any time the gliders were flying. After I'd land, I would catch myself walking around the hang glider like I was the Red Baron inspecting his biplane after a dogfight. All that was missing was the bomber jacket and a long white silk scarf. I think I had more fun answering questions and basking in the admiration of the wannabes than I actually had flying.

Soon the apprehension of flying a tangled web of tubing and cloth that I had built myself grew in direct proportion to my height above the ground. After a particularly harrowing flight off a 1300 foot cliff, I began to rethink my sport of choice. After all, if I wanted to get injured, all I had to do was smart off to Mom and she would do the rest. I began looking to unload this winged demon onto someone who didn't read newspapers and would not know of the high mortality rate for people jumping off cliffs with kites on their backs. In my search I came across a fellow who wanted to trade a small sailboat for a hang glider. I guess he was as comfortable not telling me about the risks of drowning as I was not telling him about the risks of falling out of the sky. And so my sailing career began.

This first boat I called my own was small, only big enough for one person. At about 7 feet in length, it was made of plastic. It had a 6 foot fiberglass tube for a mast and a single white sail with a big, yellow sunflower emblazoned on it since the manufacturer of this boat had given it the moniker of "Sunflower". I should have realized by the name that the sun played an important part in its enjoyment. You see while learning how to sail *Sunflower* I spent 75 percent of my time in the water and I sorely needed the *sun* to dry me out. This boat was a constant exercise in balance. From the moment I would step on to its bright yellow hull, my body would fight with itself to keep from overturning the boat, but I slowly got the hang of it and when the wind would reach about 10 knots there was nothing quite like the exhilaration of skimming across the water so fast it would make my eyes blurry. The sensation was just as thrilling but not as terrifying as the hang glider had been, I might add. But, more often than not, the wind would whisk me out to the furthermost point from land, and then abruptly die. Of course, there was no room for an oar in this tiny vessel, so I'd use my hands and spend the rest of the afternoon paddling back to shore. I was a skinny kid and the *Sunflower* made sure I stayed that way, what with all the exercise it created for me.

During the time while I was learning how to sail (and swim), I realized that the Pacific Northwest is no place to have a boat named *Sunflower* or to spend so much time in the water. Often as I struggled to get back in my boat, I felt like an errant ice cube that had fallen out of a spilled tray. I did, however, feel I had found a calling in being a sailor. The problem was *Sunflower* was built more for making me a swimmer than a sailor and I realized it was time to step up in the boat world before it was too late, so I began looking for something larger.

When I heard on the radio that the Big Seattle Boat Show was taking place in the Kingdome, my attention was piqued and I headed north to see my first boat show.

I had been to this domed stadium before to watch the Seattle Seahawks football team but it was quite a sight to see what seemed like a hundred boats crammed together on the artificial turf. It was nothing short of spellbinding. Looking down from about 20 rows up in the stands I was overwhelmed by the brightly lit arena. Bright shiny objects were everywhere; I was in a trance. The sight of all these magnificent boats was stimulating the small portion of my brain in much the same way that bright shiny objects arouse curiosity in primates. So I made my way down the stairs to the field of boats to get a closer look.

All sizes of crafts from a gigantic mega-yacht (I don't even know how they got that one in!) down to small one man kayaks were on display. There were power boats, sailboats, rowboats and dinghies and even a two man submarine! The place was packed with people lining up to get a look inside all the boats. The length of the line seemed to be in direct proportion to the length of the boat. This was fine by me, because I wasn't looking for a mega yacht. Just something a bit bigger than Sunflower so I could spend more time in the boat instead of in the water.

As I started to look around for a new ride, it quickly became apparent that a new boat would not be in my future. It seemed to me that the price of these water buoyed dreams must have included the price of electricity for lighting up the arena that the show was in. I was feeling pretty discouraged as I headed for the exit dreading another soggy year ahead of me, until I came to a rather dimly lit area near the exit of the building. There before me was the boat of my dreams! I knew this because the sign in front of me said "The Boat of Your Dreams".

It seemed about the right size: 30 feet. It had a full keel, which I knew from reading was a good thing because it meant that I would spend less time in the water. The boat seemed to have everything: a stove, a sleeping area (the V Berth they called it, since it was in the pointy end of the boat) and even a toilet! I was transfixed staring at the display near the boat that showed pictures of people actually swimming in the water around it. Their lips weren't blue and this concept intrigued me.

I jumped when a voice behind me broke my concentration asking "Looks warm, huh?"

"Sure does," I said dreamily as I turned to see where the voice had come from.

I tried to look natural as I took in the strange sight that met my eyes, for next to me stood a rather tall and skinny 60ish gentleman with mad scientist type snow white hair screaming out from his head in every direction like someone who had just bitten into an electric eel. He wore a coffee stained sweatshirt with faded blue jeans and had a name tag hanging askew on his chest that read "Nick". He didn't look anything like the other boat salesmen I'd seen on the main floor with their neatly pressed slacks and polo shirts and hair slicked back with gel giving them a bit of a car salesman aura.

Nick informed me that the people in the picture actually wanted to be in the water and they were swimming in a place called the South Pacific. There the water is warm and the sun is more than just a small dot in the sky and can actually dry you when you get out of the water.

As I talked with Nick it was apparent that the cup of coffee he held in his hand was not the first of the day. In fact, by his rapid speech and darting eyes I had to guess that Nick counted his coffee consumption by pots and not cups.

"A thousand down and we'll start laying up your hull next week," Nick stated. Nick explained he worked for "Coast Boat

Building" in Alameda, California where they would be building the boat.

A couple thoughts quickly formed in my mind: 1) I could live aboard this boat. 2) I could sail it to a place where you can actually swim in the water without getting hypothermia. The thing that really sold me on this particular boat design was that you could order it in any stage of completion. That meant that I could buy a semi-completed boat and finish it when I had the money. Finally, a boat I could afford. It seemed like a match made in heaven.

I thought, "Even I can do little trim work and then I can be sailing very soon thereafter." So the plans were made, the money put down, and I was to pick up my semi-completed yacht in Alameda CA, and tow it to my Mom's backyard in Gig Harbor. Yes-sir-re-sir, a little trim work and look out South Pacific!

After driving all the way to California, imagine my surprise when I arrived at the boatyard and not only was my semi-completed yacht not semi-complete, but it was still in the mold. Come to find out the boatyard had filed for bankruptcy that very day. I watched the telephones being disconnected and tools and equipment being removed from the yard. My thoughts quickly turned to the thousand dollars I had put down for construction of my semi-completed yacht (balance to be paid upon delivery). After a heated discussion between the yard owner, the banker, and myself (Nick of course, was nowhere to be found) as to who legally owned the semi-completed yacht, mingled with threats and counter threats, the hull was lifted out of the mold and placed on a home built trailer I had made just for this proud occasion. The deck was haphazardly placed on the hull, and secured with four bolts to assure it didn't fly off on the trip home. Off I went.

During that thousand-mile drive back home, I really didn't have time to think about what I had gotten myself into. I was pulling a 30 foot boat with a 15 foot Toyota Land Cruiser, and had lost the trailer brakes five miles out of Oakland, non-repairable, of course. On top of all that I only had three days off from work which made it imperative that I drive day and night because I could only average about 35 mph.

By the time my overland odyssey had reached the Sisskiu Mountains, the range that forms a dividing line between California and Oregon, the adrenaline that was keeping me sharp for the first 300 miles had been used up. This was unfortunate timing. As my eyes fought to stay open, night was well underway. I don't know if I nodded off or not, but suddenly there were several deer springing out of the brush directly in front of me. I slammed on the brakes without thinking about the heavy mass that was attached to the back of my Toyota. I missed the deer only because the boat and trailer whipped the truck into the oncoming lane. Sawing the steering wheel back and forth I managed to gain control just before a long downhill curve. Luckily, due to the time of night, traffic was light.

The good news was the adrenalin was back, the bad news was that the slightest movement along the roadside from then on, whether real or imaginary would have me pumping the brakes. This went on for several hours until at last I came to a long five mile downhill grade that would deposit me in Oregon, one state closer to home. At the top of this grade I started seeing several signs that read "Runaway Truck Exit". These were basically exits about 100 yards long with two feet of loose gravel the entire length. In theory, when a semi truck looses its brakes, it would veer off onto one of these exits, hit the gravel and come to a safe and complete stop. Good for them.

That might work just fine for a semi truck, but who knew what it would do to my road combination of a Land Cruiser, a trailer without brakes carrying an unfinished boat. I pulled off to the side of the road just before the crest, for one last check of the trailer, wheels, and hitch. Over the top of the hill I went. My heart was pounding and my head was light. I stayed in first gear with my foot on the brake as I couldn't afford to pick up more speed than I could control.

Slowly the miles ticked by. A sign announcing the last of the Runaway Truck Exits was coming up. That meant safety, right? It must be getting less steep. I was starting to relax a little when suddenly an overwhelming smell enveloped the cab of my small truck. Brake smell! I traveled about 200 yards before I could find a turnout. Slowing to a stop, I set my handbrake, got my flashlight from the glove compartment and jumped out into the cold night air. I couldn't believe what I saw! All four wheels had smoke pouring off of them! But it wasn't brake smoke; it seemed the brakes had heated up the wheel so hot that the paint on the rims was burning off. I was worried that the rubber would burst into flames at any moment. Grabbing an empty coffee cup, I ran to a nearby mud puddle and filled it with water then doused the front wheel. Steam and the sound of water boiling off of hot metal assaulted my senses.

It took a full two hours and all the water in that mud puddle to get things cooled down enough to continue on. The rest of the journey was relatively uneventful after that, just long and tiring.

Once the trailer was parked safely beside Mom's house, I climbed up to have a look inside my new boat. My heart sank. I was looking into an empty – not a piece of wood, not a bulkhead, not a single thru hull – "semi-completed yacht". I was thinking that what I had was a semi-completed nightmare. I had nearly resigned myself to thinking that this empty hull would make a nice tool shed or maybe even an unattached den for Mom.

Several weeks later, after a morning tour of my fiberglass echo chamber, I received what I can only describe as a sign from above. Actually, it came in the mail. It was an advertisement describing several books on building your own boat. Although none actually used the phrase "semi-completed yacht", I sent for them anyway. Within weeks I was buying screws, resin, and teak just like I knew what I was doing.

It took me two years of self-imposed exile in my fiberglass hellhole before I had a semi-completed yacht. During that time, the fumes from assorted chemicals I had to work with in a confined space took quite a toll on my brain cells. Building the boat also took quite a toll on my social life, as I devoted every spare moment to my boats completion and rarely saw friends or went out on dates.

Finally, 732 days, 6 hours and 19 minutes after I began building my boat, and with little fanfare, *Rick's Place* was lifted off the homemade trailer and placed in the cold waters of Gig Harbor.

I was amazed that: a) it didn't sink out right, b) it was more or less level in the water, and c) it even looked pretty good. "Not bad", I thought, "considering I had no construction plans and I had to make a lot of my own hardware."

However, while things were starting to go well on the boat building front, trouble was looming in the workplace. Since high school, I had worked in the neighborhood supermarket starting out as a box boy during my summer vacations. The Food King was an older supermarket. In it's hey day the store was considered cutting edge, but by modern standards it was showing its age. There always seemed to be at least one non-functioning buzzing overhead light lending a somewhat dingy ambiance to the store. The floor tiles, once scratch free and shiny were now yellowed and cracked with age.

I eventually made cashier in my senior year of high school. After a few years of cashiering, I filled the vacancy left by the retiring produce manager. The produce section was in the back of the store. The vegetable displays were also period pieces. Huge mirrors behind the vegetable bins would create the effect of endless rows of lettuce, radishes and celery. Water hoses tucked near the edges were used for wetting down the various produce. There were double doors leading to the back door which completed my little section of the store.

The store itself was located in an area of town where there was a high concentration of elderly immigrants from the "old country". After dealing with some of these people for many years (I'd started working at the store shortly after I had to give up the paper route) I realized that they were probably kicked out of the old country. They were a tough bunch to deal with. They knew the value of the penny and weren't about to waste one. As produce manager I was hoping that my face to face contact with these customers would be less than it was as a cashier, but no such luck. They were there daily, squeezing the fruit then demanding a discount because it was bruised. I knew trouble was brewing when the suggestion box at the store started filling up with hate mail about the produce manager. It seemed that these elderly people on limited incomes held me personally responsible for the high price of their tomatoes.

Day in and day out I was on the receiving end of their nasty and unkind remarks. One customer in particular decided to protest the high cost of fruits and vegetables in a unique way. I dubbed this guy Filthy Phil.

Phil Lodge was a local that had lived in the neighborhood since before the Food King was built. He was somewhere in his 70's and he'd probably been a handsome man in his prime. Phil was now bent slightly at the waist and shuffled along with the aid of a cane. He had hooded brown eyes and a puffy face. Most of his teeth were now absent. Phil was always, ALWAYS talking. He would come into the store talking to himself and then seamlessly drag others into his ramblings. By the time Phil got back to the produce, his last stop, he would be visibly worked up. His bald head would have a pinkish hue and lambasting me seemed to be what Phil lived for.

His protest consisted of taking a cucumber and two tomatoes and creating a phallic symbol in the Romaine lettuce. Phil would place his little displays amongst the rest of the produce and hide behind the end display of peaches, waiting to see my reaction. Filthy Phil and his anatomy lesson was mildly amusing, to say the least. Nevertheless, after about two weeks of his shenanigans I was beginning to get complaints from other customers. After reprimanding Phil one Saturday afternoon I came back from lunch only to find that Phil had made about a dozen phallic protests towards the high price of produce.

Unfortunately, the district manager for the supermarket chose that particular day to do a walk-through of the store. Of course, the first place he started was in the produce section. Upon seeing Phil's creation and thinking I was not doing enough to protect the citizens from Phil's health class, he asked me to turn in my apron and paring knife. My life was at a major crossroads.

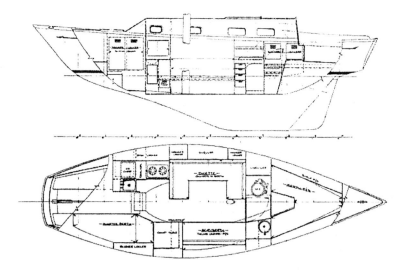

CHAPTER 2

Dock Life

"There's nothing . . . absolutely nothing . . . half so much worth doing as simply messing around in boats."

-Kenneth Grahame, *The Wind in the Willows*

Having no job and thus no income, I would have to make some major changes in my life. It didn't take Mr. Spock from the starship *Enterprise* to figure out the next logical step. I needed to move aboard *Rick's Place.* That would allow me to start saving money for my intended adventures in the South Pacific. So lock, stock and life jacket I showed up at Old Town Marina.

I'd heard from a friend that Old Town Marina might have a slip available so I rushed down there to secure it because I knew it wouldn't be vacant long. It's the nicest marina in Gig Harbor and is a much sought after place to keep a boat. A medium sized marina, it has only three docks with about 20 boats on each. It has a clubhouse, laundry and showers and it is well maintained. I knew this would be just perfect!

When I arrived, however, I was surprised to find out there are some rather stringent rules concerning live-a-boards. I hadn't considered that you couldn't just live aboard your boat if you wanted and that you had to get permission! So, to gain membership into the live-a-aboard group, I'd have to convince the harbor master of my good intentions. I was a little nervous about this meeting, because Bruce, the man in charge, was a retired Air Force Major and his close cropped, gray hair and stern eyes projected an aura of no nonsense. I could tell he was a real "tight ship" kind of fellow.

As I'd feared, the meeting didn't go so well. In fact it went something like a scene from vaudeville "I need to inspect your Y-valve" he said in a brisk tone. "My what valve ?"

"Your Y-valve", "WHY?", "yes, your Y-valve". I started getting one of those boating headaches and wondered if this was the start of the old, "Who's on first routine", so I asked him if I could get back to him in the morning.

After a little research I found the harbormaster was talking about the three-way valve used to prevent illegal overboard discharge of waste. Looking into the laws concerning waste discharge brought to light a rather interesting loophole. It is legal to use a bucket as the toilet and dump the waste overboard, whereas it is not legal to use the toilet and pump the effluant out of the boat. Not liking such ambiguity, I briefly considered mounting a toilet seat on a bucket thereby forgoing the need for a holding tank. However, I figured my friends and the harbormaster would not be too impressed with my one-man protest against this screwed up regulation.

I spent the next couple days installing a holding tank and hooking up my new Y-valve. When the Major made his next appearance, everything was in place, and he gave his seal of approval for me to live aboard my boat legally.

During this discussion, I also found out, much to my surprise, that there is a limit to the number of live-a-boards allowed in each marina. In this particular marina the magic number is 10%, and luckily they had just enough room for one more. I guess the lawmakers believe that this restriction will limit the number of jobless, deadbeat, nomadic, down on their luck boat owners from cluttering up the docks. Unfortunately, I fulfilled three out of four of these categories but my groveling and sad story on how Filthy Phil got me fired must have touched the harbormaster's heart, so I was lucky to be able to make my boat my home.

As I sat enjoying my first sunset in, or rather on, my new home, it occurred to me that I had the ultimate in waterfront property. My home may be small, but I've got the whole world for a backyard. Maybe that's the real reason for putting a limit on live-a-boards, or everyone would be doing it.

I was fortunate that my reversal in fortune took place so that I was able to move aboard the boat in the summer. This helped because I still had some interior finish work to do and it's not too pleasant to paint or varnish in a small closed up space. I'd learned during the building of *Rick's Place* that breathing too much of these noxious fumes had a detrimental effect on my brain cells.

The long, warm days of August made the boat projects easier to do, since I could spread my work area out on the deck and the dock. Sometimes I would just sit and close my eyes and make believe I was in the South Pacific. Living on *Rick's Place* was fantastic and I wished I had done it sooner. During breaks, or while waiting for glues or paint to dry, I was thoroughly enjoying meeting the other nine percent of people who lived on their boats in Old Town Marina.

The characters who lived at Old Town were as diverse as the boats that they lived on. When I was there we had a banker, an airline pilot, and a couple of business owners and then some individuals not quite as successful in life, such as myself. But there was one economic factor that made all of us equal: the almighty quarter. You see the showers and the washing machines took nothing but quarters. The showers took 25 cents for five minutes, the washing machines 75 cents a load, and the dryers seemed to take 25 cents to start up and then would run all day. Many a day someone would come by asking for change for a dollar and I would be reluctant to give up my 25 cent treasures. You'd think they were Krugerrands the way those quarters were horded on my dock!

More than once I heard the screams of agony as the shower ran out of time well before the person had rinsed off. Invariably the person had broken the one cardinal rule of the public pay shower which is: never ever go in with just one quarter. As I said, one quarter is good for five minutes of shower water, but because the hot water heater seemed to be at least a mile away it took three minutes for the hot water to finally reach the showerhead. So you had two choices: step into the ice cold water and hope that the hot water would come through before hypothermia set in, or wait for the hot water to come through and hope you could be done in two minutes.

The problem was even worse in the winter, because the pipes for the shower ran outside along the docks and this would mean that any chance for a lukewarm shower meant a person would probably have to spend a quarter just to warm up the pipes. That might not seem like much, but if you don't have the "all precious" quarter, then you are like a man in the desert without water. If the rumor mill on the dock revealed that someone was going to do their laundry, you'd see a mad rush for the showers, because you knew that there would be no hot water at all once the washing machine started. And to think that you have to pay extra to live aboard!

One great perk of living at the marina and being a cooking impaired single male was the sympathetic outpouring of food from other live-a-boards that were more skilled in the galley than I. The most generous of the "gifters" was a family living aboard *Zephyr*, a huge 50' power yacht. The husband, George, who was short and built like a fireplug, was a pilot for a major airline. I always wondered if he had to use a booster seat to see out of the cockpit when he was flying a plane. Rosie, his wife, had shocking clown-like red hair and was nearly a foot taller than George. Rosie was a stay at home boat mom who took care of their 7 year old son, Brian. Rosie was also a great cook.

Brian was a good kid, but he was sure the victim of two quite different gene pools that had sloshed together. He was built like his dad and was short for his age and very stocky. His face was dinner plate round, dotted with freckles, but the real eye grabbing feature was his flaming red hair.

Brian was a frequent visitor to *Rick's Place* and every Monday he would bring me leftovers from the weekend family feast that usually took place aboard *Zephyr*. In return for the food Brian would ask me 50 or more random questions. Almost anything he'd look at he'd ask about.

"Rick, why is that screw there?", "Rick, why did you paint that door blue?", "Rick, why........." and on and on. It wasn't irritating as you might expect, because Brian's sense of discovery and his wide eyed delight at learning was such a joy to behold.

One day during an exceptionally low tide, I saw Brian near one of the pilings. He was looking at the sea life that was stranded out of water until the next tide change.

"Hey Brian, what's up?"

"Hi Rick! I'm catching a mussel!"

"Yeah, it's a pretty low tide. We don't usually see these

guys."

"They keep squirting me. Do you think I can have one for a pet?"

Well, at least he wouldn't have to walk it. "Sure, I'll help you get one."

So I went back to the boat and got an empty quart sized can and a screwdriver. I punched holes in the can to allow water to flow through it, and then I tied a string to the top of it so he could hang it in the water from the dock.

"OK Brian lets get your mussel!"

"This one Rick," he said pointing excitedly to one particular bivalve.

"Don't worry, Brian, he's not getting away," I said laughing.

By this time Rosie had come out to see what was going on and Brian yelled with delight, "Rick's getting me a mussel to keep in this great cage we made!"

I carefully pried the selected mussel off the piling and gently placed it in the bottom of the can-cage. Brian was nearly bouncing off the boats he was so giddy about his new 'pet'.

"Right here, Rick, tie it right here next to my boat so I can see it everyday!" He exclaimed in his hardly-contained excitement.

"OK Buddy," I said as I tied the string to a nail and the can sank two feet under water.

For the next six months that kid would check on his mussel at least 5 times a day. Often he would drag me from one of my projects to see "Sam" the mussel. And for reasons I still don't understand, that mussel grew to a remarkable size in that can-cage of his. Then one day tragedy struck.

You see, we had a local sea otter that occasionally cruised through the marina. Otters are incredibly cute creatures. Small and fuzzy with near human characteristics they are charming to watch. Except when one of the little carnivores decides to snack on one's pet that is. Early one morning some crunching noises caught my attention and I looked out to see the otter floating on his back just off my boat. I was excited to catch a glance of this great creature, until I realized what he was doing. He was eating and what he was eating could only be Sam by the size of the mussel lying on his stomach! As he finished up his breakfast of Sam the mussel I thought how sad Brian would be when he found out. But quite the contrary! Brian thought it was just great. He kept feeding the otter from that day on by collecting mussels and putting them in the cancage and just waiting for the otter to come and check out the mussel de jour. Brian had a new pet.

As time went by, the majority of my indoor projects were being completed with moderate success. However, there were times when I swear the ghosts of Moe, Larry, and Curly were right beside me lending me a hand. At no time was this more evident than when I was attempting to drill a small hole through the floor pan, and ended up drilling through the hull. As I retracted the drill out of the hull, a rather hard stream of water hit me in the face. This was my first indication something was very wrong. "Hey Moooe nyuk, nyuk, nyuk".

I finally stopped the leak with a two-inch long screw. For the next year, every time a diver would clean the bottom of the boat, I was asked the same question "Do you know there is a screw sticking out of the bottom of your boat?" I would simply reply, "I had help that day", and leave it at that.

One of the most bizarre incidents happened the day I needed to go up to the top of my mast to install an anchor light. I had recruited a friend from the dock to give me a hand with this project. This was my first experience going up the mast, as well as my first experience with the boson chair.

The boson's chair was simply a rectangular length of canvas, about two feet long and ten inches wide. There was a stainless steel ring, three inches in diameter, sewn to each end of the cloth. These rings would attach to the halyard (rope) that was normally used to raise the main sail. The chair was essentially the same design as the swings found in many public schools, the main difference being that this was made of canvas and not rubber.

So to go up the mast, I'd sit in the swing attached to the halyard that runs through a pulley or sheave at the top of the mast and my friend would pull the other end of the halyard which was wrapped around a winch drum and raise me up just as you would raise a sail. This so-called chair must have been a throwback to some medieval device used for torture. After ten minutes of sitting in this alleged chair all circulation was stopped to my lower extremities. The places that weren't already cut off from blood flow were hurting like hell.

To make this job go as easy as possible I had purchased a pair of voice activated walkie talkies. I did this so that I could communicate with my friend below without having to yell down at him. I figured I could just whisper into the microphone and the guy below could hear what I had to say and send up the required tools, bolts or whatever.

The top of my mast was even with the second story of some condos built next to Old Town Marina and I had a clear view into of one of the occupied units. While working on the mast, I was occasionally dropping screws and losing them, as they bounced off the deck and into the water. I was also losing feeling below my waist because of the boson's chair. The radio conversation started out somewhat salty but quickly took on a longshoreman like quality. I started noticing a sound that sounded like a baby crying coming over the headset, and I looked down to see if my buddy below was OK. He looked fine, but then I looked over to see a woman with a head full of curlers, staring at me from the window of the condo with a look of horror on her face and mouth agape. Standing next to her was a small boy around the age of five or six. Suddenly the boy bolted, and with his hands over his ears he ran in crazy circles around the room I was looking into. I could tell he was screaming something and all the while the biggest grin adorned his cherubic face.

Within minutes, a man that I soon found out was her husband appeared on the dock, red-faced, and seemingly a bit put out. He was about my height, but about 60 pounds heavier and wearing a suit which really looked out of place on the dock. He explained that the baby monitor they had set up to keep tabs on the goings-on in the nursery was picking up my radio conversation with the deck hand. At first they thought someone was in the baby's room and this had terrified them. But when they ran in to check, they noticed me on my mast and realized what was happening. It wouldn't have been too bad, except their older son (the 5 year old I'd seen running in circles) had been overhearing all of my expletives and the kid was already parroting with great glee some of the more offensive words he had heard.

I apologized, explaining that my conversation was not meant for the public airwaves and I promised to continue the rest of my work without the headset. When my job was completed and I was being lowered back down the mast, I stole a glance into the living room of the condo that I had so disrupted. The kid was still running around at top speed with his hands over his ears yelling God knows what! From then on, whenever I met the boy and his mother on the sidewalk outside the marina he would get a big grin on his face and greet me with "That's Mr. damn-it". His mother would just roll her eyes and shake her head.

Happily, some good did come out of the mast project that day. While enjoying the view from the top, I noticed that, not far from the marina, a building was being renovated and across the front of the structure was a banner proclaiming "Coming soon! New home of Discount Marine!" After completion of my project I walked the three blocks over to see this new home for Discount Marine. It would be great to have a boat and marine supplies store nearby, because I wouldn't have to make so many trips to Seattle to buy what I needed. When I got there I saw a sign in the window that announced "help wanted apply within" and believe it or not, I got the job! The salary wasn't that great, but compared to the no salary I was now receiving, any kind of pay was fantastic. To top it all off I would get to buy all my stuff at an employee discounted price! So before the day was out I had worked on my mast, started the gangrene process in my legs, helped a youngster along the path of using foul language, and got a job at the marine store. The final piece of the cruising puzzle just dropped into place and I had one person to thank: Filthy Phil.

As winter wore on, I completed the last of my interior projects which included some more painting and installing a couple overhead lights. I was now in full cruise control, so to speak, because now the projects I worked on were directly related to going cruising and not just the building of the boat. I added a wind vane, life raft, and high seas radio for picking up weather reports. I also got out and sailed as much as possible. Winter sailing on the Puget Sound was a good learning experience and helped me get familiar with the boat. I practiced reefing, which is reducing the main sail area, changing sails, and generally working the bugs out of *Rick's Place.* Since I was doing most of this by myself I was getting quite comfortable working the boat shorthanded. Plus there's nothing like a cold shower after a cold day on the water. My job was going real well. I was meeting people, like myself, who were getting ready to cruise or that had already been cruising.

A traumatic moment did come when the store manager, Steve, called all employees together and informed us that the company was going to start using hands-free telephone headsets for intra store communications. Needless to say, this didn't bode well with me because of my past headset problems. The looks of the distraught faces of the family in the condo came to mind every time I heard the word headset. I was assured that no harm would come from the satanic electronic devices, so I relented.

One day, while stocking a shelf, a weird sensation made the hair on the back of my neck prickle to attention. Slowly turning around I came face to face with one of our more mysterious customers, a character named Allen who also lived in Old Town Marina, although I had not met him until he walked in to the store. He was truly unique in many ways. His eyes were piercing. Royal blue in color, they gave the impression of having their own light source behind them. His head was absolutely hairless. Not the kind of hairless you'd get from shaving your head, but the kind that shouts out I never had hair in the first place. He was also ageless, that is to say I could never guess his age. He could have been anywhere from 30 to 60. He had a small, almost lipless mouth and perfect porcelain skin that was void of any blemishes or moles. He was only about 5'6" and he was so thin I can only describe him as emaciated.

Talking to Allen, I found out that he had recently completed the same trip I was planning and he was a wealth of knowledge. I learned that "the coconut milk run" was the name given to the frequently traveled route through the South Pacific. However, the more questions I asked of him, the more I became suspicious of his origins. Allen had the uncanny ability to fix anything from a computer to a toilet. He also had an unbelievable, if not inhuman, memory and could recite every day and every person he met on his 3 year voyage. He seemed to have powers far beyond those of mortal man. After a particularly detailed description of his passages, it hit me that he never ran into any bad weather!

It was all beginning to add up; superhuman intellect, a vast knowledge of electronics and computers, and no concept of bad weather (after all when you travel millions of miles through space what's a little jaunt across one of our oceans?). That's right. He must be an alien from outer space. After all, he even looked a great deal like the visitors in *Close Encounters of the Third Kind.* It was this thought process that made me give Allen the nickname Alien Allen. My theory was furthered along when I would find Alien Allen on the dock, late at night gazing at the stars with a fantastic high-powered telescope. I had to wonder if he was perhaps checking on how his home planet was doing. I decided right then and there that when it came time for this guy to beam up, I wanted to be close at hand.

June 22. That's the day that I decided I would set sail and leave the rat race behind. I was purchasing charts, guide books, and spare parts as fast as my meager budget would allow. My fear of the unknown mixed with my inexperience convinced me that I needed to be able to replace or repair any or all of my boat's systems. You'd think I'd never heard of Fed Ex. This is where my role as a hunter changed to that of a gatherer, and boy how I gathered!

I purchased spare bolts, bulbs, screws, wire and rope. Then I moved on to engine parts and picked up injectors and an alternator. Soon I found myself buying spares for the spares! This was all good and well, except my boat was only 30 feet long and the actual storage space is less than that. I found this out quickly when I started buying food provisions and had to try to stuff them in with the spare parts. Canned food made up the bulk of what I was trying to store. Chili, Spam, roast beef, potatoes, fruits and vegetables. There's almost nothing you can't buy in a can. But stowing cans presented its own set of problems as they took up more space than items in plastic bags.

This is when a boat owner finds what are affectionately known as "nooks & crannies". I was putting nuts & bolts, belts and bars of soap and cans of food in places I would probably never think to look again. All the while, the stripe that marks the waterline sank lower and lower into the water with all the added weight.

CHAPTER 3

2 Live Crew

"The only normal people in life are the ones you don't know very well..."

-Joe Aneis

I once heard it said that "Life is like a roll of toilet paper. The closer to the end you get the faster it goes." If this could somehow be applied to getting ready to go cruising, I'd already used up a four pack. Just a few weeks to go and things were moving in a blur. I continued to try and stuff remaining food and supplies into my already bloated boat. Waterline? What waterline?

One detail that still needed to be settled was whether or not I was going to sail solo. In truth I never thought much about it. With all the other distractions going on around me, as well as my confidence in short handling in the local waters, I just assumed I would travel alone. It's not like I'd be the first one to sail the Pacific on my own. It was pointed out more than once by many of my friends and especially by Mom, that single handling in the Puget Sound was not the same as being at sea for the better part of a month.

One day while attempting to cram more supplies into a locker that absolutely did not have a centimeter of space to give, there was a knock on the side of the hull. Wading through cans of corn and beans I climbed the ladder and was met topside by a guy who introduced himself as Sparky.

"Sorry about the interruption", he said a bit slowly. I assured him it was more of a rescue than an interruption. Sparky was about 6'1" with blond hair, blue eyes and was a slow talker. A kind of California surfer dude, slow talker. He proceeded to tell me that he heard I was heading to Hawaii and might be looking for crew (thanks Mom). I was a bit taken aback, because no one had ever volunteered to help me with the boat before. While we were talking, I noticed he kept turning his right ear toward me. Sparky noticed my attention on him and explained that "Surfer's ear" is what he had, a partial deafness caused by something like swimmer's ear. This can be a definite negative if you're trying to call instructions out to someone on a noisy boat, but I thought I'd give him a try anyway.

His dream was to sail to the islands and surf when he got there.

"I've got ocean experience," he said. This was looking better all the time. We continued sizing each other up for a while, and then parted company, my promising I would get back to him in a couple of days. It should be noted here that being new to the cruising game, I probably didn't ask Surfer Sparky the right questions about his sailing experience.

I really didn't want to be thinking about this right now, anyway. I had plenty of other things to occupy my mind, not the least of which was having a diver come to clean the bottom of the boat. It wasn't the regular guy, so I was probably going to have to answer questions about the darn screw that was still sticking out of the hull. I think this time I'll just tell him I'd had a picture hanging there that must have fallen off.

I was spending more time listening to Coast Guard weather on the boat's radio receiver. This was a tough assignment because the broadcast is done with a synthesized computer generated voice. For me, this took a lot of getting used to and quickly became quite irritating. My radio had pretty good reception, but there was just enough static to make hearing the forecast an exercise in filling in the blanks. The blanks being those times the radio chose to go snap, crackle and pop with static. Did it say 5 knots or 25 knots? "......wind speed *crackle* knots, increasing by *crackle* knots by mid day. Swell *snap, pop* feet, increasing to *garble* feet." So it went. I took solace in the fact that according to Alien Allen, reception in the marina is usually pretty poor due to the sailboat masts, etc. and it should work much better out at sea. The funny thing is; he seemed to always have perfect reception even though he was just a couple slips down from me. Coincidence? I think not.

I also wasn't having much luck sleeping. I would wake up in an anxiety attack at least a couple times a night. Worrying about the engine, the sails, the spare parts, the weather and the screw through the bottom of my boat, amongst other things, caused me to lose sleep. This sleep deprivation led me to calling Surfer Sparky to see if he was still up for a sea cruise. That just shows you how dangerous sleep deprivation can be. Of course at the moment I didn't know what a bad decision it was to include Sparky in my crew manifest.

"Cool", was Sparky's reply when I told him he could join me on the passage to Hawaii. Truly a man of few words was Sparky.

Ten days and counting. This was getting exciting! I purchased 4 large jerry jugs to store extra fuel and water for the long ocean passage. I strapped them on to the port and starboard rails and stepped back to view my accomplishments on *Rick's Place*. What came to mind was the "Beverly Hillbilly's"! With the wind vane attached to the stern, the solar panels on the sides, the life raft on deck and now the jerry jugs, it was looking a bit "busy", to say the least. There really wasn't much I could do about it. Everything I had onboard were all necessities and safety features. Things I felt certain I couldn't leave without. So I accepted the crowded appearance of the boat and decided to quit worrying about looking like the USS Hillbilly Heaven. I discovered then and there that you can spot a cruising boat from a long way away because it looks a lot like when the Clampett's loaded up and moved to Beverly.

After the short conversation with Sparky the week before confirming his place on board, he dropped out of sight. I couldn't get hold of him and he didn't contact me. This wasn't too disturbing, because even if he ended up bailing out on me it wouldn't be the end of the world. In fact, there was something about the whole Sparky thing that had set off a little voice inside my head saying, "This is one of your little voice's and you'd better start listening to me!" Unfortunately, I kept ignoring this little voice like it was speaking in Latin.

My last day of work at Discount Marine involved a lot of good-byes. Steve, my manager and a fellow sailor, had taken up a collection from the staff and purchased several bottles of champagne to be opened when I crossed the equator or made landfall. A customer, Janis, who I had dated a couple times, even gave me a bunch of self addressed envelopes so I would be sure to write. At least the envelopes would be easy to store, but where would I stash the champagne? In return I gave everyone at the store an open invitation to join me anywhere, anytime, for a vacation. As I walked out of the store that day, my emotions were all over the map. Now it really felt like I was close to going and I was elated and scared to death.

The fear of the unknown lasted to the day prior to departure. During the morning I checked and rechecked the sails, the lines, anything I laid my eyes on I tried to take a bit closer look at. I packed my fresh foods and put a block of ice in the ice chest. I planned to stop at Neah Bay at the tip of Washington to top off the fuel, ice and fresh foods before entering the Pacific for my three or four week journey.

About three o'clock in the afternoon things started getting interesting. People were stopping by the boat and staying. Some brought beer and wine and others brought food. A regular Bon Voyage party was breaking out! Steve, his wife Yolanda, and the crew from Discount Marine came by and even the harbormaster, "no nonsense" Bruce came down after work and partook in the festivities. The Jones Family with little Timmy (the boy who learned longshoreman lingo from me) also came to say their good-byes. They were probably happy to see me go! As it turned out, George and Rosie had organized the get together and put the word out. There was a turkey that Rosie had roasted for the shindig, and I was eyeing it for some leftovers to take with me when I set sail. Alien Allen was there, of course, and I'm sure he was mildly freaking people out with that laser like stare of his.

I was in the unusual position of being the center of attention and people were bombarding me with questions. Questions ranging from how long would I be gone to how did I know how much toilet paper or toothpaste to take? Another popular question was "Where do you anchor at night?" to which I'd patiently explain that the depths in the ocean precluded me from anchoring and the boat would travel day and night.

Mom made a short personal appearance. Her main concerns were that I always wear my safety harness and contact home whenever possible. I could tell that she was both excited and scared for my impending departure. Good old Mom always supported me in whatever crazy thing I decided to do.

We continued to eat, drink and be merry, which I found out the next day isn't a good thing to do the night before heading out to sea. Live and learn. As I was passing through the crowd of about 30 on the dock, saying my good-byes, I spotted a familiar figure. I recognized the slightly hunched posture of Surfer Sparky!

"Where the heck have you been?" I asked.

"When my landlord heard I was planning on moving out he gave me the old heave ho," He slowly replied, "I've been living with different friends for the last 2 weeks and couldn't get hold of you."

So now I was back to the mindset of having crew on board. Mom will sure be happy to hear this. Sparky tossed a small duffel into the cockpit and passed me his 6 1/2 foot surf board encased in a silver bag. Well, one more thing to try and fit on board. The last of my live-a-board neighbors to stop by was Frank, the wealthy banker, who, after wishing me fair winds, quietly asked if I had any quarters to spare. Like I said before, the all-mighty quarter is a great equalizer on the docks.

The party finally started breaking up about 11 o'clock and I was feeling no pain by that time. I'm sure my state of inebriation was the reason I still was taking Sparky along even though we hadn't done any sailing together yet. While cleaning up the empty beer bottles and assorted trash I thought about what was ahead of me: warm water, sunny days, sandy beaches and exotic landfalls. And it was all going to start tomorrow! Then I threw up. Pretty auspicious start, eh?

CHAPTER 4

Aloha

"Any man that would go to sea for pleasure would go to hell for a pastime..."

-Anonymous

Just after I tossed the dock lines off, I tossed my breakfast. Thus was created my first personal rule of nautical life: No heavy drinking just before departure.

The day was clear, but windless as we motored through Gig Harbor. I silently said goodbye to the town I grew up in and wondered when I would see it again. As I passed the world famous Tides Tavern I gave a little wave to Dave Calhoun who was out on the deck singing his island style songs.

With the lack of wind, Sparky and I continued to motor the 50 miles to Port Townsend. Shortly after leaving my dock I realized that Sparky didn't really know anything about my boat. Or, as I was beginning to fear, any sailboat, for that matter. I would have guessed a "surfer dude" would know all about sailboats but it seems Sparky's experience in the water consisted of getting on and then falling off a surfboard. I took the opportunity with the light winds to help him get acquainted with *Rick's Place*. To start, I had him go down below and poke around while I drove the boat.

I had him start at the bow, or front of the boat where the V Berth is. The V Berth serves as my berth or bed when I'm not at sea. It is V in shape simply because it follows the contour of the boat and the bow is "the pointy end" of the boat as Sparky jokingly called it. I showed him that underneath the cushions that make it a comfy bed is my 60 gallon water tank plus some other storage areas that were packed full with cans of food and the never ending spare parts. There is a waterproof deck hatch over the V Berth that is much like having a skylight, plus it can be opened to pass things in or out or to let fresh air in. He liked the way I had run nets, held up by little hooks, along the sides of the V Berth to increase my storage space. They were filled with fruits and vegetables for the long passage ahead.

"Why is the bathroom called a head?" Spark asked as he moved into the next small area of the boat.

"Beats me" I yelled down.

The head was only about the size of a very small closet – about 2 feet wide with a marine toilet on one side of the space and a small sink across from it with plenty of toilet paper stored in the cabinet below it. There was a curtain separating it from the V Berth and a door that closed it off from the main salon.

Next he was looking around the largest area of the boat – it's the main living area, and thus the name, main salon. I could just barely stand erect in it being 5 foot 10, but Sparky, with his 6'2" frame, had to hunch down in this area.

"The portside settee is where we will sleep while at sea", I explained. I was really testing Sparky to make sure he knew port was the left side of the boat and starboard was the right. He looked immediately to the 6'3" long cushion covered bench that would be our seaberth. At least he passed his first test of nautical nomenclature.

Sparky then questioned why we wouldn't just use the V Berth, and I assured him that once we were out on the ocean in the waves the motion of the boat would make it pretty uncomfortable up there. There's a lot less movement in the center of the boat. Since one of us would have to be out on watch at all times, we wouldn't ever be sleeping at the same time so this one berth would be all we needed.

Across from our seaberth was a shorter settee and I'd put a fold down table between the two, so you could have a dining table when you needed one but extra space when you didn't. I had Sparky lift up all the cushions to check out the storage spaces underneath the settees so he'd have an idea of where to find stuff when we needed it. Some cruisers, a lot more organized than I, will actually make lists and diagrams of the many nooks and crannies to help them keep track of what they had. That's another thing I really should do one day, I thought.

Then he moved to the galley, or kitchen, and was amused by the two burner propane powered stove with its mini oven. Next to that was a small, single sink with a hand operated fresh-water pump and on the floor was a foot pump that could pump seawater into the sink.

"Why do you want salt water in here?" he asked, dumbfounded.

I explained again about the small water tank we had, and that we'd have to conserve it as much as possible. One way to do this would be to use salt water (of which there was an unlimited supply) for anything we could, like washing dishes. "Cool", came Sparky's usual reply.

Across from the little galley was the chart table. A large flat surfaced table that was big enough to spread out a chart (a map) to plot your position so you could keep track of where in the world you were. I told him to lift up the chart table (it was hinged with storage below it) so he could see that's where all the charts and navigation books and instruments were kept. With my VHF and Short Wave radios mounted above it, it made quite a cozy little Nav (navigation) Station. The seat for the Nav Station was the front of another long berth that ran back under the cockpit. It could be used as a sea berth, too, but I was using it for a good storage space.

"Any questions?" I asked looking in from the cockpit.

"Where's the fuel tank?" he queried. "Under the floorboards," I explained.

"So the engine must be under the stairs?"

"That's right"

"Must be pretty small," he said with a yawn.

"We may be a bit underpowered, but hopefully we won't need it much." I could tell Sparky was getting bored or tired so the instructional tour of the outside of the boat would have to wait a while.

We spent the first night at the transient dock in Port Townsend which is one of those rare towns that seems to be almost untouched by modern urban development. Most of the buildings on Main Street looked just as they did in the early 1900's. These buildings were in like new condition with several on the National Historical Registry giving a great ambiance to the small town. In the summer, Port Townsend plays host to the largest wooden boat gathering in the United States and several wooden boat building shops are still in existence there. We were lucky to get a space at the transient dock because a 3 day Jazz Festival was luring boaters from all over the Northwest, so dock space was very limited. I had a rather high level of anxiety over the trip and that kept sleep at bay for most of the night. Sparky's snoring added to my agony. My nautical rules now included asking prospective crew members if they snored like a walrus.

I awoke before sunrise and went out for a walk through the nearly deserted streets. The smell of the fresh, salty air of the nearby ocean snapped me out of my groggy daze. As soon as my head was clear, I bee-lined back to *Rick's* and woke up Sparky because I was feeling the urge to go. Right now! So we grabbed a quick breakfast of coffee and rolls in town and readied the boat.

Since the temperature was still in the 40's we bundled up in warm jackets and stocking caps to keep out the early morning chill. The sun began to rise as we cast off our lines and headed for Neah Bay, our last stop before Hawaii.

Just like the day before, there was little or no wind and flat glassy seas, so there was lots of time to talk and I started learning a bit about Sparky, including how he got his name. It turned out that "Sparky" was a name given to him in the Navy. I was surprised to learn he'd been in the Navy. It also made me realize how little I knew about this guy that I was about to spend the better part of a month with aboard a small boat. The concept that I didn't really know my crew was kind of scary. He continued by explaining that he'd been a communications officer. "I worked the radios on a destroyer until I was medically discharged because of my hearing loss," he continued. Again, I had to try to ignore the little voice in my head that kept trying to tell me something.

It dawned on me that when Sparky had said he had sailing experience, it really meant setting sail on a Navy ship, not really sailing a sailboat, so I realized I had better get busy with a crash coarse in Sailing 101.

"Hey, while we've got the time, lets go over the deck and sails a bit to get you more familiar with the boat," I offered. I saw a slight rolling of his eyes and I really hoped this meant he knew more than I thought he did.

Then came his slow response of, "Sure thing captain."

I started out by showing him which halyard to pull to raise the big main sail and a second halyard that would raise the front sail.

"I only carry two front sails for the boat and we change them depending on the wind conditions. The one on the front now is the smaller, or 90% jib that I call the working jib and the other one still stowed down below in the quarter berth behind the Nav Station is the larger one, called a Genoa that's used for lighter winds."

"What one will we use the most?" Sparky questioned.

"I expect it will be the working jib, that's why I have it hanked on and ready to go. It's made of a bit heavier cloth so it can take more abuse, you know, in case we can't get it down quickly in gusty winds."

Then I continued, "The more wind you have, the smaller sail area you want up so you have more control. So basically it's big wind, small sail, small wind, big sail."

"Got it," was his reply and his gaze went to the large main sail that was raised even though we were motoring along and he asked, "How strong of a wind before we put a reef in the main?"

I was shocked and delighted that he knew that reducing the main sail area was called reefing! There was hope for him yet! This meant there was hope for me as well.

"My rule of thumb for when to reef the main is to do it when it firsts come to mind. I've found if you sit and think about it, then things can get out of hand before you know it and you are overpowered by the wind. Better to reduce the sail and then find you didn't really need to and put it back up, then to battle the wind trying to get it down when it's already too strong. That can be difficult and dangerous."

I went on to show the two different reef points on the mainsail so we could reef the main down to the first set for semi-strong winds and then make it even smaller in the big blows. I demonstrated how you simply let the mainsail down a bit, so that the reef point you want is down along the boom and then you tie the little lines that are on the reef points around the boom.

"What's a boom?" he asked. Oh, this can't be good, I thought to myself. If he doesn't know that the boom is the long tube that runs from the mast horizontal to the boat and attaches to the bottom of the sail, we were in big trouble. I was starting to get nervous again.

So I pointed to it and said, "That's the boom," and he replied, "I was just kidding. Of course I know what the boom is," That time I know he rolled his eyes at me.

I went on talking, explaining more about reefing, "We will have the full main up in light winds, or like this when we're just motoring because it helps stabilize the boat. Then if the winds are between 15 to 20 knots we'll drop down to the first reef point. Much more than 20 we'll want to put the second reef in."

I continued on with, "Spark, remember when we reef the main, the boat leans on it's side less and steers easier and is much more comfortable down below in the cabin."

I think he absorbed most of what I said just before that ten thousand mile stare of his set in and I knew the sailing lesson was over for the time being.

My lack of sleep from the night before was catching up to me and I thought it might be a good time to see how Sparky could manage the boat on his own. It wouldn't be too difficult since we were just motoring along. So I gave him instructions to stay on course, watch out for ships or anything else in the water and to call me if he had any questions. I went below and flopped into the sea berth and the drone of the engine put me right to sleep.

I woke up an hour outside of Neah Bay and everything seemed fine after my absence on deck, so I was feeling much better about my choice in crew. The little voices in my head were quiet again and a sense of comfort settled in.

Neah Bay was in stark contrast to Port Townsend. Gone were the quaint buildings and throngs of tourists. Here there was just one run down motel in town and a dingy diner that only served breakfast and lunch, no dinner. And, due to it's exposure to the nearly constant prevailing west wind coming off the Pacific Ocean, all of the trees were stunted in growth and leaning in an Easterly direction. Neah Bay is one of those strategically placed stopovers that offer you diesel, water and little else.

We ended up waiting in Neah Bay for two days while a Southerly blew itself out. South was the direction we needed to go, and it's difficult to make much headway when you have to tack back and forth into the wind. It would go much smoother to wait till the wind would come from behind or even to the side of the boat to start our long passage.

Neah Bay is a way for God to tell cruisers to get going on their voyage, there's nothing for you here. After several calls to the Coast Guard weather people, as well as NOAA (National Ocean Atmospheric Association), the time seemed right to make the big plunge into the big ocean.

The plan was to stay about 50 miles off the Washington Coast and head due south until we were at the approximate latitude of Los Angeles, then we would make a right turn and head to Hawaii. I also reviewed the safety rules I'd adopted for the passage. Safety harnesses, the tethers that attach us to the boat, would always be worn when in the cockpit or on deck. We would have constant look out with 4 hour on and 4 hour off shift change. I was again a bit concerned about Spark's hearing deficiency, but the knowledge that he'd been in the Navy helped alleviate my fears.

As we rounded the tip of Washington with a cloudless sky and 15 knots of wind on the beam, a wave of relief flooded over me. The years of preparation were finally behind me and I was actually realizing my dream. It was like a big weight was lifted off of me, and I was anticipating an uneventful crossing.

The first lesson learned was that the t shirts and shorts Sparky and I had been able to wear during the afternoons while in the protected waters of Puget Sound would not cut it out here on the open ocean. We'd have to stay bundled up in our fleece the whole day because the temperature never seemed to get above 50 degrees. As we shivered, I hoped we would catch up to the warm climes very soon.

At sunset the coast of Washington was still in sight, as we were only 10 miles offshore and heading in a Southwest direction.

The GPS was slowly ticking off the miles to the waypoint that would announce that we were 50 miles offshore and could then turn to a Southerly heading. We had a reef in the main and a 90% working jib on and were moving at a comfortable 5 – 6 knots. It couldn't have been better. But as the darkness set in so did a new sensation. The boat felt like it was speeding up and the 6 foot waves looked to be growing. The darker it got, the bigger the waves appeared. There seemed to be a direct correlation between how dark it was getting and how bad the conditions were becoming. The illumination of the moonlight on the waves didn't help, making them look much larger than they really were. The sound of the ocean seemed to be amplified in the night. While unnoticed during the day, the seas roared at night and would often sound like a train bearing down on us.

When it came time for Sparky to take over I could tell he was nervous and a bit out of sorts. "I'm not feeling so hot," he said. I decided to stay in the cockpit with him and things remained about the same for the rest of the night.

When the first rays of sun poked over the horizon, I was nearly giddy with excitement. The boat and I had survived our first night at sea, and all was right with our little world. Before daybreak I sent my crew member down below for rest in hopes his mal-de-mar would subside. The sunrise was phenomenal, as was the rest of the day. The wind remained constant and so did the boat speed. I called Sparky for his mid morning watch, but got no response. I figured he needed a bit more rest, so I made some breakfast. I was now standing watch and cooking, which was somewhat inconvenient. When the food was ready to be served I had to shake surfer boy to wake him up. This was the point when I knew the hearing thing was going to be more than just a nuisance. I wish I had listened to those little voices that kept trying to get my attention before our departure.

When I finally got him out on deck he looked pale. What happened next was so random that I was completely caught off guard. "Where's the shoreline?" came his whispered voice. "About 30 miles east," I replied. "But we need to see land," was his strained reply. "You're putting me on, right?" I asked with hope in

49

my voice, but I could tell by his appearance that this was a real problem for him.

"Well, Sparky, I begged the last island we passed to follow us to Hawaii, but it had other commitments. Seriously, buddy, you must have looked at a map or a globe or something to get an idea where we were sailing to? You do know we're going to Hawaii, right?"

Before he could answer, Rick's Wrecked Eggs (one of my specialties) were occupying a place on the cockpit floor, instead of being in Sparky's stomach. I felt bad for him, so I just had him stand watch while I cleaned up, then I sent him down to his bunk while I read and enjoyed the gorgeous day. Sparky spent the majority of the day below, with only brief visits to the cockpit. His sea sickness seemed to be getting worse.

Now I asked Sparky some things I should have asked him back at the dock, such as, "Just how much offshore experience do you have?" When he replied it was only on big ships, I asked him if being out of sight of land was bothering him and I got a resounding, "Hell Yes!" It seems he spent his time in the radio room on a big ship and didn't know if he was away from land, or even if it was day or night. "So Sparky, just what are you trying to tell me?" And his reply while leaning over the rail to feed the fish was devastating, "I'm scared to death of being in the middle of the ocean at night!" Why hadn't I listened to those little voices?

I tried talking with him to get his anxiety level down. As night approached I channeled my nervous energy into making sure the boat was in order and that we were on course. I also tried to track down what was making some mysterious noises that only seemed to happen at night. I figured that once Sparky got over the sickness his outlook would improve. Thankfully it was another star studded beautiful night. The same sensation of speeding up and the waves seeming to be monstrous was occurring again, but I was already getting used to it. Unfortunately Sparky wasn't.

Sparky spent most of the night in the only bunk available below. One thing I had been counting on with the planned 4 hour on, 4 hour off watch system was that only one person would be down below at any time. Thus, we would only need one place to sleep. We could "hot bunk" it as they say in the navy.

The adrenaline that had been coursing through my veins for the first 36 hours was starting to wear down, so I kept an egg timer with me on watch to jar me awake should I drift off. Generally the night passed relatively fast. I knew things were going to get uncomfortable and unsafe unless I got my crew healthy and active and I was able to get some sleep.

By the next morning I'd developed a simple three-step plan to get Sparky back into the watch rotation. I realized he needed fluids and food, activity and fresh air to bring him around. It was one thing to single hand the boat to Hawaii, but totally different to single hand plus take care of and worry over a sick and scared crew member.

So I got Sparky out of bed with an early morning breakfast which I served in the cockpit to get him plenty of fresh air. I gave him orange juice and lemonade to get his fluids up. He was doing well and was able to keep it all down, so I moved on the next step, activity. I disconnected the wind vane and told him I needed him to steer the boat for awhile. The wind and swell had both dropped a bit, so steering a compass course would be easy enough. The concentration required for the task kept his mind off how bad he'd been feeling and he was improving by the minute.

After a couple hours I reconnected the self steering. Sparky was in much better spirits by this time and he had finally been able to keep his breakfast down. This was good since I was too tired to wash the deck again. I was feeling very smug about the success of my plan so I put on some music and laid down in the cockpit for much needed rest. I told Sparky to keep an eye on the course and I fell dead asleep secure in the knowledge that Rick's three-step anti-seasickness plan was a huge success.

Sparky woke me two hours later when the sun was getting ready to set. I could tell that he was getting apprehensive about the coming darkness. I tried to talk to him about what his fears were and all he could say was "the unknown". It was my shift so I sent him below to get some rest and assured him that when it was time for him to take over I would stay in the cockpit during his watch. He looked very relieved by this. Of course my staying on watch while Sparky was on watch wouldn't exactly get me any rest.

Once again the night was nearly flawless and I was getting very comfortable with night travel. In fact I was enjoying it. The phosphorescence trailing from the stern and the flashing of the fish swimming along the side of the boat was a constant source of entertainment for me. Never had I seen so many stars and shooting stars, in my life. Mother Nature was serving up a 24-hour extravaganza and I felt like her sole audience.

When the sun rose the next morning, the light revealed many more clouds than we'd seen in previous days. It was a beautiful sunrise, but I was reminded of the old adage "red sky at morning, sailors take warning." What would today bring?

By mid morning the wind had freshened to 20-25 knots and the direction had shifted to the Southwest. We adjusted our course to make travel a bit more comfortable, which put us on a Southeasterly heading, or back toward the coast. I was glad we had 50 miles between us and land in case we had to keep to this course for very long because running aground in the night would be a very bad thing.

Rick's Place was now pounding into shorter, steeper swells. The boat would hit every third wave out of rhythm and a shower of water propelled by the wind would spray the entire length of the boat. Fortunately, one item I added before leaving home was a cockpit dodger. This was simply a canvas "windshield" with clear plastic windows that was situated over the main hatch to keep water from spraying down below. It also provided a nice shelter to huddle behind when out on watch.

As I concentrated on the rough seas, Sparky yelled up to me, "Hey, you better come down here!" with great concern in his voice. My adrenaline immediately kicked in and I practically dove down through the hatch thinking there was a serious and immediate problem.

"Listen, do ya hear that?" he asked.

"No," I said looking around at the mess that the rough weather was making. Just about everything that had been on a shelf was now on the floor.

"There, there it is! Listen!"

A mild groan had come from the mast and the sound was transferred acoustically down below. This sound had been with *Rick's Place* since we launched over a year ago.

"Don't worry, Sparky, we're OK."

I could hear cans of food rolling back and forth in rhythm with the waves that passed below us. The commotion that was going on below was overloading my senses and I was starting to feel queasy.

"I gotta get some air," I told Sparky and I disappeared up the stairs. I couldn't take a chance on both of us being sick, and besides, who would clean up after me?

The waters were getting pretty lumpy, as well, but the weather report on the Coast Guard channel didn't seem too serious. I was still doing fine, but my crewmate once again took a turn for the worse. When Sparky came up in the morning, instead of saying good morning he threw up at my feet. I instantly came up with a new three-step-plan to remedy the situation 1.Get him off the boat 2. Get him off the boat and 3. GET HIM OFF THE BOAT!

I immediately started plotting the way to San Jose, or rather San Francisco. When I presented this option to Sparky he was all for it. He wanted to get to shore ASAP. There was one obstacle however, that would stand in our way to the Golden Gate: The Big Weenie. That was the name I'd given a stretch of ocean that is circled in red on the pilot chart and the shape is that of a fat hot dog. It indicates an area off the California coast that is prone to steep and confused seas because this is where the California current and the continental shelf merge together. To reach San Francisco from our position, we would have to sail directly through this zone which I'd always hoped to avoid. The weather forecast wasn't particularly menacing, so I altered course to head to San Francisco and The Big Weenie.

Once we set off to our new destination, Sparky went down below and I feared by the pale and scared look he had that I wouldn't see him for the rest of the trip. Luckily the steering vane was guiding us without a problem and our speed was a steady 6 knots. I placed a 2nd reef in the main and left the 90% jib on and we were traveling very comfortably. If the conditions would hold like this it would be a quick trip to land and the end of my nightmare called Sparky.

As we neared the coast the seas began to pick up. We were definitely in The Big Weenie. I don't know how big those seas were, but they seemed like skyscrapers to me. When we'd drop down into the trough, the winds would decrease and there would be a weird silence. Then we'd rise up to the top of a mountainous wave and the wind would howl like a Banshee.

I watched with morbid curiosity as the gigantic waves would loom above *Rick's Place*. I called for Sparky several times to come up and lend a hand but either his lack of hearing or his fear kept him from responding. Night was falling and I was actually glad. I wouldn't have to see those massive waves any longer! The boat was taking care of itself, so it was like I was just along for the ride. Unfortunately it was Mr. Toad's Wild Ride. I went below to get my foul weather gear and clean up some of the cans and things that had popped out of cupboards and were rolling around the cabin. I was relieved to see Sparky hadn't left me anything on the floor that I also would need to clean up.

After picking up the noisemakers and wedging some dish cloths and papers between some rattling items, things were much quieter downstairs. I started spending my time sitting on the companionway steps, so my body was down below and a bit warmer, but my head was out where I could keep a good eye on things. I felt like I was sitting in the passenger seat of a Winnebago careening down a dark mountain road without a driver. How Sparky was sleeping through all of this, I'll never know.

At about 2:00 am, the nearly full moon came out in splendor from behind the scudding clouds. The boat also seemed to be riding better but I wasn't sure if this was just wishful thinking or maybe I was just getting used to the crazy motion. By sunrise I was certain we were through the worst of The Weenie. The faithful GPS was telling us there were just 35 miles to the outer makers entering San Francisco Bay. That would mean we should be able to anchor before nightfall.

I knew a bit about the Bay Area from talking to other cruisers and from a road trip I'd made several years before.

Sausalito would be a good anchorage until I could get my cruising plans put back together. This was my first lesson in always keeping cruising plans flexible, because there are so many things that can force you to change them. Sparky did make a brief appearance on deck at this point, but he only mumbled something incoherent and went back down to his nest.

With the sun beginning it's descent in the west; the diminishing rays were lighting up the Golden Gate Bridge and creating a brilliant spectacle. I knew then I'd made the right decision coming into The Bay. I was glad I had a copy of "Charlie's Charts of the West Coast" for extra guidance into this unplanned landfall. Being late on a Saturday afternoon there were hundreds of sailboats tacking back and forth along with several freighters thrown in the mix. This heavy traffic combined with my lack of sleep on the way down the coast made our passage under the famous Golden Gate more chaotic than reflective. Things seemed nearly out of control all around us especially since I hadn't had to worry about things such as right-of-way for some time now. Didn't these boats all realize I'd made a long hard passage on the Pacific Ocean from Washington?

Once under the bridge, I turned on the engine and took down the salt encrusted sails and made a beeline to Sausalito. I dropped the anchor as the darkness was creeping in around us. After seeing that the anchor was securely set, I moved a couple sail bags out of the quarter berth and collapsed from exhaustion. The stillness of the boat actually caused me to wake up in a start several times that night. It was such an unnatural feeling after what we had been experiencing the past week.

At dawn I was awakened again. This time to the smell of breakfast cooking! Sparky was feeling so good now that he was once again near land that he took it upon himself to fix a meal. The first he'd managed to do during the whole voyage.

After enjoying the much needed breakfast that Spark had dubbed his "Surfer's Surprise," I set about making plans. It would be good to get into a marina for a while so the provisioning and the small improvements I planned to make would be a bit easier to accomplish. I began calling on the VHF to all the marinas I had on a list to see if I could find a berth, and after several no's I finally hit a BINGO with Emery Cove Marina on the Oakland side of the bay. Diane, the harbormaster, said I could get in that day and stay for a month if need be.

We hauled anchor and headed across the bay. After we found our slip we stepped ashore to the first solid surface we'd been on in a week. The funny thing was it didn't seem solid. The ground seemed to be swaying under our feet and I felt like I might fall down. The feeling was a lot like spinning in circles when you were a kid and then trying to walk. I was afraid now that Sparky was on land his seasickness would turn to land sickness.

We started cleaning up down below and Sparky went up to the phone and came back to announce he'd gotten hold of some friends in the area and would be spending the night on shore. That was a relief. I was really looking forward to having *Rick's Place* back to myself. He said he was sorry he let me down, but I assured him that this was just a minor sidetrack and I was kind of glad to get to spend some time in the Bay Area. I was feeling pretty good about how the boat preformed and most of all how I was able to adapt to the passage. I'd decided that when I set out for Hawaii again I'd be doing it single handed.

I walked Sparky up to the parking lot where his ride was waiting for him. I gave a quick call to Mom to let her know of my little detour and she was just happy to hear from me so much sooner than expected. Surprisingly, I felt a twinge of loneliness as I walked back to the boat, so I busied myself washing *Rick's Place.* I hosed down the sails and lines and just plain putted around. There was still plenty of fresh food and beer aboard, so I would be content for the next couple of days. Sitting in the cockpit reading and listening to music, I dropped off to sleep. When I turned over to get in a more comfortable position, I opened my eyes and found myself staring into the big green eyes of a rather large tabby cat curled up near my head. It was such a shock I let out a yelp, but that didn't even faze this cat. It just laid its head down and went back to napping.

A short time later, an attractive looking woman who appeared to be around my age, in her late twenties, walked over to my boat. I'd seen her on the dock earlier, when we were first pulling in. It was hard not to notice her because she was taller than average and had beautiful long blonde hair. She also had a unique style in clothing that I can only describe as modern day hippie. Standing there in a peasant dress and sandals, she introduced herself as Sheryl. She went on to explain that she was a live-a-board from the next dock over and was looking for Jack, her cat. After a brief description of Jack I knew her cat was the interloper who had decided to take a nap with me. He wasn't in the cockpit any longer so we assumed he'd traveled on or headed home. We talked for a bit before she continued her search for her wayward cat. That night when I went below to go to bed, I was startled again by Jack who was now curled up on my V-berth.

Jack was a regular visitor to *Rick's Place* after that. He was such a mellow cat, unfazed by sudden noise or movement that sometimes I wasn't even sure if he was alive. Once after one of his regular visits I made a rather surprising discovery. There was cat poop in my toilet! The next time I saw Sheryl; she confirmed my observation and told me that Jack was toilet trained. She explained that it wasn't all that hard to teach him to use the head. But, of course, he couldn't flush. But hey, no litter box is a great thing on a boat. I have friends that aren't that well trained.

CHAPTER 5

Aloha (again)

"And Jesus said, take the boat out..."
-Mathew 14:22

Two weeks passed with blinding speed. I had a few projects to keep me occupied since the trip down the coast (especially the crossing of the Big Weenie) had exposed the problem of not having things secured safely below. It was truly a good shakedown cruise. The need for additional latches, tie downs and more storage nets became glaringly apparent. Hopefully my improvements would lessen the number of flying cans of corn, falling books, and the mysterious sticky stuff that seemed to accumulate on the passage. I had Sparky to thank for this unexpected stop that would surely make the rest of the sail to Hawaii much less trying and more enjoyable.

On one of my trips to the local chandlery to obtain parts for my numerous projects, I learned that a race was due to leave for Hawaii in a couple weeks. I wasn't up to entering a race, but I thought it would be great to head out a bit before them so I could kind of tag along until they left me in their dust, or their wake, as it were. That way I would at least know there were other boats somewhere nearby. Maybe I would even be able to talk to one of them occasionally on the VHF radio.

During my stay at the Emery Cove Marina, I was happy to have Sheryl and Jack as frequent visitors to *Rick's Place*. Our common interest in boats was turning into a common interest in each other and I don't mean Jack and me. These feelings were making for mixed emotions concerning my immanent departure. In fact, we'd even discussed having her join me on the trip, but Sheryl had just recently opened up a small flower shop in San Francisco and couldn't leave at that time. Timing is everything.

My last project, just two days before leaving, was the purchase and installation of a radar detection device. Much like a radar detector for cars, this black box let out an alarm and indicated on its small screen if the boat was scanned by a ship's radar. It was called a Collision Avoidance Radar Detector, because it would alert me to ships in the area that I might not see, thus avoiding an unexpected bump in the night. For a single handed sailor it would act like an electronic lookout while down below sleeping, cooking or chasing down all the junk rolling around on the cabin sole.

Departure day arrived with a glorious blue sky. The weather was forecast to be rather benign, so I was good to go. Sheryl made us a great breakfast, but our conversation was somewhat stunted, due to anxiety, excitement and a sense of loss at leaving. This was my first experience of what I later learned to be one of the hardest parts of cruising, always saying goodbye to new found friends. I also felt that if Sheryl and I had a bit more time together our relationship could easily develop into more than just friendship.

As we walked down to my boat, my stomach felt more like I had been eating butterflies instead of scrambled eggs. I told Sheryl to say goodbye to Jack for me and give him some catnip. She tossed my lines to me as I pulled out of the slip and I promised to call when I reached Hawaii. Once again I was on my way; this time alone. As I motored under the Golden Gate Bridge and began to raise my sails, I hoped it was true that God protects the ignorant, for I surely fell into that category.

I was soon clearing the coast under a full sail and I set the wind vane, for a course of West-Southwest. The wind vane was a lifesaver, because it was like having another crew member. It would steer the boat on any course using wind as its source of power. And this crew mate didn't require feeding and would never get sick.

The butterflies in my stomach were replaced by a bit of queasiness, but nothing serious. I would have to cross out of the shipping lanes before I could completely relax. The first day passed quickly as I read, snacked and listened to music. That night I spotted several lights from ships on the horizon, and I made it a point to call and identify myself. I was also curious to know if they were able to spot me on their radar. I was comforted to find they were easily picking me up at about 4 miles, the same distance I would pick them up on my radar detector. Now I just had to hope all the ships would have their radar on.

Bundling up in long johns I spent the night in the cockpit catching quick cat naps and drinking hot cocoa. The wind was out of the Northwest and the boat was pushed along at a very comfortable 6 knots so I was quite content. The dawn broke revealing gray skies and the wind was a bit stronger and the seas steeper. I reduced sail to the working jib and a single reef in the main, which would prove to be the sail configuration I would use for most of this passage.

My morning ritual was to walk the deck, check for chafe and wear and tear, then go below and check the bilge area under the floor to make sure it was dry and I didn't have any leaks. It was easier to detect potential problems and take care of them during the day then to wait for the calamity of a middle of the night emergency. When I went in to the head I received the shock of my life. There was cat poop in the toilet! Hoping beyond hope that the toilet was just regurgitating a little, I flushed it and went back out and sat in the cockpit. Going through my mind was the old saying about denial isn't just a river in Egypt. Fear of what I would find, kept me from doing an all out search for Jack. If he was aboard, would I have to turn back after such a successful start to a long voyage? That was a decision I just didn't want to have to make.

It was hunger that forced the issue. Not mine, but Jack's. He finally crawled out from behind some sail bags, stretched, sat down and began crying for food. "I hope you like tuna," I told him, since I obviously hadn't come prepared with any cat food. It really surprised me how well adapted Jack seemed to ocean travel. The thought of turning around to take him back to Sheryl was quickly pushed out of my mind. Heading back into the weather and seas for some 100+ miles would be completely nuts. So, just as I had with Sparky, I welcomed Jack aboard with some trepidation. Once again I had a crew member aboard *Rick's Place*.

On my morning deck walks, I began finding squid that had been washed aboard the deck by waves and flying fish that had met their fate while flying out of the water only to find my deck rather than another wave. These unexpected treats were well received by Jack for his morning meal. The rest of my routine involved doing any projects that needed doing followed by a mid-morning nap. After the nap, I would plot my position and put a big X on the chart and calculate my miles made good. Occasionally I would pull out my sextant and practice getting my position "the old fashioned way" and compare it to my GPS position. I have great respect for those who traveled the oceans with only a sextant and a compass, and I feel it was important for me to be able to use these skills as well. I was also very thankful that I didn't have to rely on it. One of my problems with the celestial navigation was having to be down at the chart table for long periods of time doing the sight reductions. I don't know if it was being below or having to do the math, but I always got queasy.

After my shipboard chores were done, I would then relax in the cockpit with a good book and follow that with another nap. Then I would check the weather forecast and do any sail adjustments I felt necessary. Jack and I would have an early dinner, so I could get the dishes done before dark. The cat proved to be much less trouble and just as much help as Sparky had been plus Jack kept his meals down. At night I tried to keep a pattern of 2 hours of sleep and 2 hours of watch. When morning came I'd start the routine all over again and the days began to blend into each other. Jack was content to stay below until about our 5th day out when he came out to explore. I realized then that I needed to make a harness of some type for him. So I got some webbing out of my sail repair bag and fashioned a tether and harness that would keep him in the cockpit. Jack, with his laid back demeanor, took this new harness in stride, not like your typical cat that rebels against any kind of change. I'd noticed a large shark trailing some distance behind the boat for the last few days and I didn't want my new crew member to become the Cat de jour for Sharky. This also inspired me to be even more diligent about hooking my tether on at all times.

By this time, the boats in the San Francisco to Hawaii race had already caught up and in many cases were passing us. A few times I was able to talk to the closer ones over the VHF radio (that has a range of about 15 miles). These guys were amazing, as were their boats. There were all sizes of boats in this race ranging from 27 footers to the big 72 foot yacht owned by Roy Disney. The big difference between these boats and *Rick's Place* is that they were built for speed so they were very Spartan on the inside to keep the weight down. The lighter the boat, the faster it will go. They'd run with full sails and even spinnakers, that are normally just used in light winds since they are so big. They would have these unfurled all day and all night with little regard to the wind strength just to get another few knots out of their boats.

One night near midnight I was talking to a guy flying along under his spinnaker and his boat broached! That meant that the boat got overpowered and was driven sideways into the sea. Becoming broached is a very radical and potentially dangerous incident. He treated it like an everyday occurrence and hardly missed a beat. My stocking cap was off to these guys.

I was also able to get word back to Sheryl through their radio schedule with the race committee, and let her know Jack's whereabouts. This was quite a relief, as I knew she'd be worried. They also passed word back to Mom for me, as I knew she'd be worried as well even though she doesn't even know Jack.

At 10 days out I had to start making more sail adjustments because the weather was slowly changing. Even the water was changing: both in color and temperature. Fatigue was catching up with me and I was having to sleep for longer stretches of time. Birds began to land on the boat and stay and rest for a couple days at a time. They were a welcome distraction from the daily monotony. Jack agreed and he would sit eyeing them for hours.

Another subtle change was the length of the daylight. Heading south, the days had begun to get shorter, but I hadn't really noticed since it had been so cloudy. Then, one morning, after a clear night, I was excitedly anticipating a beautiful sunrise around 6:30 am. When the sun hadn't come up by 7:30 I ran downstairs and checked my ships clock and it told me the same thing. By eight o'clock I was in complete panic. Where was the sun? Had there been some cosmic catastrophe I hadn't heard about? It finally dawned on me that in addition to the shorter days, I had already crossed several time zones without adjusting my clock or watch. All was well with the world after all. If I had I been getting a bit more sleep, I don't think I would have experienced such confusion.

And then it happened. I was finally in the fabled trade winds! The sailing was now nothing short of pure magic. The winds were a steady 15-20 knots from behind and the seas were a gentle rolling 6-10 feet. The days were warmer and I was able to get rid of the long johns and stocking cap. Jack's treat of flying fish were more plentiful now and he enjoyed at least one every morning. You have to feel sorry for the poor flying fish. Here they are taking flight to avoid some danger in the sea, and they unluckily end up landing on the deck of my boat and becoming feline food instead of back in the water where they belong. Jack did not share in my concerns.

Three days out of Hilo, Hawaii I was reading the sixth novel of the passage. I glanced around the horizon in my constant search for ships (or anything!), and I spotted a strange sight. It appeared to be a jet coming right at me at about 50' off the water! The jet was flying about as slow as he could and still stay in the air. I waved as he went by and was surprised how clearly I could see the pilot. Once by me, he climbed nearly straight up; barrel rolled and came back for another low pass. It was the strangest encounter of my entire trip and I couldn't figure out what he was up to. Was he just out joy riding and wanting to get a look at what kind of crazy fool is out here in a small boat? It wasn't until later in Hawaii, chatting with a group of other cruisers, that had made the crossing at a similar time that we pieced it all together. We'd all had the same experience: he'd buzzed all of us, and word had it they were actually searching for a particular overdue boat.

That same evening I had another experience that really shook my day. The channel that I had been getting my weather from was coming in with lots of static. I wasn't too worried, since the weather had been pretty consistent since I'd hit the trades. Then, through the static, I heard something about a hurricane. Hurricane? Where? Hurricane? Not exactly a forecast to ease a person into the night.

I spent the rest of the evening trying to get better reception and tuning into the forecast every hour. It took about 4 hours, but I finally pieced together the whole report. As it turned out, this hurricane was about 300 miles off the Mexican coast. It was heading this way, but it was at least 5 days behind me, so it was no worry unless the wind left me completely, which wasn't likely in the trades.

Not likely? My mistake. I woke in the night to the boat wallowing with limp sails in a windless sea. Just great. Nature seemed to be trying to teach Mr. Smug a lesson. I thought things had been going just a little too easy. We rocked uncomfortably all day with no wind and not enough fuel to motor any real distance. By sunset my nerves were shot and I was feeling sick for the first time on this passage. 1200 miles traveled, less than 300 to go, and now this. I didn't get much sleep that night.

My worrying about the storm that was gaining on my position, still 1000 miles away, was intensified by the lack of wind. My brief thoughts about sacrifices to the "wind gods" must have been telepathically picked up by Jack, because I didn't see him at all during this windless period. I knew he was still onboard, as evidenced by the occasional kitty deposits in the toilet.

For the next 48 hours, time seemed to be standing still. The wind was a series of fits and starts. One minute we were moving at a respectable rate and the next we were becalmed. Being this close to Hawaii I was now getting more frequent and better weather updates on the high seas radio. It seemed the hurricane was on a fairly direct course toward the islands and had intensified. It was still over 800 miles away from Hawaii but it was obviously headed towards the islands and me. I figured my lack of wind was the result of the storm to the east. Even though I promised God that I would reserve Sunday for church, give up any and all bad habits and donate to the United Way, the wind would not fill in.

The boat carried about 30 gallons of diesel fuel, and the inboard engine was a small, one cylinder British model which was a bit under-powered for the boat's weight. Regardless, I decided that if the wind did not pick up by sundown, I would run the thing until I was either out of fuel or in Hilo. If things got really bad weather wise, I thought I'd rather be in port, and Hilo was the closest option. I guess I felt better about being smashed against the rocks then simply crushed by big waves and sent two miles down to the ocean floor. Go figure. I couldn't find Jack to get his opinion on my decision.

Sundown came and true to my word I started the engine. 3 – 4 knots was the going rate. More rain squalls were besieging us now, and as usual they preferred to attack at night. The first sign of a squall was when the stars would disappear, and then the rain would come and I mean hard rain. Having grown up in the Seattle area, I thought I knew hard rain, but these tropical outbursts took the phrase to a new level. The 3 inch diameter drains couldn't always handle the volumes of rainfall entering the cockpit and I would find myself standing in several inches of water during some of these showers. The one saving grace was that it wasn't cold.

The wind would vary with each of these occurrences so you never knew what to expect. Sometimes the squall would just bring a slight change in wind speed or direction, but the other half of the time the wind would increase anywhere from 15 – 30 knots and could be a complete change in direction. Then once the system passed, it would die out completely and then return to what it had been before the squall. This kept me pretty busy dropping and resetting sails and I was getting exhausted on top of my increasing anxiety.

Things seemed to have moderated a bit and I was sailing along with the engine running with a full main and large front sail out. The engine vibration lulled me to sleep in the cockpit for a much needed rest. Suddenly a squall overtook the boat from behind, and unfortunately this micro weather system packed some major winds. The boat was immediately knocked down by a gust that must have been about 40 knots. The rain was pelting down so hard it sounded like rocks hitting the cabin top and it made it difficult for me to see. I managed to release the sheets and halyard and this brought the boat back upright. I lowered the sails from the cockpit and they didn't drop all the way down, but there was no way I was going out on deck in this mess to do anything about it.

After 20 minutes of this weather terror, things began to calm down and the stars were visible again. With this calm after the storm I was able to go below to check things out and maybe catch a bite to eat. I was shocked to see that some water had found its way into the cabin and was mixed with the inevitable montage of books, cans and that damn sticky stuff that gets on everything, but comes from who knows what. I spent the next several hours cleaning and straightening up below and searching for Jack, who had found a cozy space between some sail bags and seemed completely unfettered. I could take some lessons from my feline friend.

The continued windless conditions forced me to motor sail for about 12 more hours. By daybreak it was evident that I would not have enough fuel to motor the rest of the way to Hilo. With my binoculars I could just make out the cloud tipped peaks of the Big Island: Hawaii! I was still 35 miles out, with no wind, a hurricane on my tail and only enough diesel to last me about another hour of motoring since I needed to reserve the last 5 gallons for the harbor entrance. When the hour of motoring was exhausted it became eerily quiet when I had to shut down the engine. The only sounds were the creaking of the boom as it slogged back and forth and the beating of my heart.

It was maddening to actually see land for the first time in so many days and not have the wind (or fuel) to get me there. I had been pouring over the harbor charts and studying the entrance charts for days now—anytime I had a spare minute. Making landfall at night would be foolhardy and dangerous and could cause the loss of the boat. My mind set, along with lack of sleep and my general run down state, made me feel almost desperate not to spend another night at sea. The wind continued to be light and I was only moving along at about 3 knots. The swell had gotten longer in period, which is to say the time between wave crests had grown. This was a result of the hurricane which was now about 400 miles away. High clouds had begun obscuring the sky during the day, another sign that trouble was on its way.

By noon it was evident that I had a decision to make: either stay off shore for the night, or make the harbor entrance after sunset. While studying the chart, yet again, and wishing I could get in tonight, it suddenly struck me that other cruisers may be anchored in Radio Bay, which was my destination in Hilo. If I could reach someone I could get information on entering the harbor. With great excitement I went to my VHF and called out to anyone in Radio Bay and asked them to please respond. I continued to try every half hour and had just begun to feel discouraged when I finally got a response! It was still a couple of hours before sunset and we were only about 10 miles out from the entrance, so there was hope. The boat that replied was named *Cetus*, and they were in Radio Bay. Hearing another voice (one that didn't emanate from my own head) was really exciting.

Terry, the skipper, explained the layout of the entrance and gave me GPS coordinates to get in. He had come in during daylight hours (as we all should), but he didn't seem to think it would be much of a problem at night, stating, "It's well marked and lit with flashing entrance lights, so talking you in should be no problem." Knowing someone was in there waiting for me was reassuring, and knowing he would be standing by the radio to help gave me the courage to break one of the great rules of cruising: never enter a strange port in the dark.

So I started picking out landmarks and making my way into the harbor as the last of the sun's rays were being obscured by the horizon. As the natural light began to fade, new lights began to appear; lots and lots of lights. The lights of Hilo were coming on: bright lights, dim lights, red lights, green lights, blinking lights, big lights and small lights. Against this background of seemingly hundreds of lights from land, it was virtually impossible to distinguish the navigation lights I needed to enter safely through the breakwater.

I was becoming overwhelmed by fear and confusion. Every time I thought the right lights were in sight, something would make me doubt their validity. I started the engine with precious little diesel left, and motored near what I guessed was the entrance to Radio Bay. Trying to line up those entrance lights amongst all the other lights after not seeing any lights at all for so long, was really doing a number on my rods and cones. I radioed *Cetus* with my dilemma, afraid to get much closer in case what I thought was the entrance, wasn't. Terry explained he felt coming out to try to find me in his dinghy, in the dark, may be hazardous to his health.

Jack and I were in wholehearted agreement, even though we wished for some help. About this time I thought I heard the engine misfire reminding me I didn't have the fuel to keep motoring back and forth out here. I'd need some fuel to get out of the harbor if it turned out I should spend the night at sea and make a fresh try in the morning. Just as I resigned myself to doing the safe and sane thing and started to turn the boat back out to sea, the VHF crackled to life, "*Rick's Place, Rick's Place*, this is *The Happy Hooker* calling." That's all I needed right now was some kind of demented joker calling me on the radio, but it came again, "*Rick's Place*, this is the fishing vessel *Happy Hooker*, come in." Looking quickly around and hoping against hope he wasn't calling to warn me of our immanent collision, I replied to his call.

The skipper was a local heading out for a night of fishing, and he had overheard my conversation with *Cetus* and knew my predicament. He was heading my way and would drop a friend of his off on my boat who could guide me in. "Fantastic!!" I shouted. I think I had tears in my eyes at this time. His instructions were I was to stop *Rick's Place* where I was and within an hour, *The Happy Hooker*, along with my guide, would be there. I was ecstatic.

Jack must have thought I'd lost my mind as I zoomed around picking stuff up and straightening up the boat. We were going to have company! Even watching for the approaching boat lights, I was shocked that I didn't see them until he was only about a quarter mile away. Looming out of the background lights of the city, the 50' fishing boat motored to within 100' of our position. I hadn't considered how my guide would get on board, and it was clear that with the differences in boat size and the swell it would be impossible to pull up next to each other.

Tony, the skipper of *The Happy Hooker*, called over for me to stand by. I figured they must be planning to drop a dinghy into the water and soon I heard a splash and some laughing, and then silence. Straining to see what was in the water, I soon saw some movement, but it wasn't a dinghy, it was someone swimming from the other boat! Dumbstruck, I willed myself into action. I started tearing through the cockpit locker trying to locate the boarding ladder.

Moments later there was a knocking on the side of the hull followed by "permission to come aboard." Looking down I saw a big white toothed smile on a deeply tanned face surrounded by dark shoulder length hair floating around the head. It was an odd sight, indeed.

"My name's Ben, and I will be your waiter for the night," he said as he handed me a float bag he had tied around his waist. In his other hand he had a small line that lead back to the power cruiser. He passed that to me then with little effort, he pulled himself out of the water and onto *Rick's Place*. When he was finally in the cockpit, I handed him a towel.

Ben was short with elaborate tattoos covering his heavily muscled arms. He then turned toward the other boat and yelled to Tony, "Throw the jug". I was mystified when a splash sounded and Ben proceeded to pull on the small line he'd brought with him. Attached to the other end was a jerry jug full of diesel! He truly was a lifesaver. After hauling the jug on board, Ben pulled out one more surprise. "Here you are skipper," he said as handed me a six-pack of beer that he brought over in the float bag! Ben's grin was as wide as my eyes. So we sat in the cockpit, talking over our beers, and I learned that Ben was a local who also owned his own commercial fishing boat. He and Tony had been listening to my conversations with Terry, of *Cetus*, and since Tony was getting ready to head out anyway they knew they could give me a helping hand, in the spirit of aloha.

We poured the 5 gallons of diesel into the nearly dry tank, started the engine and headed for Hilo. On the way in, Ben informed me that the hurricane I'd been running from had been downgraded to a tropical storm and was expected to loose even more force in the next 24 hours. Thankfully I wouldn't have to worry about losing my boat to a hurricane, at least not yet.

With the ruckus on deck and a new voice on the boat, Jack came out to investigate. Ben and my feline stowaway soon became fast friends, but Ben had some ominous news for me. "Don't get caught bringing a cat to the Islands," he warned. I explained the circumstances about my unwanted, but much loved, crew member and Ben said the authorities would be unmoved. At best I would have to pay for a long quarantine at a veterinarian, but sometimes they destroy the offender. I wasn't sure if it was me or Jack that was the offending party, but I didn't want that fate to befall either of us. Ben advised that if I keep Jack on board at all times I shouldn't have a problem. Just great, I thought. The reason this animal is 2000 miles from home is that he won't stay on his own boat. Why is it that just as you think things are going good, some new problem like this pops up?

Ben skillfully guided us through the maze of navigational lights and before long I was tying the boat up to the seawall in Radio Bay! Terry & Heidi Sparling from *Cetus*, along with their 5 year old daughter, Carly, were there to greet me and take the lines. It was nice to put a face to the name and voice that had been my lifeline during that long night.

Terry was about my height; in fact his features were similar enough to mine that he could have been mistaken for my older brother. His brown hair had a few flecks of gray and I guessed his age to be somewhere in his mid thirties. His wife, Heidi, was probably about the same age with shoulder-length blonde hair, an infectious smile and an easy laugh. Heidi had made up a pitcher of Margaritas in honor my landfall. Apparently anytime a new cruising boat comes in it causes a celebration among the cruisers and many showed up for the impromptu party on the seawall. I told some tales from my trip and listened to others, but due to the late hour of my arrival, the party didn't last long. I thanked everyone for their help: the *Cetus* crew, *The Happy Hooker* (via radio), and a very special thanks to Ben for being my "waiter for the evening."

Land sickness was starting to rack my balance, along with the beers and margaritas playing their part. Closing the hatch I staggered down below and promptly threw up in the sink. Another rule of passage making: Never drink right after completing a long passage.

CHAPTER 6

Hellhole Hilo

"Here's to swimmin' with bow-legged women..."
-Robert Shaw, *Jaws*

After a "dead to the world" sleep, I woke to the rain pounding on *Rick's Place*. I poked my head out of the hatch and was shocked to see cargo containers where I expected to see palm trees. And not just a few of them, but probably a thousand of them stacked in walls about five stories high! What had been veiled in darkness the night before and unknown to me was that Hilo was a major shipping port for the islands. The walls of containers were stacked on three sides of Radio Bay, blocking view of any buildings or vegetation. This was certainly not the white sand, palm tree lined beaches I had fantasized about. Never having been to the Islands, I didn't realize that my first landfall in paradise was going to be so wet, either. Where were the sunny skies I'd dreamed about? Certainly not in Hilo. Talking with the other cruisers that had been here a bit longer, I learned that although it always rains some in Hilo everyday, the fizzled out hurricane was adding more moisture to the mix.

I'd made a decision on my long passage to Hawaii that I would always spend at least as much time in an anchorage as it took me to get there, This decree somehow made it easier to endure the hardships if I had a good reward awaiting me at the end. Hilo wasn't appearing to be that great of a reward, so I was thinking I may have to amend my new rule.

My first task that day was to check in with the harbormaster as all incoming boats are required to do. The harbormaster's office was hidden among the maze of containers from all the cargo ships that use the bay and I wondered if I should be leaving a trail of breadcrumbs so I could find my way back. Once I finally found the office at the end of the maze I filled out the required paper work for entering the islands. Luckily, the question of pets on board didn't come up at this meeting, so Jack was safe for now. The rain had momentarily stopped, so I asked directions to the local market and off I went in search of fresh food.

After I left the industrial area, I followed a well worn path through several vacant lots on my way to the grocery store that was about 6 blocks away. These vacant lots were absolutely amazing to me because they were filled with plant life unlike anything I'd ever seen. The lots at home would have some tall grass and Scotch Broom, but these were virtual jungles with broad leafed plants six to ten feet high. Colorful, exotic flowers and palm trees filled the open expanses. I thought that if the vacant lots were this fascinating, I couldn't wait to see a real jungle. Then the rain started up again, bringing me back to reality.

I returned to the boat with my bags full of fresh fruits and vegetables and my stomach full thanks to the great greasy hamburger stand I'd found on my journey. I began to think maybe Hilo wasn't so bad after all. But then the rain started pounding even harder than before. During my time in Hilo, I became good friends with Terry and his family on *Cetus*. Their daughter, Carly, was instrumental in helping to keep Jack on board and entertained. Carly was the cutest little six-year-old with wildly curly white blonde hair, impish grin and unlimited energy.

While Heidi and Carly would be busy each day with home school, Terry and I would help each other work on the never ending list of boat projects each of us seemed to have. When he wasn't out on an extended fishing trip, Ben was also a frequent visitor to the boat. His local knowledge was invaluable in helping us locate hard to find parts for our projects, because this was Terry's first visit to Hilo as well.

I did look into flying Jack back to Sheryl in San Francisco, but I found out I would have to produce quarantine papers and it was just too risky. After all, I still didn't know which of us would be destroyed if we were caught messing with the rules. I figured by the time I reached Honolulu I would have a plan to get my hitchhiker back home.

The *Cetus* crew was getting ready to leave. The Sparling's

were anxious to get to the dry side of the island and see what paradise really looked like. With their impending departure I began to get the itch to move on, as well. This itch was intensified by the rather soggy life I was leading. Due to the daily, nearly constant, rain showers, I spent a lot of time closed up in the boat. And it wasn't just wet, like I was used to back home, but it was hot and humid, to boot. It was time to go. So much for the rule of staying somewhere as long as you'd traveled to get there.

My next destination was Kealakekua Bay on the Kona (read DRY) side of the island. This is where the legendary Capt. Cook met his demise. James Cook was considered the greatest navigator of his time and he came to Kealakekua Bay after discovering Australia. Upon his first arrival, he was received as a God, but returning to the same spot a few weeks later he was killed on shore over a misunderstanding with those same natives. Hopefully things would go better for me. I just had to make about a 24 hour trip, first traveling down this side of the Big Island of Hawaii then up the other side. After the long passage I'd just been through, this should be a piece of cake.

Boisterous trade winds greeted *Rick's Place* as we left Hilo. Unfortunately it took some time to gather my sea legs after being in port for two weeks. I found myself feeling a bit queasy once again. I was several miles offshore and the boat was flying with a double reefed main and a working jib. Shortly after sunset I saw a sight that I'll never forget. Mauna Loa Volcano was in the midst of an eruption, and though I couldn't see the volcano's crater in the darkness, I could see the red glow of the hot lava as it was being blown hundreds of feet into the sky by some unseen force and then the river of molten rock meandered down to the islands shore. From my position I could just make out the steam plumes that signaled the lava's plunge into the ocean. It was a spectacular sight and watching this amazing phenomenon helped take my mind off my mal de mar. I knew there would be no napping on this passage since I was so close to land and it was important I stay alert.

Around midnight I finally rounded the most Southern Tip of the United States, which also happened to be the southern tip of The Big Island of Hawaii. I then turned north heading up the Kona coast, leaving the choppy seas and strong winds behind me; I was gliding over smooth water. It was a whole different world on the western side of the island.

The contrast between the two sides of this island was eye opening. Gone was the lush green vegetation packed on every square foot of earth on the rainy side and replaced with a much drier environment with tall, dried grassy fields and palm trees. With binoculars, I could see the beautiful white sand beaches I'd been searching for. On the Hilo side there was only black sand beaches due to the volcanic activity. I could also see small coffee plantations scattered on the hillsides as I sailed closer. Sport fishing boats were now a common sight. They'd take their load of tourists out to sea several miles to fish for Mahi Mahi, Wahoo and Sailfish.

By midmorning the anchor was down and Spinner dolphin were performing their aerial acrobatics nearby. I was so enthralled with the beautiful clear water (I could clearly see my anchor chain at 35 feet!) and the graceful dolphin playing so close, that I grabbed my dive mask and jumped over the side. In the nano second before hitting the water, it dawned on me that I had failed to lower the boarding ladder. I put it out of my mind though, as I floated around the boat in the warm water surrounded by the squeaks and whistles of the leaping mammals nearby. When I'd swim under water the dolphin would glide past me. Although they seemed to be as curious about me as I was about them, they always stayed just out of arms reach. After about 10 minutes the dolphin left the anchorage and my thoughts returned to the problem at hand: getting back on board the damn boat.

Trying to climb the anchor chain was a joke. I knew I'd seen it done in the movies, but I couldn't get even half way out of the water. Swimming to the stern I saw the paddle to the wind vane was still down. I knew it was either climb back up on this or suffer prune skin for a very long time. After the second try my foot found a bit of a niche and I was able to pull myself up and flop over the top of the wind vane. Then the quiet anchorage was punctuated with blood curdling screams: even Jack came out to see what was going on. It was just me. I'd pinched and lacerated a good portion of my groin climbing over the gears, pulleys and hose clamps on my way back on to the boat. The salt water dripping into my injuries was excruciating. I wouldn't forget to put that boarding ladder out again. Jack, as usual, was of little consolation to me.

After several days at anchor I realized there were two things I could always set my watch by while anchored in Kealakekua Bay: 1.The dolphin coming into the anchorage in the morning and 2. The tourist boats from hotels in a nearby bay. These boats were loaded with gaggles of swimmers anxious to snorkel with dolphin in one of the most beautiful bays in The Islands. I was able to enjoy snorkeling near Cooks monument and with the dolphin any time I wished, and these people were paying about $40 a head for a short trip there. I figured I saved myself about $800 going there on my own boat. All I had to do was build a boat, cross the Pacific, outrun a hurricane and not run aground going in to Hilo. Pretty good deal, huh?

Another great thing that came out of my stay in Kealakekua was the creation of Kealakekua Bay Punch. When a few other boats came into the anchorage one day, an impromptu potluck was soon in the plans. This seems to happen anytime two or more cruising boats find themselves in the same anchorage. As usual, I was at a loss as to what I could bring since my culinary skills aren't the best. Then I remembered a bottle of rum I had stashed away for just this sort of celebration; actually for any sort of celebration. I dug through the cupboards for something to mix with it and I found a jar of Tang and I thought, "Well, it can go to the moon, it can certainly go to a potluck!" So I mixed up the Tang, added some rum and squeezed a couple limes into the mix and voila! My meager contribution was the hit of the party. Of course, it's not all that hard to be a hit when you bring the alcoholic libations.

After a week I was ready to move on. Having studied the cruising guide books, it seemed the Big Island was somewhat limited with regards to protected bays. Maui seemed the place you'd want to be, so I loaded up the boat to head to...Lahina. Actually, I would have to head further up the Kona coast before crossing to the other islands to take advantage of the trade winds. I would go up to Kawaihae and then cross the Alenuihaha Channel to Maui. The distance between the islands was short, a mere 50 miles, but the tall mountains on both islands created a venturi effect. High school physics reminds us that a venturi effect is caused by the squeezing of airflow which increases the speed and density of said air. The advice from the locals is to listen to the weather reports and when the trade winds are predicted to lighten up, leave immediately that night.

Motoring up the Kona coast to Kawaihae I didn't give much thought to the upcoming channel crossing. After all, I had just crossed the Pacific Ocean. How bad could these 50 miles be?

Once anchored in Kawaihae, I rowed to shore to explore the town. Kawaihae was a lovely little town that didn't seem to be a tourist stop. The town was clean with one supermarket, one laundromat and four bars; like I said; a perfect town. There was a small crowded marina that held the many tourist fishing boats I'd been seeing along this side of the island. These boats would speed down the coast to the large hotels about 10 miles to the south, pick up the fishermen, fish all day then return to Kawaihae by nightfall with the tourist's trophy fish. The balance of the small bay was crowded with sailboats. Some were cruising boats waiting for weather so they could continue on to other destinations, but many were decrepit, derelict boats that hadn't been touched in years.

I enjoyed getting together regularly with other cruisers for gab fests at a great little Mexican place nearby; Tres Amigos. We wiled away the time trying to one up each other's sea tales over cold beers. This was how I spent my time instead of stowing loose items and making sure my tray table was in its upright and secure position, so to speak. Several days later the weather word came down, calling for diminished trade winds, hence less venturi effect, less wind, less waves on the seas and thus a good crossing.

I scrambled during the remaining day light hours making ready, or so I thought. I pulled up anchor at the same time the sun was dipping below the horizon, which kinda gave me the creeps. Having spent so many nights at sea didn't prepare me for actually leaving at night. It just didn't seem right. The wind was 10-15 knots on the beam and the rapidly fading light permitted me my last glance at the Big Island.

Ahead, about a mile out, I could see the clear division between calm blue sea and white frothy tormented water beyond. Looking back, the harbor entrance was already indistinguishable. Not wanting a repeat of the Hilo Folly, I chose to keep going and not attempt to enter another harbor in the dark. For about an hour I meandered in the twilight zone between calm water and wild waves. I kept the boat speed down, hoping things would some how change by the time the bow crossed over to white water.

Pandemonium is one way to describe what happened next. Scared breathless is another. Terrifying, gut wrenching; take your pick. The boat immediately went on its side and the water was cascading down the decks. Even with the trades blowing somewhat less, the wind was still 25 knots through here. The seas were steep and extremely choppy. It was a hell of a bumpy ride. But the one thing that was most disconcerting about this crossing was the fog like mist. The visibility, if you could call it that, was just a few feet past the bow!

The boat was heeled, so the rail was in the water, we were doing 6 knots, but it felt like three times that speed. The sensation was like careening towards a concrete wall that I never quite reached. Due to the strong wind, I chose not to engage the self steering, which meant I would steer by hand for the entire crossing, or at least till things settled down a bit. The sound of crashing books, cans and whatever else was a noisy reminder that I should have stowed more and partied less before my departure from Kawaihae. My imagination was running wild and my eyes were sore from the strain of trying to pick out anything that might impede my progress, such as a freighter, logs, half submerged containers, or other small boats.

I kept conjuring up all of these potential disasters looming in the thick mist. I even thought I was hearing voices. It reminded me a bit of the feeling I had watching the old movie "The Fog". What dangers were out there that I just couldn't see?

Rick's Place was swallowed up in an envelope of dark mist and at times heavy rain and the daunting sea. For the first time since leaving Washington, I was very concerned that the boat would be lost without a trace. The hand steering forced me to concentrate on the task at hand, so to speak. If I got the wind on the wrong side of the sails, or back winded, through a mental lapse, something would surely get destroyed. Back winding causes the boom to crash uncontrolled to the other side of the boat, with such force that it could cause severe damage to the boom or sail or both.

The minutes crept by with an agonizing slowness. My hands were fatigued from administering a death grip on the tiller handle and bracing my legs across the cockpit for stability was causing my old back strain problem to resurface along with some painful leg cramps, as well. Four hours into the channel crossing (or butt kicking), nature was calling, in fact screaming, for me to take care of bladder business. Reluctantly I hooked up the wind vane, while sending up a prayer that it wouldn't get over powered leading to an accidental jibe. I'd considered relieving myself over the side, but I'd heard too many stories of boat drowning victims being found with their flies down, having been swept off the boat doing just what I had in mind.

To protect my night vision, the only lights I have on at night are the navigation lights at the top of the mast. To find my way around when going below, I use a flashlight with a red lens (accomplished with a little red fingernail polish. An idea I picked up from a helpful sailing magazine). The red beam of light cutting through the darkness of the interior revealed a sight that seemed straight from hell. The only thing missing was a guy with a pitchfork and a pointy tail.

In addition to the disarray of books and other items that had emptied out of one of the lockers, there was lots of water sloshing around. "Another fine mess you've got us in", I said to myself. Luckily it wasn't coming from some leak in the boat, but rather from one of the ports that hadn't been dogged down tight enough, basically a leaky window. I tightened the port down completely, but left the rest of the mess, knowing things would need to calm down a bit before I could even think about cleaning up down there. Checking on the cat, I found him in his usual spot in the v-berth, wedged between the sail bags. For the first time since he came aboard, I could tell Jack was having about as much fun as I was.

I also checked the chart and made a quick plot of my current position. The good news was the crossing was going faster than anticipated, but the bad news was that the crossing was going faster than anticipated. What made this bad was that near the end of the passage I would have to cross between two islands, Kaho'olawe and Molokini, only a couple miles apart, one of which is uninhabited and would be totally unlit. For safety and sanity's sake, I wanted to traverse these waters during daylight, but my current speed would place me there well before dawn.

I needed to slow the boat down a bit, but if I slowed it too much the ride would get worse and control would be difficult. I took my chances and dropped the main sail. I didn't want to risk going up front to take down the jib in these seas. It worked well and I still had good control. I was still moving along quite smartly with just the small working jib out. During the rest of the night and into the early morning hours, I strained to see any change that would indicate the coming dawn. I was in a race with the sun, one which I really wanted to lose. Passing between the two islands before sunrise would just be too much strain on my already stressed out nerves. I kept a constant plot on my chart and knew the islands would be close before daybreak. This was also showing me, as was my course over ground on the GPS compared to my compass course, that the strong current through this area was making me travel nearly sideways, drawing me closer to the rocky shores of Kaho'olawe than I cared to be. I kept adjusting my course to take this current into account and avoid another boat destroying bullet, but not being able to see the island really had me spooked. At least there was a big light on Molokini, so I had some point of reference. The closer I got to Lahina, the smoother the seas got as I was now on the lee side of Maui. So the conditions improved and the sun came up at about the same time. Just as I had experienced while sailing around the Big Island, the morning brought on a whole different world than the terrifying night.

This time I didn't have to worry about making a channel entrance and the guide books added a new phrase to my vocabulary: Open Roadstead Anchorage. Loosely translated this means that you just anchor in some shallow water out in the ocean.

You are completely exposed to wind, waves, flotsam, Jetsam, and anything else Mother Nature decides to send your way. So I anchored in the roadstead off of Lahina, Maui. The wind would come up, the waves would come up: but I loved it.

After I spent the first day cleaning and drying the boat out, I discovered Lahina Town was a great place to hang out. Lahina still reflected its whaling town past. At the turn of the century the whaling ships that plied the waters, would stop in there to give the crew an opportunity to get to shore after their months at sea. Unfortunately, European disease came to shore with the sailors decimating the Hawaiian population.

Many of Lahina's original buildings have been restored and the town was a quaint touristy town, in many ways like Port Townsend back in Washington. Nice restaurants and bars dotted the street and whale watching tours drew people from all over the world.

When I wasn't walking through town, I was in the warm turquoise waters just off the town where *Rick's Place* was anchored. That was where I first came face to face with a sea turtle! He swam gracefully by me while I was snorkeling; startling me at first because it was the first time I'd encountered something that large in the water, other than the dolphin. His shell looked to be nearly two feet across and his green eyes darted around, probably searching for his next meal.

Dolphin were around in abundance; their whistles and clicks constantly echoing through *Rick's Place*. One other sea creature that caught my attention in a not so pleasant way was the Portuguese Man O'War. The Man O'War is a jelly fish that has a very bad attitude. Traveling on the ocean currents, these guys can grow to be a foot in diameter, with tentacles that can be as long as thirty feet, packed with stinging venom used to ward off enemies. When these tentacles come in contact with human skin it can produce huge stinging welts and can even throw the unlucky victim into shock. The tentacles are nearly invisible as they float through the water, leaving little chance for avoidance.

There are a couple ways to relieve the pain once you are stung by one of these tentacles, the first being Adolph's Meat

Tenderizer. The second is to use uric acid, or more simply put, urine. You simply urinate on yourself, and the acid neutralizes the venom. Being that I was stung on my back when I came in contact with one, the peeing option didn't work for me, so I had to do my best with the meat tenderizer, but it had mediocre results. I suffered a burn like welt for over a week.

Eighteen other boats were in this roadstead and I was happy that *Cetus* was one of them. The majority of the boats were anchored closer to shore in about 25' of water and some of them were lucky enough to have secured one of the few treasured mooring buoys available. I had to put the anchor down in 50 feet of water because I didn't want to crowd into the pack. I always feel more comfortable with some distance between me and my neighboring boats.

Lahina had a small boat harbor, but it was filled with local fishing and tour boats, so very few transient boats were lucky enough to get a space in there. One of my favorite pastimes is walking around marinas and looking at different boats and different people. The optimum word here is "different". I could tell this marina would be good one for finding the unusual. Perusing the dock, I stopped to admire an older wooden ketch. It may have been 30 years old, but it was in beautiful, like-new condition. Suddenly, out of the companion way hatch, a woman appeared, then, without a sound, seemingly glided up to the bow of the boat. She was statuesque. She was wearing only a small bikini over her deeply tanned skin, and I mean deeply tanned. In fact, I think she'd been in the sun a bit too long because she was sporting some rather deep sun wrinkles, making it hard to pinpoint her age. She was probably younger than she appeared, but maybe not. Her boat was tied up with its bow about 6 feet off the dock with ¾ inch lines secured to the dock cleats. With the stealth of a ninja, she walked across the dock lines as if they were a tight rope! When she stepped from the rope to the dock we were suddenly face to face about a foot apart, and I noted that she was at least a good 3 inches taller than me. Placing her hands on her hips and tossing her long sun streaked blond hair back she announced in her thick French accent, "I am Françoise." I stared speechlessly at this French toasted Amazon. I couldn't think of a thing to say. She then informed me, "Zee vater, it ez too warm." My brain was pleading with my mouth to say something clever and I managed a witty, "Uh...." Nice job mouth. She then continued, "Zis ez hurricane weather. When the water is zis warm it brings the hurricanes." And with that she spun on her heel and strode away. I stood there rooted to the dock, unable to comprehend what just took place and unable to move. There was that "H" word again, the same one that had struck terror in me on my long passage to the islands. But what could she know? She doesn't look like a weather forecaster, at least not like any I'd ever seen before. "Too much sun on the brain, more than likely", I decided. No one else seems concerned about the water temperature or approaching hurricanes. Yeah, just the ravings of someone who doesn't like nice warm, really warm, seawater.

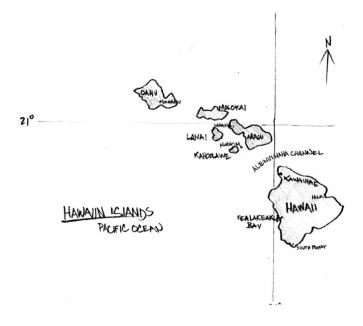

CHAPTER 7

Rick, Jack and Iniki

"And this too shall pass."
-Old Sailing Adage

Unbeknown to most people in the Hawaiian Islands, a major event was happening 400 miles to the east out in the warm ("it ez too warm") waters of the Pacific Ocean. This event, TS9, or tropical storm 9 would soon impact them greatly. Before long, by virtue of an increase in wind speed, the World Meteorological Society gave TS9 a name and proclaimed "Iniki" a category 1 hurricane as the wind speed was a modest 75 mph. During the next 24 hours, Iniki would blossom to a category 3 hurricane boasting wind speeds up to 130 mph. To me the difference between 75 mph and 130 mph is just splitting hairs. You're just as screwed no matter which one you're caught in.

The approaching storm was really not a surprise to me. Since leaving Washington I made a habit of listening to a weather forecast at least once a day on the high seas radio. This ritual was done whether I was sailing or at anchor. Plus I'd had the ominous warning from the beautiful French woman just days before. Iniki was on a collision course with the islands, but nothing was being said by the local news media. My guess was that because of the tourist industry, things like hurricanes and the black plague are down played and information is given out on a need to know basis. This is one of the reasons the local boaters call the weather service there "The Liar's Club".

I determined that if Iniki stayed on her present course, the roadstead would be a nasty place to be anchored. But where should I go? How do you out run or hide from a storm that could change direction at any time? So I cornered the harbor master in the small boat basin in Lahina. He laughed as I expressed my anxiety about the approaching storm, saying "It will never happen."

"The storm systems always veer away from the islands.

There's no need to worry," he added.

"But, what if?" I asked.

"In that case, we'll cram as many boats behind the breakwater as we can. But it won't come to that; trust me. The most we'll experience here is a bit of heavy rain," he assured me.

This conversation awakened the little voices that had been sleeping in the dark recesses of my brain. Walking away from his office I tried to convince myself that this local knew what he was talking about, and Francois had been wrong with her proclamation that "Iz hurricane weather."

Another matter, this one closer to the heart, involved Sheryl. Last week we had talked and made arrangements for her to spend some time with me in Maui. Being together in this tropical paradise would allow us to renew our friendship. Hopefully absence was making her heart grow fonder, plus, with any luck we could figure out a way to get Jack back to his home in California. This whole scenario was now in danger of coming undone. Sheryl's flight was scheduled to land about the same time as hurricane Iniki would come close to the islands. Timing is everything.

The monster storm was around 200 miles away and was starting to affect an area nearly twice that in diameter. Forecasters seemed equally divided on its future course. Some had it veering to the south, while others thought a brush with the islands was in store. That night, trying to sleep, my nerves felt raw. Would tomorrow bring Sheryl back into my life, or would nature conspire to keep her just out of my reach? I didn't need to wait until morning to find out. About 3:00 am. I was rudely awakened from my fitful sleep, as the boat rocked hard and tossed me off the settee I was laying on. The boom was creaking loudly as the boat rocked side to side and Jack was pacing around the cabin; not a good sign, I knew. I had learned on our voyage together that Jack had a sense about things especially bad weather. Roadstead anchorages are unprotected and can get a little rolly, but this was a different feel than I'd experience since I'd been here, so I thought I should check it out. Bracing myself as I worked my way through the darkness, I finally got to the hatch and opened it up to take a look. It took a minute for my eyes and my brain to correlate the scene in front of me. Six to ten foot rollers (waves that were not yet breaking) were marching through the anchorage toward shore. These hills of water had long periods of time between each peak. During my passage to Hawaii, when I was being threatened by an earlier hurricane, waves just like these had rocked my small boat. This was not a good sign.

Scanning the horizon, I could see the lights of about 6 large ships steaming out to the open water. The Navy was getting out of Dodge. They weren't taking a chance that Iniki would devastate the fleet in Pearl Harbor as the Japanese had done in 1942. Again, not a very comforting sign.

The lights from the small boat basin appeared clearly from about a mile away and I decided it was time to head in. At mornings first light I would haul anchor and haul ass to the protection of the breakwater. I turned on the VHF radio to try and pick up a current weather report, but was devastated by what I heard. It wasn't an official weather report, but rather a conversation between two other boats. "There are waves breaking at the entrance to the harbor," came a strained voice. "We were the last boat in before they closed it." So much for listening to the harbor master. Next time someone gives me that "trust me" line I'll immediately do the opposite.

Before I had a chance to feel sorry for myself, another voice came over the radio. The guy sounded very sleepy, or hung-over, or both. He explained he was a crew member on the 50' sailboat *Wolf* anchored about a mile and a half from me. He was wondering why he'd just gotten thrown out of his bunk. "What's goin' on?" he asked. An unidentified woman's voice came on and explained that the hurricane had changed course and was passing about 75 miles SW of Maui and was causing the unusually steep waves. "That's news to me," came the response from *Wolf* You're not the only one, I thought.

The good thing was that although the rocking and rolling was a bit uncomfortable, the boat, cat and I were not in any present danger. The wind was only blowing about 15-20 knots, almost normal tradewind conditions. I checked to make sure the dinghy was still securely tied to *Rick's Place*, and wished I'd taken the engine off earlier. I wouldn't be able to in these conditions. It would come in handy, though, because I planned to use it to set a second anchor when the sun came up. I already had a 35# plow anchor down and I was silently thanking Alien Allen for his good advice to get the biggest anchor my boat could carry and use all chain to connect it to the boat.

Dawn seemed to be coming a bit later due to the heavily overcast skies. When there was enough light to see, I knew going to shore would not be an option. The waves had now grown in size and were beginning to break farther off shore than normal. My 3 hp engine on the dinghy would not keep me ahead of the waves; I would be swamped trying to make it to shore. Jack and I were quickly running out of options.

Normally the waves would break right at the shoreline, in about 6 feet of water, but with the increased size, they were curling and crashing about 100 yards from the norm. Half of the anchored boats were now dangerously close to the breakers as these rollers were rapidly moving farther out. This in turn would put more vessels in danger of having the waves crash directly on to them. I got the second anchor all set to put out and went below to check out the weather information on the radio. The wind was now up to 25 knots and gusting to 35. Through the shrieking wind I heard a voice and then a knocking on the hull. "Who could be crazy enough to be out here?"

I stuck my head out the companion way and saw a 20 foot bright orange inflatable with a huge outboard engine bobbing beside *Rick's Place*. The lone occupant was a bushy bearded, wild haired individual who was yelling over the howl of the wind, "You want to go to shore?" I thought about it for about 5 seconds and responded with an excited "Hell yes! But can you get through these waves?"

"No sweat," was his simple reply. I was happy he didn't add "trust me."

I told him I needed to set a second anchor, so he motored around to the bow of the boat, took the hook from me and slowly motored off. When he was several hundred feet off the bow, he tossed the anchor and chain over the side. I pulled on the ¾ inch line that was connected to the chain and set the anchor in the soft sand. I wrapped the line around a cleat, then added some chafe protection and felt that the boat was reasonably secured for the present conditions. Hurrying down below, I grabbed a canvas bag and threw the boat papers, my passport and wallet inside. I closed all the sea cocks, made sure every hatch and port hole was tightly closed and then it hit me: Jack!! What should I do?

I thought that if something should happen to the boat as this storm passed through, I would feel pretty bad if my clandestine crewman was lost at sea. There were howls of protest as I roughly jammed him and his harness into the canvas bag. Zipping up the bag I knew Jack would be fine for awhile in his cozy confines. Handing the bag to the guy in the inflatable, I tried to time my jump between the two wildly pitching crafts. As I landed half in the boat and half in the water, my rescuer grabbed my collar and hauled me in.

He introduced himself as Doug and handed me a lifejacket to put on. Doug had already taken several people off anchored boats and really knew what he was doing. He shouted over the wind that the Coast Guard helicopter was on its way to evacuate everyone who was still on their boats. Being so close to the water, the waves looked absolutely monstrous. I took a short piece of rope and tied it to the handle of the canvas bag and the other end to my wrist just in case we should go for an unexpected swim on our way in. The beefy outboard roared to life as Doug yelled to me, "Hold on!" We quickly rode through the swells, going from peak to valley on a ride that would rival any roller coaster. We reached the area where the waves started breaking and Doug slowed the dinghy down, which put us in a trough behind the breakers. The wave in front of us pitched up, crested, and then broke in white water and foam frenzy. At that second, the motor again whined in protest as we shot through the foam and swirling water toward a boat ramp that looked like a good place to land.

Glancing behind me, it was clear what we were running from as the next wave was towering some 10 feet above our small boat. We raced to stay ahead of it, and I was unconsciously leaning forward trying to coax as much speed out of the craft as possible. The unstable wave crest cascaded down just a couple of boat lengths behind us and we were suddenly surrounded by a tremendous amount of boiling white madness. With this surge of water, the little orange inflatable was now traveling at break neck speed. Jack chose this time to poke his head out of a bit of unzipped bag and got clobbered with a gush of water. He moaned and retreated back into the relative safety of the bag. Jack liked being on the sea, he didn't enjoy being in it.

Doug cut the motor as we closed in on the boat ramp. We surfed up the ramp and when the water receded we were there high and dry! We jumped out and drug the boat as far up on the shore as we could. Doug thought it was getting too hairy out there to continue taking people off boats. I thanked my rescuer profusely and wished him luck because his boat was out there riding out the storm, as well.

Pushing my way through the gathering crowd, I ran up to the telephone booth on the road. I anxiously dialed Sheryl's telephone number knowing if she answered things weren't good because she should be in the air by now. As the phone began to ring I was silently hoping there would be no answer. Ring.... (Don't pick up!), ring......(Please, don't pick up), ring.....(She must be on her way!), ring...... "Hello?" Damn, my heart sank.

"Hi Sheryl, it's Rick."

"Rick, are you all right? The news says the hurricane is right over the islands!"

"Jack and I are fine. We're on shore and right now the boat seems OK, too."

"Rick, the airlines have cancelled all flights to Hawaii until further notice. I won't be visiting you after all," she said with disappointment in her voice. I was just trying to come up with something clever to say in an attempt to hide my own disappointment, when a collective gasp came from the crowd gathered at the boat ramp. "Hey, I'll call you after this thing settles down a bit," I replied hurriedly. But before she could answer the phone line went dead. "Miserable, stinking, rotten storm," I mumbled to no one in particular.

94

A surreal scene greeted me when I returned to the water's edge. Abut 100 yards off shore, a wave, bigger than the others, came crashing down directly on an anchored 40' catamaran. When it receded, pieces of wood, a few cushions and a sail were all that remained of someone's home. Of course, the obvious question of whether the boat was occupied was quickly answered by the emotional breakdown of a nearby couple. Luckily, Doug had taken the husband and wife off earlier in the morning. There was another multi-hull moored near where the catamaran had been and it, too, was in dire straights. The 35' boat would ride up on the face of the wave and its deck would be nearly vertical before the boat was snapped back to horizontal by its anchor and chain.

Luckily no one was on board this doomed vessel, either. A wave, one bigger than its predecessor, picked up the boat, and as it went vertical, the bow was ripped off! The hulls went past the point of no return and seemed to hang in midair. As the wave crested and broke, it flipped the boat upside down and delivered a knock out blow. When the water flattened out, the only visible sign that the boat had even been anchored at that spot was a 6 foot section of the bow that was still tied to the mooring buoy. It was a gut wrenching sight.

A deep, resonating thunk, thunk, thunk announced the arrival of the Coast Guard helicopter. With the wind now at a steady 45 knots, the pilot had his hands full trying to hover. Lowering the rescue basket from 75 feet above the water, the rescuers began taking the remaining occupants off the vessels closest to the raging surf. The skill of the pilots was nothing short of superhuman. The wind was buffeting the aircraft side to side as well as up and down.

One occupied boat was a problem for the rescuers. The lone crew member refused to abandon his ship. It was almost amusing to watch this war of wills as the helicopter pilot would repeatedly lower the basket and bump the cabin top as gently as if he were knocking on a door. But the guy in the boat, just wouldn't answer. He'd rather take his chances with the hurricane than take a ride on a gyrating rescue basket 75 feet into the air, and I couldn't blame him a bit. Within an hour, everyone else had been taken safely to shore and deposited in a make-shift landing zone at a nearby ball field.

While the helicopter drama was being played out, amongst the destruction and tremendous loss, a lighter moment took place as a truck with surfboards fastened on racks skidded to a stop nearby. Six young men, several looking like locals, piled out and began readying themselves for the awesome waves. They were able to run down a nearby wharf that extended about 400' out into the water. Climbing down a ladder, they were soon surfing in the midst of boat cushions, sails, coolers and all the other junk floating from the destroyed boats. The waves had increased in size and intensity making it seem like pure suicide to be surfing. Another boat, this time a mono hull, broke from its mooring and drifted into the surf line and was immediately crushed. This was apparently the sign the intrepid adventurers needed to get them out of the water. As I was walking near their truck, a familiar voice called out, "Hey, Rick dude." When I turned I was astonished to see Sparky, the crew I left in San Francisco!

"What the hell you doing here?" I inquired while shaking his hand.

"I've been on Maui about a month living with friends and surfing," was his reply.

Sparky's friends were urging him to get in the truck. They were heading to better surf near the Hilton Hotel. I guess there were too many boat parts in the water here. We promised to get together for beers, and then he was gone with a wave. As their van weaved through the debris that covered the road, the thought hit me that Sparky must have flown over and I wondered how that went. I suspect he must have indulged in some form of self medication so he wouldn't realize he was out of sight of land or did he just keep the window shade closed?

This brief encounter made me realize I was feeling a bit lonely, somewhat isolated and really scared. All the while *Rick's Place* rode the waves, disappearing in the troughs except for the top of the mast, and then reappearing triumphantly on the next crest. So far the dinghy was still hanging on behind her.

While I was feeling self pity, Jack was feeling really pissed.

He had been in his canvas travel bag for over an hour, and I could tell by his hollering and fidgeting that it was time to let the cat out of the bag. Searching around, I found some protection from the wind and blowing sand near a group of condominiums. A small brick wall provided what appeared to be a safe place to let Jack cat stretch his kitty legs. Placing the harness on the terrified cat was no fun. Hooking up the short piece of rope to the harness, I coaxed him out of the open bag. His urges finally got the better of him and he came out, only to immediately lie down and start howling. As we sat there together, amongst the on going mayhem, I couldn't help but think what an absurd situation this was. This cat really wanted to take care of nature's calling, but wanted a toilet to do it on! While trying to calm Jack down I felt a presence behind me. "Is that your cat?" Came a husky female voice. Oh oh, I thought. We're busted and we'll both end up in jail, or worse.

I looked up and saw a cute, smiling, 40ish woman with short brown hair and glasses. She was holding a bag of groceries in one arm and was reaching down with her other hand to scratch Jack behind the ears. "Yeah, he's not very happy with his surroundings," I said, trying to smile.

"You're not off one of those yachts, are you?" she queried.

Here it comes, she's going to turn me in to the cat patrol and that will spell curtains for us. So without much thought I blurted out, "I'm just visiting!"

"Poor thing," she said looking at the ill tempered cat. Letting my guard down I explained that he was out of his element, "He's trained to use a toilet and doesn't know what to do without it."

"You're kidding me, right?" she said with a laugh. "No Ma'm," I replied.

"I'm Liz. My husband and I live in this condo complex," Come on up and get out of the weather. Our power's out, but it's warm and dry. Plus we have a toilet," she said with a grin. Relieved that she wasn't here to arrest me I introduced myself, and Jack. Without hesitating, I crammed him back into the canvas bag, thus sustaining another series of scratches on my hand and arm.

Entering the condo, all the sounds and feelings of havoc

from the storm suddenly stopped. It was so quiet. I just stood rooted in the entryway thoroughly enjoying the absence of the outside stimuli. My trance was broken by Liz yelling out, "Tom, I brought home another stray cat!" Tom, her husband, was nowhere in sight. "Hon, you hear me?" Suddenly a CD player came on and I immediately recognized the song "Trying to Reason with Hurricane Season" by Jimmy Buffet. "Very funny, Tom," Liz called out. "Hey, get out here. We have guests."

Her husband appeared from an adjoining room. He was about 6'2, a full foot taller than his petite wife. He had a warm smile and gentle lines around his eyes that showed he smiled a lot. He was sporting a University of Oregon T-shirt and looked at me a bit puzzled and said, "He doesn't look like a cat."

"Rick is off one of the boats out there. The cat's in the bag and he needs a toilet." When Tom started to direct me to the bathroom thinking I was the one in need, Liz pointed out, "Rick doesn't need the bathroom. The cat does." More confusion showed on Tom's face and slight exasperation was showing on Liz's. Jack's patience was clearly running out, as evidenced by the moving canvas bag.

"Rick, just take Jack down to the bathroom and I'll bring Einstein up to speed."

After making sure the lid was up and the seat was down, I left Jack in the bathroom to do his duty, so to speak. Wandering back to the living room, I was inundated with questions from Tom and Liz.

"Did you lose your boat in the storm?"

"Where are you from?"

"Are you alone?"

I was anxious to get outside to check on *Rick's Place* and determine if I had indeed, lost my boat in the storm, so I answered their questions without much detail. I suppose under the circumstances I should have been more polite. After all these folks had brought me in out of the storm and had given bathroom privileges to Jack, but all I could think of was my home being smashed to pieces by the hurricane.

I asked if they would mind if the cat stayed in their

bathroom for a while and Liz was enthusiastic about having cat company. They made me promise that I would spend the night at the condo and I suspect that may have been because they were afraid I wouldn't come back for Jack cat. So I went back out into the maelstrom that was called Iniki. The wind was about 50 knots, but it was now blowing from the opposite direction. It was still raining, but not as hard as before. I quickly located *Rick's Place*. At first it appeared the boat had dragged anchor, but then I realized it was just because the wind had changed direction by 180° so it was just riding in a different position. That was a relief. But a quick count revealed that two more boats were missing from the anchored group. The frontage road that runs along the water's edge was closed due to the amount of debris from a combination of boat parts and pieces mixed with fallen palm trees. I found a rock to sit on because it was just too damn hard to stand up.

Night was falling and everything I owned was bobbing up and down in the hurricane's swell. As I watched, it became very dark very quickly due to the power outage in the area. *Rick's Place* was disappearing in the gloom of the night. I strained to see any hint of how she was holding out there, but it was futile and just caused me a bad headache.

I wandered back up to the condo, not knowing if I'd have a boat in the morning to continue my adventure, or if it would all come to a crashing end. As I climbed the stairs I said a little prayer to Moe, Larry & Curley to protect *Rick's Place*. Tom opened the door and I saw Jack curled up in Liz's lap. He's such a suck up! Liz had already fed and brushed him, more pampering than he'd had in a long time. Tom had just made up the couch for me to sleep on and had begun mixing up some drinks. Liz was curious about how I happened to be here during the hurricane, so I did a brief recap of my life:

> Born to a Humphrey Bogart fan.
> Plundered and pillaged as a kid.
> Learned to sail and swim at the same time.
> Put life savings into a semi-completed dream boat/nightmare.

Lost job due to Great Genitalia/Vegetable Scandal.
Got a new job that paid a few cents more than it cost to work there.
Taught a local boy to talk like a longshoreman.
Became King of the Quarter while living at the dock.
Took cold showers and paid for the privilege to do so.
Met an alien and a surfer (who the alien had probably experimented on).
Sailed down the coast and left a surfer in San Francisco.
Met a girl and a cat.
Left the girl and took the cat to Hawaii.
Got help coming in to Hilo that was beyond the call of duty.
Learned what it's like to be in a hurricane.

"So that about sums up all the bizarre seemingly unrelated events that through the Chaos Theory, you know the one that says something about a butterflies wings in South America fluttering and resulting in a wind storm in Kansas, brought me to this place and time," I said in conclusion.

"That's one wild story. Do you really hear the Three Stooges talking to you?" was Liz's reaction and Tom was nodding in agreement.

After finishing Tom's great Margarita and my long story, I was suddenly very tired. The stress and lack of sleep of the last few days hit me like a brick wall.

The next thing I knew, my eyes popped open and it was nearly sunrise. I had slept soundly through the night. I threw on my T-shirt and ran down the stairs outside. My heart was pounding, my stomach was in a knot and I was afraid to look. What would I find? Will there be pieces of my boat washed up on shore with the rest of the rubble? Will there be no trace of my boat, or will it have drifted out to sea with its anchor dragging through the water as the boat *Wolf* had done?

CHAPTER 8

Return to the Sea

"If you haven't been aground,
you haven't been around..."

-Unknown

At the Lahina Roadstead, only 8 of the original 16 boats that were anchored there prior to the hurricane remained. Fortunately for me, *Rick's Place* was one of the survivors. *Wolf* was blown out to sea, but was recovered a day later with a very frightened crew member on board. *Cetus*, which had been anchored near *Rick's Place* before the storm, had nestled herself into a small protected harbor on the nearby island of Lanai and, thankfully, had also come through unscathed.

Reports said Iniki had sustained winds of 130 mph with gusts to 145 mph. Eight thousand people lost their homes, five people (including 2 surfers) lost their lives. The damage from Iniki was being estimated at 1.8 billion dollars with the majority of the Hurricane's destruction centered on the Island of Kauai; where the fast moving storm suddenly slowed and decided to spend some time.

After I saw that *Rick's Place* had survived the hurricane, I went back up to the condo and pried Jack out of Liz's lap as I thanked her and Tom for their hospitality.

When Jack and I arrived at the boat launch, we bummed a ride out to the boat. Stepping aboard *Rick's Place*, it was quite shocking to see how much dust and wind blown dirt had found its way on the decks and even down below. The halyards had taken on the reddish hue of the hills of Lanai, some 15 miles away. Other than being dirty, the boat was in great shape. Even the dinghy and engine were still attached and floating quietly off the stern! I was so relieved and I thanked The Stooges for watching over my little home.

The weather had turned quickly back to the beautiful sunny days with ten knot trade winds keeping the temperature on Maui very comfortable. Two days after the hurricane shook up our little world I sat in the cockpit thinking about it, and realized how stressful the days had become for me. The only time I really forget about the weather or boat repairs or my stowaway cat is when I am snorkeling. That's why I started spending so much time in the water.

I was beginning to question if I wanted to keep doing this. I never imagined I would be on edge so much of the time. I found myself listening to weather reports three times a day, for fear I'd get caught off guard by some incoming storm. I also felt like I had to spend way too much time fixing things on *Rick's Place*. There wasn't anything major to repair but I just felt like it was all work and no play and found it very annoying.

Suddenly I was pulled out of my deep, morose thoughts by a big splash right next to my anchored boat. There, to my delight, was a group of ten to twelve Spinner dolphin frolicking all around *Rick's Place*! They'd dive down deep into the sea and then shoot straight up about 10 feet into the air. They played so close that it seemed they were going to jump right on to the deck, just like a flying fish. I think about an hour went by as they put on that amazing show but suddenly they started drifting further away from me and their whistles and clicks receded until I once again sat in silence.

Then a comforting warmth spread through me and a big smile enveloped my face. The Spinner dolphin answered the questions I'd been pondering and the answer was, yes, I will go on, because no matter what the hardships, moments like that make it all worth while.

The next couple of weeks since my epiphany with the dolphin went quickly with a mix of boat projects, swapping stories with other cruisers and just enjoying the beauty of the world around me. One of those boat projects was a real problem, however. I had to tear the toilet apart because something was blocking the outlet hose, which renders the head inoperable. "Damn it, "I said under my breath to no one in particular. So, that gorgeous day, instead of snorkeling with friends, I had to work on the worst boat repair possible. Jack watched my contortions with mild curiosity. I knew the cat was somehow involved with the toilet's dysfunction, but I just didn't know how.

The longer I worked on the malfunctioning appliance, the more nervous the cat seemed to get. I'm sure Jack was afraid I wouldn't get his toilet operational before it was time for him to go. To work on the head, I would have to twist into what I call "The Pretzel", trying to reach some almost unreachable nuts and bolts. The cat, naturally, picked that time to cozy up to my face. Not wanting to lose my grip on the nut, I had to tolerate the cat rubbing up against my face which was making me want to sneeze. Finally I got the offending nut free, uncoiled myself and shooed Jack away. I placed the toilet out in the cockpit to gain some working room in the cramped quarters.

Looking over the disconnected hoses that remained, I finally found the cause of the blockage: The catnip filled toy that Liz had given Jack was lodged solidly in the outlet hose! So it was Jack after all!

I scurried up the companionway to make quick disposal of the prize plug, and stopped dead in my tracks when I reached the cockpit. The cat was now sitting on the toilet, in the cockpit, answering natures call, apparently for the second time!

"You couldn't have waited another fifteen minutes until I had the toilet hooked back up, could you?" I bellowed at the cat. He neither understood, nor cared and just completed his business, scratched and went on his way. But he wasn't finished punishing me just yet.

As I was busy cleaning up the mess outside, I heard the sounds of screws, springs and other parts, associated with the toilet, tinkling as they hit the floor downstairs. Dropping what I was doing, I ran below and there, to my horror, was Jack playfully pawing at a small pile of parts I had left sitting near the sink. After a quick inventory, it was apparent that some of the tiny hardware was gone. Scanning the floor, I found some of the pieces, but, unfortunately, a few of the screws and one very important spring had disappeared down the sink drain.

Now I'm going to have to locate the rebuild kit I purchased and stowed away back in Washington. This was one of those times I really regret not taking the time to make an inventory list of where I stashed things.

"Damn, damn, damn!!" I lamented, as I tore the boat completely apart, looking for the parts I needed. It was getting late in the day and I desperately wanted to get this project done before nightfall. "I've got to get this done soon! Today! Before I get any older; before I need to use the toilet myself."

Two hours and thirteen minutes later I found the parts. Yeh, I kept track of the time. The whole interior was now littered with boat parts, food, cans, nearly everything that was stowed in the cabinets and settees. Then I finally got back to the task that I started before Jack decided to help me out. I noticed it smelled terrible out in the cockpit, thanks to Jack's indiscretion and the tropical heat. Finally, after 3 screws, 1 nut, a really important spring, and most of the daylight hours, I finished the task of getting the head operational. I'd originally estimated this project to take me an hour at most to complete, but I should have realized that there are no one hour projects on a cruising boat. So much for the lazy days of cruising in paradise!

The head was working fine and I'd completed all the little projects on my current "to do" list. I felt good and decided it was time to continue on, so three weeks after the hurricane, we were off to the nearby island of Lanai. I'd heard a lot about Lanai from the *Cetus* crew when I talked to them on the VHF radio a week before as they headed on to Honolulu. The family had really enjoyed their stay on the lovely little island, despite the ugly hurricane that had bludgeoned it.

I anchored out in the small bay on the lee side of the island. There's a dock at the head of the bay, but it was full, mostly with local fishing boats. At least there was a good place to tie the dinghy when I got to shore.

Lanai was simply beautiful. The only building disrupting the landscape as I looked from the boat was a small cinderblock structure just up from the rocky beach and near the dock. It was the harbormaster's office. Beyond that are rolling hills, and a forest of palm trees: quite the contrast to Maui's beaches which are lined with large hotels and condominiums.

I rowed the dinghy in, because I didn't want to use the

outboard and disturb the quiet beauty. Then I just stood on shore looking all around. Gazing back across the water to Maui, where I had been anchored just hours before, I saw the familiar bellows of grey white smoke from the huge, controlled fires on the sugar plantations. The plantation operators burn down the old dry stalks in order to make room for the new plantings. It was much nicer to be viewing it from this distance, because I wouldn't end up with the layer of ash on the boat as I did while anchored in the Lahina Roadstead.

I walked along the dirt road that led to the larger bay on the other side of the island and it was a delight to my senses. There was a variety of flowering tropical plants all brightly colored with powerful scents. The area was striking with the soil having a distinct rusty red hue, a characteristic I became familiar with when Iniki sent a coating of it to *Rick's Place* just a few weeks ago.

Emerging from the small jungle of palm trees, I was greeted by the roar of crashing waves on a beautiful white sand beach. It is amazing how drastically different the two sides of the island are, even though there is only a twenty minute walk between them. While *Rick's Place* was anchored in a quite little bay on one side, the other side is bombarded by the large ocean swell that marches unimpeded to shore and crashes in a brilliant sparkling spray.

And there were people! I saw sunbathers, kids building sand castles and others playing in the surf. When I walked closer to the water I spotted a large resort a short distance away. That explained all the vacationers. It didn't look like the towering hotels on Maui, as its buildings were only a few stories high, and it is spread out over the hillside overlooking the bay. I found it very intriguing and couldn't wait to hike up there and check it out.

As I wandered on to the resort grounds I realized it was unlike anywhere I'd ever stayed in my life. There were two large swimming pools and one even has a swim up bar with seats just below water level with a thatched roof over the counter area. Two rather sun burned tourists were sitting at the bar drinking fancy fruity drinks as I walked by. Beyond the pools there was a huge building and I wanted, no, I needed, to see what was beyond those large, ornate double doors. I tentatively opened one and when I entered, it was immediately clear that this resort was for the rich and famous. The long hallway was lined with paintings, which to my untrained eye, appeared to be old masters. As I walked along the plush carpet, a comfortable coolness enveloped my body and I enjoyed the simple luxury of air conditioning after the hot walk up the hill. Passing a full length mirror, I caught a glimpse of myself and realized that my faded shorts and t-shirt weren't exactly the "resort wear" I'd seen on some of the guests.

I came to a door with a gold plaque on it that said "Library." I just knew that any second, my presence in this exclusive hotel would be detected and they'd throw me out, but a little voice in my head told me to take a peek at the Library before I was banished. So, I opened the door as casually as if I owned the place and a gentleman sitting at a desk near the door looked up, smiled and said, "Hello, my name is Reginald, if I can be of any help, please don't hesitate to ask."

"Thanks," I replied as I glanced around the elegant room, richly decorated like a study in an old mansion.

"Newspapers and a selection of periodicals are on that shelf, and if you're interested I can have any of the reading materials sent to your room," Reginald went on.

"That won't be necessary; I'll just read them here." I responded, thoroughly delighted to be allowed to sit in this luxurious space and read. Being an avid reader, this appeared to be a little piece of heaven, so I smiled at Reginald and found a comfortable chair near the floor to ceiling window over looking the resort and the ocean beyond. I spent the afternoon catching up on world events, finding out which celebrities are doing what to whom and just plain relaxing.

Two hours flew by with my catching up on the news and making small talk with my new pal, Reggie, but I realized I'd better get back to check on my boat. As I made my way to the door, Reginald said, "Have a pleasant afternoon, sir."

"Thank you, Reginald, I'll see you tomorrow," I respond as I closed the door behind me.

Stepping out of the building, the hot humid air hit me like a slap in the face, because I'd gotten used to the comfortable air conditioning in the Library. Back on the beach I took a quick dip in the ocean to cool off before heading down the dusty red road back to *Rick's Place.*

The next day I returned to the comfort of the library and my new friend Reginald, and it became a daily ritual for me on my stay in Lanai. I'd also snorkel every day, the waters weren't as clear as they had been in Maui, but I still enjoyed my time in the water. The five days I spent in Lanai were wonderful and the time sped by too quickly. I would have spent more time on that idyllic island, but I felt the need to push on. I knew I would miss my daily visits to the library. I'd also miss Reginald and his cheerful greetings, just like I was an old lost friend. He always gave me a sincere, "Do visit us again," as I'd leave and he never knew I was an intruder that wasn't really staying at the resort.

"Jack, today we're going to Molokai," I said with excitement, but Jack, as usual was unimpressed. I, however, was enthused to be heading off on another adventure. I had heard that every island in the Hawaiian chain is quite different from the next, each with its own unique characteristics, and I was finding that to be so true. I couldn't wait to see what Molikai, with its intriguing history as a leper colony had to offer.

After hauling up the anchor I motored out of the cozy little harbor and turned to take one final look at the fascinating island. I was shocked to see Reginald waving goodbye to me from the rocky shore! I imagined he was saying, "Do visit us again." I guess I didn't fool him after all. I'd need to keep in mind that I'm not quite as clever as I thought.

Once the sails were up we were bombing along at 6 knots. The sun was out and it was a glorious day. I saw a whale breeching not too far from us and I was completely agog at the wonders of nature around me. The time went fast on that short passage and soon I was scanning the water ahead for the harbor entrance buoys that would lead me into a protected bay on Molokai. I had heard that the hurricane had displaced some of the markers here, as well as elsewhere in the islands, so the path through the coral to the anchorage may not be as easy to locate as it was previously.

The sun was behind me, making identification of the different water depths fairly clear. The dark blue water indicates the deeper water in the channel which is where I wanted to be. Shallow water is much lighter and the coral heads will show as brown and the darker the color the closer they are to the surface. From experience I know *Rick's Place* can travel safely in 6 feet of water because the bottom of the keel is about 5 ½ feet under the water.

As I approached Molokai I took down the sails and fired up the engine. I could see a long pier running out in the small anchorage from the shore. There's a dock at the end of the pier that looked like it had room for about 4 boats. As I'd feared, the entrance buoys were gone, so I proceeded with caution through the dark blue channel. The channel was getting shallower all the time and suddenly it split in two! It wasn't clear which path I should take, so I did a mental coin toss and stayed to the right. The depth was down to 8 feet but I was almost to the pier.

I was scanning ahead looking for the best place to tie up, when suddenly it felt like a giant hand slowly picked up *Rick's Place* and we stopped dead in the water. Looking down at the depth sounder I saw that we were in 5 feet of water! Why wasn't I watching the sounder? I quickly put the engine in reverse hoping to back out to the deeper water, but I still wasn't moving. I felt my face starting to sweat. At least is seemed to just be sand I was stuck in and not a hull damaging coral head! I continued to gradually give it a little more throttle and then, yes, we moved just a little! Clouds of sand were being kicked up by the propeller and I was worried that the sediment would get sucked into the engine cooling water.

Just as suddenly as we stopped, we were backing up, breaking free of the muck's solid hold. It was difficult getting back to the fork in the channel because that direction put the sun in my eyes instead of over my shoulder, so I had to strain my eyes to see the safe path. Very slowly, I picked my way back to where I thought the channel split was and I did see a marker that I hadn't noticed on my way in, because it was just below the water line instead of floating on top where it should have been. I hoped that it marked the fork so I turned sharply, yet slowly into what I presume to be the correct course. The sun was once again behind me, but the water colors weren't as distinguishable as they had been. Looking back I saw the problem. The sun was already beginning to drop to the horizon and I realized I'd been messing around out there for several hours. I really needed to get out of the channel before I got lost and the sun set. My anxiety level was really climbing at that point. The pier was so close I could have swam to it, but getting *Rick's Place* safely there through the underwater maze was another problem.

I was keeping a close eye on the sounder to avoid another grounding and it held steady at 8 feet. "Just about there, Jack," I said, trying to calm myself. Then it dropped to 7 feet but there was only about 25 yards to go. My heart sank as I felt the boat noticeably slow down, but it was temporary as *Rick's Place* pushed through a small mound of sand and then we continued on our slow journey.

Finally we were in deeper water again as we left the channel and maneuvered around the pier in the anchorage. There were a couple signs on the dock and squinting, I could make out one that said "Barge Tie Up Only" and the other sign said "Pleasure Boat Tie Up". It's confusing because the arrow on the pleasure boat sign seemed to be pointing to the barge sign, and that seems a bit incongruent. But darkness was rapidly descending upon us and Jack and I were both quite hungry, so I pulled up and tied to what I assumed was the correct spot.

I decided not to take the long trek down the pier to shore that night and would save my exploring for the next day. I fixed us both dinner, turned on the local radio station and began to read.

I came awake with a jolt at a little after 11 pm. I had fallen asleep on the settee while reading as all the tentative maneuvering through the channel earlier that day had really drained me. There were bright lights outside illuminating the dock like it was the middle of the day and there were voices shouting and a loud engine noise from a boat.

I scrambled up to the cockpit to see what the heck was going on out there and I saw a 200 foot barge coming toward the small dock I was occupying! It was being pushed along by a tug boat. There were huge mercury vapor spotlights lighting up the entire area and a group of men on the dock taking lines from the tug's deck hands. They performed a wonderful choreography that placed the huge barge gently alongside the dock with the tug on the outside softly easing the massive container closer and holding it fast. I could see that the barge was really a floating horse corral with about 30 horses nervously moving around in their limited space. And boy, did they stink!

A ramp was swung into place and a semi truck with a large horse trailer came down the pier and pulled up next to the floating corral. As the men coaxed the horses off the barge and into the trailer I saw that the sign on the trailer said "Molokai Horse Rental", and I realized that these horses must be for the tourists to take the advertised horseback tours of the island.

Then I noticed one more thing. The sign that said "Pleasure Boat Tie Up" really said "No Pleasure Boat Tie Up"! The failing light upon my arrival and the dust on the sign had obscured the key word "No", so I had placed myself right where I shouldn't be. That seems to be kind of a re-occurring theme with me.

After a few hours of a fretful sleep, I decided to forgo exploring the island because there didn't appear to be much to see within walking distance of the pier and I was parked in a no parking zone. So I sheepishly picked my way out of Molokai's lagoon at first light because I didn't want to wait for an official to ask me to leave. Next stop Honolulu.

We had another nice short passage between Molikai and Honolulu and we were able to tie up to the transient dock in the Ali Wai Harbor in Honolulu. It's a very enjoyable and very unique place. It seemed to be the global crossroads of the cruising community. Boats from Europe, Australia, New Zealand, and parts unknown tie up here. *Cetus* and many other boat friends I'd made during my stay in the islands were also there at the time. And, In the back of my mind, I knew it was time to start thinking about what to do next. Those crazy voices were nagging at me again, and one would think I'd learned to listen to them because, in retrospect, they sure seem to know what they're talking about.

Carly, the youngster from *Cetus,* came over immediately upon my arrival to play with Jack and continued to do so every day to keep him occupied. She did point out to me on her first visit that my cockpit "smells kind of stinky, like cat pee."

"Yeah, I'm going to have to work on that," was my reply as I remembered how Jack abused my hospitality that day I had to rebuild the toilet. So I began spending my days scrubbing the cockpit teak trying to get rid of the stink and hanging out on the dock swapping stories and comparing notes with the other transients in the Ali Wai.

"Blah, blah, blah, Rick, blah, blah, blah." When I heard my name I poked my head through the hatch and saw Terry, from *Cetus,* standing there with a young man who looked to be a local. "Rick, this is Sammual Hanamoka Jr., Sammual, this is Rick," he said. I shook hands with the heavyset Hawaiian who appeared to be in his early 20's. He sported a wide toothy smile accompanied by bright brown eyes.

Terry interjected, "Sammual has a problem that I thought you may be able to help him with." He went on to say, "You see….well…., hell, you explain it Sam."

"My father, Sammual Sr., died last week after a long illness. He loved the sea as much as he loved Hawaii. Before he died, he made me promise that I would scatter his ashes on his beloved ocean," Sam Jr. said with a hopeful look on his face. OK, now I was wondering where this was going and why did it involve me?

Terry helped him along by explaining, "The boat that was chartered to take Sammual Jr. and senior out to sea had engine problems so the deal fell through." Ah, then I understood where it was leading. Terry continued, "We would take *Cetus*, but we're blocked in by those boats behind us." OK, OK, "So what do I need to do?" I asked a bit hesitantly.

"Just motor out about a mile and we'll spread dad over the water along with some flowers," was Jr's reply. I thought that sounded easy enough, though the idea of taking a dead body on the boat made me a bit queasy, even though he was already in the form of ashes. As Terry and Sammual were leaving, Terry turned and said, "I think your cat has been pissing in the cockpit – it doesn't smell so good."

"Great, thanks for the heads up," I replied sarcastically.

The next morning, my eyes involuntarily squinted at the bright tropical sunshine flooding in through the open hatch. I was looking to see who was knocking so early in the morning. "Rick, wake up! Time to go!" Although we hadn't set a time to cast off on the last sail for Sammual Sr., I didn't realize 7:00 am. was even being considered.

Standing on the dock were Terry & Heidi, Sammual Jr. (holding a porcelain jar I presume to be Sammual Sr.), and another, older Hawaiian dressed in bright robes, whom I assumed to be a man of the cloth. Terry and Heidi's daughter Carly was spending the morning on another friend's boat while we headed out to sea. So the group hopped on to *Rick's Place* and we slowly motored out of the breakwater into the nearly flat, windless sea.

The robed man was called Kahalooi and he was, indeed, a Hawaiian priest of ancient ancestry. He stood out on the bow, by himself, and started a low moaning chant as he stared at the turquoise water with seemingly vacant eyes. He kept chanting and moaning, chanting and moaning and Sammual Jr. explained to us that the Shaman was calling the Goddess of the ocean to accept the ashes of Sammual Sr. Chant, chant, moan, moan; it was getting kind of eerie and I asked Jr.,

"Sammual, we've been traveling for an hour. How much further?" "Kahalooi will know," was his reply.

"We'll know before Kahalooi when we run out of fuel," I retorted.

As if he had heard our conversation above the engine noise and chanting, the High Priest turned and with an almost imperceptible nod, signaled that this was the spot where Sam Sr. wanted to be. As I turned the engine off we slowed to a lazy drift and Kahalooi turned up his volume. Sammual Jr. walked Sammual Sr. up to the bow to join the medicine man. The rest of us waited solemnly in the cockpit and watched the mysterious ceremony. Flower leis were thrown into the still water as they prepared to commit Sr. to the ocean but it appeared Sammual Sr. had other ideas.

Sammual Jr. opened the container and began to gently spread a handful of ashes when a gust of wind came up out of nowhere and the ashes were all blown back on the boat! Undeterred, Jr. waited for the wind to die back down and tried again to extricate his father from the vase. Again the wind simply blew his dad on to the deck and Kahalooi seemed infuriated and his chanting and moaning were reaching a crescendo.

I'm not sure how much time went by, but I was feeling pretty creeped out. Each handful of ashes went over the side, only to be blown back up onto the boat. With agonizing slowness, Sammual Jr. finally concludes that he needs to just pour the rest of Sammual Sr. over the side as quickly as possible, thereby fulfilling, at least in some small part, one of his father's last wishes.

The service came to an end and Jr. returned to the cockpit with his empty jar indicating that we could now go back to the dock. We motioned for Kahalooi to join the rest of us in the cockpit for the ride home. As he stepped to the stern area, Kahalooi wrinkled his nose ever so slightly and began a barely audible, almost whisper chant. I hoped he was asking the gods to do something about the terrible smell in the cockpit. Between this smell and the ashes they'd tracked, I felt like the boat was one big litter box.

Back at the dock, after everyone had disembarked, I hooked up the water hose to wash down the boat. As I rinsed, I watched the majority of Sammual Hanamoka Sr.'s earthly remains flow down the scuppers and mix with the oily sheen and murky harbor water. I realized the strong odor Jack had left in the cockpit seemed to have faded away. Did Kahalooi have a hand in deodorizing *Rick's Place*? Who knows, but I silently thanked the Cosmic Controller for bringing me together with the Hawaiian High Priest.

CHAPTER 9

Time to Go

"The only difference between an ordeal and an adventure is your attitude."

-Bob Bitchin

I woke up after a rather restless night's sleep. It was one of those times, before being fully awake, that I didn't know where I was. Just as the mental fog was starting to lift, the cat, occupying his customary position near my head, stretched. With claws fully extended, he gave me quite a wake-up scratch across my forehead. I yelped, Jack yawned, and the promise of another day was upon us.

I performed my morning ritual of stumbling up the stairs, with cocoa in hand, to try and get a feel for the coming day. Sitting in the cozy cockpit, I closed my eyes and listened to Honolulu come to life. The rush hour was just gearing up in the distance and the whine of a passenger jet engine caught my attention. As I followed its approach to the airport, I couldn't help but wonder how many tourists it would disgorge in Paradise today.

It finally hit me why I wasn't sleeping worth a damn as of late. The anxiety of not having a clear plan had manifested itself into sleepless nights.

That all began to change when I met Capt'n Joe. A sloop that had obviously been sailed hard was tied next to me when I got back after spending some time on the beach. The guy who popped out of the cabin looked to be 170 years old. He had a slight hunch and a noticeable limp. I wouldn't have been surprised to have seen a wooden leg on this old salt. By the looks of his skin he'd spent a lot of time in the sun and didn't believe in sunscreen or moisturizer. He had a bulbous nose with a web of broken capillaries. That was Capt'n Joe.

Escape was the name that was hand painted on the stern of his 35 foot wood plank boat. Rust stains were streaking down from the fasteners that were obviously installed a very long time ago. There was a crazy hodgepodge of items strapped on to *Escape's* deck: a crab trap, a BBQ, rubber dinghy, 2 fishing poles, 4 fuel containers and 2 sail bags. I don't know how the skipper could even walk on deck, let alone sail this mess. Obviously he didn't care about keeping up appearances. I was curious to hear his story, so I invited him to join me for a drink that evening.

Sitting in the local bar not far from the Ali Wai, I was enjoying a cocktail or Sundowner as we've come to call them in the cruising community, with Capt'n Joe. It seems Capt'n Joe is a regular here and quite the ladies man, at least in his own mind. He would flirt non stop with the waitresses and any female patron that ventured too close to our table would get an invitation to come down to his boat to see his etchings.

"You'd be plenty surprised how women love a sailboat captain," he whispered a bit too loudly. His breath was so heavy with alcohol it almost knocked me over.

"So where ya going next, kid," he asked, but before I could answer he looked past me and called out to a nice looking redhead passing by, "Hey hon, want a free tour of the bay on a sailboat?" She smiled politely and kept walking.

Once his attention turned back to me, I answered his question. "Well," I said, "I haven't thought much past Hawaii, but Tahiti and maybe Fiji sound good." He then let out a kind of disgruntled sigh. I should emphasize here that cruisers all seem to be overly opinionated on any subject especially destinations. He went on to say, "You're a fool."

Oh, great, here comes this guy's unsolicited rantings. "Here's the way I see it"…" I knew it, I just knew it. "You spent all that time building your boat, you fitted her out, you sailed from the west coast," at least he had been listening to me when I told my story. "Which, all in all, is no small feat. But you're telling me the best you could come up with is going to another place that has jumbo jets landing hoards of tourists every other day? You should just save your time and money and fly to those places. It's a hell of a lot easier." My quick witted response was, "I like sailing," oh, thanks brain.

"Then get a day sailor and sail on lakes."

"I like the adventure," another great comeback.

"Look," Capt'n Joe said a bit more quietly, "I'm just trying to tell ya to get off the beaten track. Expand your scope. You seem smart enough. For every place like Tahiti or Fiji, there are 5 places that don't hardly see anyone.' He went on with, "Don't be afraid to poke your bow into places that aren't in one of those damn cruiser guides."

"I'm not too enthused about putting everything I own up on the beach." Now I was rolling.

"Common sense!" Now he was shouting, "Being aware of what's around you. Taking nature's signs when she gives 'em. Hell, I've sailed 50,000 miles and never felt in a life threatening situation. Look, you're going south, right? Go to Fanning Island. It's on your way and it's an easy enough coral pass to get some experience on."

A week later, *Rick's Place* was charging down azure Pacific swells, heading for a place called Fanning Island. It was ideal weather conditions: blue skies with 15 knots of wind on the backside of the beam. I am always amazed at how quickly Jack gets his sea legs, especially since he's got to get 4 legs coordinated to my two. At 50 miles out my body was once again starting to adapt to ocean travel. A visual sweep of the horizon behind me revealed that the two boats that started out with me from Honolulu were now well out of sight. Now that's another interesting story.

After my encounter with Capt'n Joe, and while I was preparing to leave Hawaii, fate brought me in contact with two other single handers with similar plans to head south. Both of them had Palmyra as their first destination. Palmyra is an uninhabited atoll just west of Fanning Island. While talking over beers one evening, one of them proposed that we travel together. It was suggested that we form a sort of caravan, or boat-a-van, as we called it. The thought was that if we stayed together, only one skipper would need to be on lookout at a time, letting the other two get some rest. (I really must stop making travel plans while drinking.) Anyway, rotating watch and keeping radios turned to the same channels, extra eyes watching for ships and squalls; it sure seemed like a good plan at the time. Once again I should have listened to the little voices in my head that were saying that it seemed too good to be true.

When the three of us met up outside the Ali Wai channel the trades were light, so it was easy to maneuver close enough so we could have one last face to face. Now a word about my two new sailing companions. Dick was 50ish, pleasant, easy going with about the same experience as me. He had sailed from L.A. in a 32' boat. It was a very traditional looking boat with lots of teak trim on the outside, giving it a pleasing and distinctive appearance compared to modern production vessels.

Ron, the other skipper, was the complete opposite. This guy is why decaffeinated coffee was invented. He was a bit younger than Dick and he never stopped talking. He had started out from Portland, Oregon, with crew on his home built 38' boat. He got to Hawaii and his crew said good-bye. I would understand later why they did. Suddenly single handed, Ron had pushed for the three boat concept as a security in numbers thing.

As we sailed along and the boats got closer, the big surprise was that Ron had placed a 55 gallon drum of diesel on deck! "Kind of extreme, isn't it, Ron?" I shouted. With a smug smile he replied, "I can motor all the way to Tahiti now."

My guess is that no one told Captain Ron about the trade winds. The whole time I was thinking, "Why in the world would someone put that much fuel on the deck of a sailboat?"
"Ron, the winds should be pretty steady on the way down, "I was yelling to be heard over his engine.

"You're right, I'll be ready", was his reply. He hadn't heard a thing I said. "Oh well."

Leaving the lee of the island, the trades started picking up to about 10 or 15 knots. Dick's boat, as well as *Rick's Place*, had full main with 90% working jibs. Ron, on the other hand, had 100% engine and 90% throttle. While Dick and I sailed along at a comfortable 4 knots, Ron would plow ahead and then, without warning, would turn back toward our two boats. He'd circle around us then shoot on ahead again. This went on for about 12 hours. He was scaring the hell out of me! Half the time his boat would be heading back to our position with no one at the helm, passing uncomfortably close. He was also constantly on the radio, talking

121

incessantly. He just wouldn't shut up. And all the time circling, circling, circling.

The final straw came after hearing his dissertation concerning how the moon landings were faked. And since they were filmed, supposedly, at Disney's Studios, they needed to knock off Mr. Disney to keep the whole thing hush-hush. I grew up with Walt; I loved Walt and no one takes his name in vain.

"Enough is enough!" I shouted at Jack, my crew member. Then I picked up the microphone and said, "Ron, Dick, can you hear me?"

"Loud and Clear Rick," came the response.

"Hey guys, the wind is forcing me to bear off a bit." My little white lie to get away from this bizarre convoy had been made. "I'll be moving away from your course," but I'll try and stay in touch as long as possible." I guess that was another little lie.

Dick acknowledged with a detectable disappointment in his voice and Ron said, just as hyper as ever, "We'll be here! Give us a call."

Not bloody likely was my thought. And as *Rick's Place* was slowly pulling away, Ron was still circling, circling, circling.

Waking up on the morning of the tenth day and 1000 miles later, a small dot appeared on the morning horizon. Thank you dear GPS. Soon I could detect the turquoise glow in the sky as it reflected off the large lagoon just as Capt'n Joe had told me it would!

Fanning Island: my first landfall in a foreign country and my first coral lagoon pass was lying before me. Several hours later, I was searching the shoreline with my binoculars, trying to locate the pass that was supposed to be so easy to navigate.

Finally, I spotted a break in the palm tree lined shore. As if on cue, several small canoes could be seen making their way out to the open ocean.

Would this be my long dreamed of greeting by scantily clad natives? With calm winds, I motored over to where the small boats were grouping just outside the surf line. While approaching the gathering, I noted that hand carved paddles had been replaced by modern outboard engines and Nike T-shirts and Chicago Bulls jerseys replaced loin cloths. As I slowly motored closer, it became apparent by their body gyrations that they were urging me to the pass that I could not yet see. The surf looked as if it stretched across the entire beach. Certainly these small boats didn't just come through the 5' high breaking combers? Suddenly, as if by magic, a 50' wide path of wave free water appeared! It was funny how you couldn't see the pass you until it was right in front of you.

I turned 90° to the shore to line up the pass. The sun was now behind *Rick's Place,* exactly where I needed it for navigating through coral. A brilliant explosion of turquoise assaulted my eyes. I had gained a bit of experience in Hawaii regarding what different colors of water indicate in the way of water depth and presence of coral heads, but I was completely unprepared for what I was seeing here. The depth sounder was measuring 80 feet as the boat started through the pass, then 60 feet and quickly to 45. Looking over the side I just knew the depth sounder had to be giving me false readings. The coral heads, schools of fish and even the lone manta ray looked just too close to be 45 feet deep! It looked closer to 10 feet, but the sounder held steady at 45. "I've gotta get this thing recalibrated," I said to an empty cockpit. Then I noticed that my "Speed over Ground" on the GPS had dropped from 5 knots to a mere 2 knots. That had to be wrong, as well. After all, I could see water flowing by like I was still doing 6 knots. What the hell was going on with my instruments?

One of the motor powered outriggers came up beside my boat and the occupant had the old outboard throttled wide open. It was belching out a blue smoke cloud that L.A. would be proud of. The guy was yelling something, but his words were being drowned out by the noisy overworked Johnson. Out of frustration, he moved closer to my boat and grabbed the life line and then shouted for me to follow him.

All of this was happening while I was trying to navigate my first coral pass with instruments I couldn't trust and this native guide's outboard still on terminal blow up. My speed was now down to 1 knot and the coral heads were closing in as the pass narrowed. I quickly dismissed the idea of making a U turn and heading out to the safety of open water, as there didn't appear to be enough room for that at this point. Sweat was starting to sprout from my forehead and my anxiety index was climbing. I am sure my death grip on the tiller was going to leave a mark. Ten minutes stretched to 20 minutes, but the palm trees on the beach that I was using to measure my progress seemed to stay in one place.

The throttle was open all the way to its stops and the tiny diesel engine was putting out as much power as it could. I found myself leaning forward silently urging the boat on. After 30 minutes of seemingly being in one spot, I looked over the side and finally saw a different patch of coral. I was moving!! In fact, we started to pick up speed; 2.5 knots and then a little later it reached 3 knots! I was going to make it!

My grip started to ease on the tiller handle, the blood started to flow, and I was starting to breathe again. Just then the engine's high temperature alarm sparked to life! With no temperature gauge I had no way of knowing if the tiny overworked engine was just a little over heated or approaching the China syndrome. My options were limited at this point. The pass was still too narrow to do a 180, I dared not leave the helm since I had no autopilot so I just had to listen to the alarm as I tried to guide *Rick's Place* through this gauntlet.

About that time, Mr. Jack sashayed up the companion way and in to the cockpit. He was probably drawn out by the smell of land for the first time in over a week, and with great curiosity he propelled himself onto the deck. The last thing I needed to worry about right then was my nomadic sailing mate falling overboard.

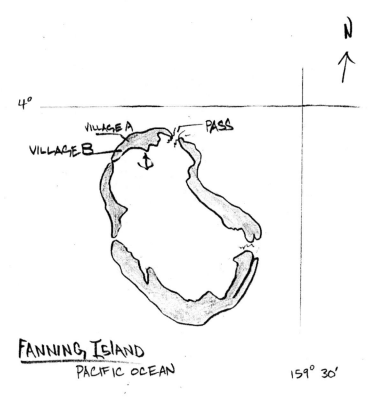

FANNING ISLAND
PACIFIC OCEAN

CHAPTER 10

Fanning Island : Paradise Found

"Life is really simple, but we insist on making it complicated."

-Confucius

The shriek of the high temperature alarm brought me back to problem #1; the engine was going to melt down if I didn't act soon. My hand went to the throttle and I slowed the engine down, hoping this would eventually help cool the thing down. As I did this the boat lost its forward momentum and just stayed in one spot. A minute later the alarm went silent with the boat hovering in this state of equilibrium for about 11 minutes. Then I noticed that the out flowing water was slowing down and I was once again starting to make progress through the half mile long pass. About forty minutes later I was anchored in 15' of water. The anchor was clearly visible and finally I was able to turn the engine off. After 3000 miles, a crew member that mutinied, a stowaway cat, being pursued and caught by a hurricane and a Hawaiian burial at sea, I was finally in my first foreign anchorage. I jumped into the warm turquoise water, but not before putting out my boarding ladder.

While floating around *Rick's Place*, I could tell that the water was clearer than anything I had encountered before. I figured this out because I'd just tried to retrieve a beautiful sea shell that looked to be only about 6 feet down on the sandy bottom. I couldn't get to it in just one breath, so I knew it was much farther away than it appeared.

"I'll be damned," I said out loud as I broke the surface for a gulp of air. I had just realized the depth sounder must be OK after all. It was an optical illusion of shallow depths created by the clarity of this water. Diving under the boat again I checked the knot meter sending unit, the little paddlewheel that measures my speed through the water, and it looked fine, as well. It was another illusion, created by the strong current flowing through the channel out of the lagoon that made me feel like I was going faster than I really was. Another mystery solved.

Fanning Atoll is what was left of an ancient volcano that sank until all that remained was the outside rim. The water filled crater of the volcano is what forms the lagoon and it is about 5 miles across. The rim forms a barrier reef with intermittent stretches of dry land, called motus. There are breaks in the reef where the passes are located, some deep enough for large craft and some you couldn't get a flat bottomed boat through.

My chart of the Atoll indicated there were two villages, both located on the same motu. I was anchored between these two small hamlets. Capt'n Joe had told me there were about 120 people living on this island.

Upon arrival I was required to raise my yellow quarantine flag and wait for customs officials to come out to the boat and clear me in. They were probably going to take a dim view of me bringing a cat that was uncertified and completely without papers, into their country. So I rounded up Jack, gave him some food, put him in a box and buried him under several bags of sails. Thirty minutes later a vintage World War II landing craft was maneuvering straight for me. At the last minute the lumbering vessel executed a perfect turn that brought its 45' bulk alongside *Rick's Place*. With their 14' high craft idling next to me, I couldn't help but think how silly this must look because the landing craft was so big compared to my smaller vessel. They lowered a rope ladder over the side and before long four smartly dressed officials were climbing down and squeezing into the tiny cockpit of *Rick's Place*.

The government of Kiribati, which controls Fanning Island, was well represented. Agriculture, Immigration, Customs and a mysterious fourth man that remained unidentified, all jammed into the small space with grace and courtesy. Within 40 minutes they completed their "look around" and filling out all of the forms. They stamped my passport and the landing craft was called back out and the foursome disembarked and for a while I was alone with my thoughts. I couldn't keep from staring at that stamp, simple black ink on blue paper, but to me it was a symbol of success; a trophy, my first place award for the craziness that made up this cruising life. Before I had a chance to break my arm patting myself on the back, the cat announced his displeasure at being cooped up. For some reason, maybe Jack knew he could get in trouble; he had been silent while the authorities looked around. Now that they were gone, Jack wanted out. I agreed and it was time for Jack and me to party! Ahhhhhhhhhhhh.... nothing like warm beer and stale chips for a celebration. At the time, nothing could have tasted better.

The next day was spent getting the boat back in order, doing some laundry and launching the dinghy. Having completed my boat duties, I rowed to shore and found a path that led in to the heavy vegetation. After a short walk I came to a road that I knew from my chart connected the two villages. What I didn't know was that by choosing to go to village A instead of village B, I might set in motion a series of one up man ship between the A's and B's. Perhaps a short history lesson is in order at this point.

Fanning Island's true name is Tabuaeran Atoll, as it is the territorial possession of Kiribati, a multi-island nation which is located some 1000 miles to the west in the South Pacific. When the other islands of Kiribati were becoming over populated, the powers that be decided to send out a colony of people to the remote uninhabited island of Fanning. The government paid the people and helped build some housing and a dock for supply ships. The group that came over consisted of both Catholics and Protestants. When the group landed on the island that was to be their new settlement, they just naturally divided by their religious beliefs, and two villages were formed. Over the years, the competition between the two villages became serious stuff. They have traditional native dance contests, fishing competitions; competition in nearly every aspect of daily life. And when an unsuspecting boat crew comes to shore, the first village they happen to visit, gains bragging rights for some time to come.

So I found myself at a crossroads: literally. Being an unsuspecting boat crew I had no idea that the decision to go right or left made any difference at all. So off I went, soon to be a lost soul to one group, bragging rights to the other. Before I had a chance to make the wrong or right move, as the case may be, divine intervention stepped in my path. Actually it was one of the officials that had come to *Rick's Place* upon my arrival. His name was Robert and he asked that I please follow him. I was immediately concerned, as I had let Jack out to lie out on the deck. Could he have been spotted? It seems everywhere we go I am on the verge of getting in deep kitty litter because of that cat.

After about a quarter mile walk through the steamy heat of the day, we came to a clearing. In the middle of the clearing was a structure obviously built to hold a large group of residents. It was about 75 feet long and 25 feet wide. The roof was thatched and there were large log supports in each corner but the sides were open. Later I saw that there were curtains made of palm fronds that were rolled up on the sides and ends to provide ventilation. These could be let down and secured to form walls in inclement weather.

Robert and I walked into the oversized hut with a sand floor, and the only "furniture" inside was a large table, rather like an alter, in the center of the room. On this "alter" was a 27" RCA television vintage 1980. Next to this relic was a top loading VCR, which had to be early 80's as well.

"What the heck?"

These two vestiges of the so called modern world looked so laughingly out of place! Robert must have figured out my next thought as he broke the silence saying "generator" and pointed to a small shack about 50 feet away.

Robert explained that one of the high points for the 2 villages was Wednesday movie night. For on that night the people from both villages would gather and put aside their differences and watch movies together. Robert went on to explain that the supply ship that came every three months would bring a few movies and cruisers that would stop at Fanning would also leave VHS movies for the islanders to enjoy.

"It has been broken for two weeks"

"The TV?" I asked.

"No the machine to play movie", Robert replied.

Bingo! The light in my head goes on and "the voices" are stirred awake. They're saying fix the machine and bring religious harmony to the island, at least for Wednesday nights.

"Whoa….," says the voice of reason," you don't know a

thing about fixing vintage VCR's!"

"Yes, but I could just take a look," another voice says.

"OK, suit yourself," reason responds.

Oh great, now the voices are fighting amongst themselves!

I hurried back to the dinghy and rowed to the mother ship and collected everything I thought might be useful in my pending project. A small screw driver, tape and an electric current tester was what I came up with for fixing something I knew nothing about.

When I got back to the long hut, I was shocked to see a gathering of 10 very old men, the village elders. There were also half a dozen children running around laughing and hitting each other with sticks. Every so often one of the men would reach out and whack the closest kid to him, trying to get them to settle down. I really wasn't looking to have an audience watching as I tackled the task ahead. Whack! Another kid feeling the wrath of an elder broke my concentration. Just like kids everywhere, this just seemed to get them going even more.

Back to business, I looked at easy stuff first. No broken cords or obvious loose wires on the outside. With as humid as the air was, I was surprised anything electrical worked on this island. I knew it was time to get down and dirty. I removed the screws holding the outer casing and gently started lifting up, being so careful not to mess up the circuit boards.

"Easy, easy does it," the voices were telling me. WHACK! Another kid screamed so I lifted my head up to see the commotion and came eyeball to eyeball with an older, toothless, dark skinned guy who was 3 inches away from my face. He had that look in his eye. The one that says, "You are so over your head!" But, I pressed on. I must unite these poor souls at least for one more Wednesday night.

The cover came off and there was nothing obvious, nothing catching my eye. I asked Robert to start the generator. After a brief belch of black smoke the old machine rattles to life. Reaching into my tool box, I pulled out my AC/DC tester which, until that time, I'd never really used. I handled it like it was the Holy Grail. The audience was with me now, they were expecting great things. They were all craning their necks to see what would happen next.

As I checked the incoming power cord, I somehow got my finger in the wrong spot and promptly got shocked. It's just the kind of shock that's really irritating, but by no means dangerous and my involuntary muscle spasms seemed to delight both young and old. Needless to say I had Robert turn the generator back off. After a bit more investigation I found the problem: a wire that had the tell tale green patina of corrosion! I cleaned and reconnected it and then it was time for the BIG MOMENT. Generator back on, I hit the power button and much to my surprise the top popped up! There were smiles all around.

The group collected closely around while a tape of "Planet of the Apes" was inserted, the TV turned on and the screen came to life.

"Get your hands off me, you damn dirty ape" blared out of the tinny speaker. This was followed by lots of hand shaking and back patting. I was relieved. Failure was not an option on this one.

Soon the coconut telegraph had spread the word and a celebration was in the making. Children were given the task of sweeping the sand floor of the long hut, using palm fronds. Colorful table cloths were spread on the long low table and mats were laid down to sit on. As the villagers arrived they each placed their offering on the table and it was looking like quite a feast. There were colorful reef fish, tuna, lobster tails, coconut crab, and what appears to be a big favorite, corned beef hash right out of the can! Mounds of vegetables that I couldn't identify were on the table and pork cooked while wrapped in banana leaves seemed to be a popular dish. Green coconuts with a hole cut in the top provided the liquid refreshment and there was some type of coconut pudding for dessert.

There were about 30 villagers there by then and only the men were sitting cross legged on the mats around the table, the women stayed in the background and served the food. They won't eat until all the men are finished. The children remained outside where they were running around non stop playing some high-energy game.

While we were eating, a group of teens that compete in

inter-island dance competitions began a short show for us. It was a very stiff and formal traditional dance and they all looked very serious as they performed the graceful hand movements telling a story about a legendary island princess. I was so full I couldn't even think about eating another bite. Then the men began to drink some kind of after-dinner concoction. I was handed a cup and all eyes were on me while I tried my first taste of what must be some type of island moonshine. It was a most unpleasant taste, which they must know, because when I gagged slightly they all broke out into laughter. I asked what kind of drink it was and I was told it is made from the sap of a coconut palm tree. After collecting the sap, they ferment it in a jar buried in the sandy soil and after a few weeks it turns into this strange after dinner liqueur. Palm bark would have tasted better!

I spent little time on the boat after my success with the VCR. The people of both villages, Catholic and Protestant, took me in, in a way that I never would have imagined. Rarely did I eat any meals on *Rick's Place,* because I was always somebody's guest. I would go out fishing with the locals, come back and help with the things that needed to be done around the villages. It was a wonderful existence.

Of course, it was discovered that I had Jack as a sailing companion, but luckily here it wasn't a problem and we weren't going to be destroyed as had been the threat in Hawaii. The kids were always swimming out early in the morning to see him and Jack was growing fat from all of the attention, not to mention all the fish they would bring for him.

Snorkeling became my passion and I would do it for hours on end. The pass into the lagoon that was so terrifying during my entrance was now a wonderland. I'd motor the dinghy outside the entrance during slack current, then I would don my mask and slip into the water and hold on to the side the small boat. The incoming current would propel me back into the lagoon and because of the water clarity I felt like I was flying over some beautiful undersea world. I would drift for about a mile before the current would peter out, then I would hop in the dinghy and do it again, and again.

The beauty of the coral was simply indescribable with its

long spires reaching for the sunlight. There were millions of colorful reef fish and graceful manta rays, easily the size of my dinghy, all seemingly within reach. It seems every time I snorkeled I would see something unexpected. Wolf eels with their large teeth and beady black eyes would pop out of coral crevasses like a jack in the box, grabbing a quick meal then retreating back to their hiding hole. Schools of bright blue neon fish, each less than an inch long, would suddenly appear from a coral head and just as quickly disappear back into it as I approached for a closer look. I could poke my face within inches of where they were hiding and not be able to spot them. A small octopus had me following it around for an hour, squirting out its purplish black ink whenever it felt threatened by me.

One day I was an unwitting participant in a fish hunt. I was snorkeling near my anchored dinghy when a school of small silver fish came between me and the inflatable. The fish were momentarily spooked and confused. Within seconds, several frigate birds that had been flying overhead started dive bombing the hapless fish. From my under water vantage point I had a rare glimpse of Mother Nature in action as the birds would plunge into the water and grasp a fish in their beaks.

I'd also learned about sharks from the local kids. The kids often accompanied me snorkeling and were quite amused at my reluctance to share the vicinity with the sharks. At first, when a shark would appear, I would rocket back into the dinghy bringing peels of laughter and cat calls from the younger ones. They showed me how to distinguish the good sharks from the bad as if there is such a thing as a "good shark." Luckily it was rare for one of the "bad" open ocean sharks to come into the lagoon and the reef sharks were treated with total disregard by the locals. Their dogs even chased them when they came close to shore.

Things were not always spits and giggles on Fanning. One day while on shore, a squall line moved in and before I could get back to the boat the wind was blowing 30 knots. A nasty swell was rocking *Rick's Place* like a hobby horse. The rain was coming at me sideways and stung like buckshot and after nearly being swamped by a big wave I finally made it out to the boat. Getting on the boat was another story. The dinghy and the mother ship were rocking in two different rhythms which resulted in me loosing my footing on my first attempt to get aboard and left me hanging from the life lines (very appropriately named) with my feet dangling between the dinghy and the water. The next attempt I got on, but lost the rope used to tie up the dinghy, so I jumped back into it before it could be blown away. OK, third times a charm. Just as the two boats synchronized I clamored aboard with a death grip on the dinghy rope, or painter, as I had learned it was called.

Since I was anchored in such shallow water, the wind made the waves very steep and when the bow of the boat would go down, a wave would crash on deck and roll down the sides. After I tied off the dinghy, I looked below just as a wave washed over the front hatch. Apparently the hatch was not fully tightened down, because water was rushing in through it and everything below was getting wet. My berth was soaked and the cat was super pissed off having been on the receiving end of one of the incoming deluges.

It took me several days to get things cleaned up and dried out, and that included Jack. That squall served as my wake up call. I realized that I had spent four weeks on Fanning which was about two weeks longer than I had planned. It had been so easy to forget about moving on with my new found celebrity, the kindness of the people, the hours in the water and the ease of life here on this beautiful island. Put it all together and you get a case of what I call "passage block".

So the preparation began; time to move on. Wake up voices! I need some guidance. But where to? I hadn't even crossed the equator yet, so there was a whole hemisphere awaiting me.

CHAPTER 11

On the road again…

"Got out of town on a boat, Goin' to Southern islands."

-Crosby, Stills & Nash, *Southern Cross*

Two days out from Fanning, Jack and I were finally getting our sea legs. It amazes me how much of a workout my body gets when making a passage. The bruises and strained muscles are the norm for the break-in period of about three days or 300 miles, whichever comes first. This is due to the pitching of the boat in the ocean swell. Always moving side to side, forward and back, my muscles are constantly working to compensate for the movement and it just wears them out. None of that mattered; the BIG event was nearly here: The Crossing of the Equator!

I'd been watching the GPS count down the degrees of latitude as the sun began to set. We were moving along at a comfortable four knots with the wind off the port. I decided several days earlier I would aim for Tahiti which was now about 1000 miles from my current position. I realize that by going to French Polynesia I am breaking the rule that was laid out for me by Capt'n Joe just before I left Hawaii. He stated: "If you can get someplace in a Jumbo Jet, take the jet, it's easier."

One thing with having Tahiti as a destination is that to get there I would need to travel east into the prevailing winds and current. This could prove to be very wet and slow in a small boat because I would be heading into the waves. So, as a back up, in case the weather gods were not smiling down on me, I had about 6 alternate stops I could make, each a little more west than the last. So it seemed like a win-win situation.

Jack was on his leash in the cockpit with me, when suddenly he stiffened as something caught his eye behind me off the stern of the boat. I should mention that his wide eye terror look doesn't do much for my nerves. It was the time of night when I tended to hear strange sounds in the water and basically want to run away and hide under the covers. I slowly turned around, fully expecting to see a set of teeth or a long tentacled arm breaching the surface of the sea, but instead, we saw hundreds of twinkling lights flashing by under the water. The lights are accompanied by clicking sounds: Dolphin! As they swim through the water the bioluminescence is activated creating the twinkling effect. It appears as if the dolphins are encrusted with diamonds and it reminds me of Tinker Bell flying through the sky leaving a sparkling trail of Magic Dust behind her. There are about a dozen Tinker Bells flying around, beside and under the boat. With the bright phosphorescence trails we could see them coming from 50 feet away!

I hooted and whistled and they clicked back at us. Jack and I watched this show for over an hour. He tried to run around the deck to see as much as he could. I'm quite sure that without the tether and harness he would have ended up swimming with the dolphins.

When the magnificent mammals finally did their last roll on the bow wave and the sparkles disappeared, I went down to check our position. The GPS was reading 000.6 <u>SOUTH!!</u> We were a half mile into the Southern Hemisphere: The South Pacific! Just writing those words in my log sent chills up my spine. I opened a bottle of Champagne given to me by my friends at the Bon Voyage party back in Gig Harbor. Then I opened a can of tuna fish for Jack and proceeded to toast some of those who helped me get this far: Alien Allen, Sparky, Mom, Capt'n Joe, The Voices, Jack Cat and Sheryl. How I wish Sheryl was here right now! With the radar detector set, I fell into a blissful sleep below, with Jack lying near and then on, my head.

It may have been the drink or just the satisfaction of finally getting into the South Pacific, but I awoke 5 hours later with the first rays of sun poking through the ports. Five hours is about three hours longer than I usually nap during a passage. While doing my usual scan of the horizon, something didn't look quite right. On the southern horizon, right were I was headed, was a dark, no, BLACK line right where the sky meets the sea. During the previous months at sea I'd seen lots of clouds, but these were so different. The cloud band stretched from east to west without a break. It was slowly eating up the blue sky that it bordered and I was heading straight for it at warp speed (well, actually about 5 knots). I quickly calculated that no, it is not cyclone season, but the black ink that was looming in my path had me on edge.

Suddenly the radar detector started beeping announcing that a boat's radar waves were invisibly sweeping over *Rick's Place*. Scrambling up on deck, I quickly spotted a freighter on the horizon coming out of the wall of darkness. I got on my VHF radio and tried calling ship to ship, but got no reply. Now my imagination was starting to raise its ugly voice and I was saying out loud, "you know, Jack, maybe nobody is left on board and that's why they don't answer the radio? Maybe they all abandoned ship!"

Great, I think to myself. Now I'm rambling to the stowaway cat trying to get answers. With the ship just a couple of miles off my portside; I grabbed the handheld radio and tried to make contact one last time. Suddenly a voice came back, catching me so off guard that I nearly dropped the radio. The voice was Australian and cheerful sounding which was reassuring. We chatted about the normal mid ocean stuff; where I was going, where I had come from, how long I'd been at sea. Now came my turn and the big question was "What the hell did you just come out of?"

"That, mate, is a trough," came the almost too cheerful response. Right then I knew I'd missed a chapter in my weather book, because I didn't know what a trough was and I was pretty sure I didn't really want to find out.

"What can I expect?" I queried. "

Well, it's a pretty big area of low pressure and packing quite a wallop: 12' seas and 30 knot winds with gusts to 35. Best batten down. It's pretty messy out there."

Oh great, just great.

"Do these troughs show up often?" I asked with a little fear in my voice.

"Not too often, I mean they develop periodically but not always this nasty," he said, trying to sound reassuring.

"Mate, can we do anything for you? Do you need anything? Can we contact anybody for you?" I gave him my mom's number as well as Sheryl's phone number in San Francisco and he said he would call and report that all was well aboard *Rick's Place*. I just hoped that wasn't a premature prophesy.

After bidding final farewells with the Aussie on the radio, I immediately stepped into action. The first order of business was to start the engine to fully charge the batteries. I stowed some lose items below and secured cupboard doors. Moving up to the cockpit I could see that the cloud cover had blocked out about two thirds of the sky in front of me. It was apparent any attempt to try and outrun the weather would be futile. The wind that had been pushing me along so reliably for days had dropped off to non-existent. I knew what would happen next: a big blow. What I didn't know is which direction it would come from.

I took the opportunity to quickly change sails. I dragged my smallest, but strongest built storm sails from below. I hanked on a storm jib that looked even smaller than I remembered. Taking down the main, I opted for my never before used storm trysail. I was so thankful that I had a bit of warning of the upcoming wind because it took me about 45 minutes to get the main sail down, the boom lashed and the heavy duty trysail up the mast. Trysails are often made of orange fabric so that a boat is easier to spot by rescuers from airplanes. A distinction not lost in thought during my battening down process.

The wind was now starting to pick up, right on the nose, from the direction I wanted to go. Daylight was running out and there would be no stars to steer by this night. Over the next couple of hours I could feel the waves building. As the wind increased in strength, I let the bow fall off, while still trying to make the general direction of Tahiti. I really, really hate to start a night shift with the onset of terrible weather. The wind vane was working well and I had my hot cocoa, but it was going to be a long dark night.

At first light I was stunned at the sight outside my little cocoon. The waves looked monstrous with the tops being blown off by the wind creating a white spume. The boat would struggle up one side of the swell, get blasted by full wind, then slide down the backside where the wind would almost be non existent because of the height of the waves. The Aussie said 12' waves, but from my perspective, so much closer to the water than he was in that big ship, they looked twice that size.

A word about my traveling companion, Jack the Cat. He seems to be able to sense when bad weather is on the way. His system shuts down and he will not move from the pilot berth until everything is calm again. This time the weather must have snuck up on him and his system didn't shut down in time. Jack made several gallant attempts to use the toilet, but about the time he would get somewhat comfy he would get thrown off until finally he retreated to the pilot berth and just howled. It took me a while to figure out what the problem was, but after I did, I picked Jack up and deposited him in the sink. I could almost see the relief in his kitty eyes as he did his business and jumped down and resumed his watch from the comforts of the pilot berth. I realized I'd given him a bad idea and would have to keep an eye on the sink. But first there was a storm to worry about.

The roller coaster from hell continued through the daylight hours with no relief. My trips to the deck were getting less frequent now. I would poke my head out for a few minutes then quickly retreat back to the relative quiet below. Cooking was out of the question. Just standing took immense effort. Opening cabinets had to be done with the right timing or else the entire contents would take flight when the boat would pitch. I managed to pick up a weather forecast for the area within about 100 miles, but no mention was made of the craziness going on outside.

I felt another long night was in store for us. Lying on the pilot berth, I would try to catch a catnap, just to be jolted awake when the boat would fall awkwardly off a swell. This seemed to happen about twice an hour. I would then be obliged to go up to see if things were still in order. Luckily they always were.

It seemed just before dawn the motion as well as the sounds started to settle down. I awoke to Jack practically sitting on my head trying to get comfortable. It took me a minute to realize that he was now out of his storm hole that he always occupies in bad weather! The first rays of sunlight were poking through the port holes and I raced up the stairs delighted to be met by blue sky. We survived our first "trough" at sea!!

The wind was now around 15 knots from the east; the trades were back. The seas, however, were confused. Left over storm waves colliding with the Easterly tradewind directed seas, made things rather sloppy for the rest of the day. I was finally able to take out my chart and put an X at our present location, something I hadn't been able to do in the past 48 hours.

All of the Easting that I had made since leaving Fanning had evaporated because a sailboat doesn't have the ability to travel directly into the wind. With my limited amount of fuel aboard *Rick's Place* motoring into wind and seas for any length of time was impractical. Thus, going to Tahiti was out of the question, as we would be bashing against the elements trying to get there. I was plain tired of bashing at this point. Plus, there were no guarantees that we wouldn't encounter more inclement weather.

Bora Bora was now right in front of us; only 250 miles away, with an excellent point of sail. We could be there in 2 or 3 days! At least my plan of having several stops spaced close together seemed like a wise idea right now. I found some literature about Bora Bora in a guide book I bought back in Hawaii. Club Med, good snorkeling; a regular tropical paradise.

Fifteen days and 1200 miles after leaving Fanning Island, Bora Bora was in sight. Unfortunately it was late afternoon with about 15 miles to go. There was no way I would be able to make it in before dark, so I was resigned to just hang out until daylight. This meant I would have to sail back and forth near enough to the entrance so we could get in the next the morning. I would need to stay awake to keep an eye out so *Rick's Place* didn't pile up on the rocks. In some respects this is harder than making a passage. It was another long sleepless night.

"The night seemed so damn long," I muttered. Jack was rather uninterested in my rambling. I had actually gotten him out of his cubby hole because I needed company to stay awake and the cat would have to do. Hearing the surf crash on the shore all night had completely frayed my nerves.

Day break revealed a beautiful island with its extinct

volcano rising up out of the water. It is quite a different look from Fanning Island, not just the mountains but the lush jungle as well. The entrance was easy to spot as it was wide with entrance markers on either side. There was no nasty current this time, either. As *Rick's Place* glided in through the pass, Jack and I were surprised to see young Polynesians surfing 25' off our starboard side. I raised the quarantine flag as we motored through the lagoon. That was also a reminder to get Jack into his hiding spot. This would be my first encounter with the French and an international incident was something I didn't need.

Unfortunately, Jack didn't see things my way. The overload of smells coming from the land was driving him crazy and he wouldn't listen to reason. I put him in his canvas cat cozy, placed some sails over him and reto head for the customs dock. Ten feet away from the dock and Jack started to meow like he was being murdered! Instantly I turned the boat away from the dock and headed back out in the lagoon so I could see what the hell was bothering the four legged wind bag. He greeted me with fully extended claws when I opened his bag. True, it had been a while since we did this drill, but he's usually pretty good about going under cover. He walked around a bit and I opened some tuna for him, but he didn't touch it. "Time to try again" I decided. More displeasure, more scratches, but he had quieted down.

Jack waited until just before we got to the dock and then he resumed yelling. Out we went again. Anyone watching from shore must have wondered what the crazy American was doing. This time I plopped Jack on the toilet and he did his business while I patiently explained to him we would be in BIG trouble if I got caught bringing a pet to the islands. Well, third times a charm and we made it to the customs dock where a man took the dock lines and helped tie *Rick's Place* up.

"Having trouble?" he asked in a heavily accented voice.

"The engine was acting up," I lied. He looked kind of skeptical and walked away. Then I noticed my arm. In my haste to get docked I didn't realize that Jack had tattooed me with several blood letting scratches. The stranger that had helped me probably saw the dried blood and wondered what kind of madness was taking place on that boat.

The pier appeared to be just a road that dead ends at the water. The difference between the street level and the water level was about 7 feet, so instead of stepping off the boat as I usually would, I actually had to climb up off of *Rick's Place* to get on to the dock. It was apparent that this landing serves the much larger inter-island supply boats, because there were large truck tires hung as bumpers all around for protection.

Looking around from street level, the first thing I spotted was the small white church with the tall red steeple that the guide book had me use as a point of navigation when I first entered the lagoon. Closer to me were several small tourist type shops and some vendors with carts filled with bananas and other local fruits and vegetables. There was so much to see and so much activity with the cars and bicycles driving down the very nicely paved streets, I felt overwhelmed. It was a far cry from the stark simplicity of life on Fanning Island. There I felt I'd stepped back in time and here I felt like I could have just stepped off a cruise ship.

Finding the gendarme was the easy part of checking in, because it was just a short walk down the street and the customs office was very well marked. However, making sense of his grunts was the hard part. I knew no French and the official checking my papers knew no English or at least not that he'd let on to. Unlike the customs crew on Fanning that treated me like a long lost friend, this guy appeared to be very put out about my wanting to visit the country to which he was caretaker. In time I would learn just how different the two cultures were.

French Polynesia requires the posting of a bond at check in. The cost is an amount equal to the price of a one way airline ticket out of the country. I guess this is so a cruiser can be bled of every last dime and still not be a burden on the country when it came time to boot you out. Plus the banks charge a fee to change dollars to Francs on entry and then a fee to change it back to dollars on the way out. Nice little racket they've got going here.

Fortunately I had heard about this bond stuff while I was in Hawaii. So before leaving I located a travel agent in Honolulu and had him write a letter guaranteeing a one way plane ticket would ready for me at the drop of a phone call. I gave him a credit card number in case I did need a ticket and he gave me the document. With this paper in hand I managed to circumvent the French bonding rule! Later, talking to other cruisers, I learned I was the only one to get away with this. Most people enter the country in Tahiti where they are very strict to the rules, but here in Bora Bora they just don't see many check in's, so I was fortunate that the trough blew me here.

Another bright side is there would be no official visit to the boat! Jack and I dodged another bullet. Probably a lot more literally than I cared to admit.

Now, it was on to the Bora Bora Yacht Club that I'd heard so much about from Capt'n Joe. We picked up a mooring buoy in front of a thatched roof bar that was the so called yacht club. Free moorage and fresh water are available, but they do limit your stay to 3 days, I presume to give everyone a chance to have the opportunity to enjoy the facilities and spend their money in the expensive restaurant. This would be a great place to get the boat and the crew into post passage mode. Jack was happy to get outside in the sun and immediately nestled in to his "at anchor" spot laying stretched out in the sun on the boom.

Getting the dink into the water, I once again opted to row to shore instead of using the outboard. There were outdoor showers available and I took full advantage of the glorious feeling. I was having the usual land swaying episodes and these hit especially hard when I would close my eyes while standing in the small enclosure.

Fully refreshed and clean I stood and stared out at the beautiful blue lagoon of Bora Bora. I was struck once again in the difference between this island and Fanning. They are both atolls which were formed by volcanoes that sank back into the ocean, but Fanning Island just had the rim of the cone remaining and Bora, being much younger, geologically speaking, has yet to sink all the way. So Bora Bora has a large central landmass that is quite mountainous with its prominent and famous twin peaks rising out of the dense jungle. A coral reef surrounds the island; save for the narrow channel that all the watercraft entering the lagoon must traverse. This keeps the lagoon free from the influence of the ocean swell.

Along the reef are many motus, or small islands, some only 100 feet wide, others big enough to hold a large resort with their quaint bungalows built out over the lagoon. The water was clear and I could see coral heads near shore and there were colorful birds flying around the thatched roof bar. I was lost in my thoughts when it suddenly hit me: I was 5000 miles from Gig Harbor, standing in the Bora Bora yacht club and I sailed there in a boat I built myself. I could not contain the grin on my face.

I ordered a beer at the bar, but looking at the prices on the menu I quickly determined that eating there was going to be out of financial reach for me. A simple hamburger was nearly $15 and the prices seemed to skyrocket from there. So I sipped my expensive beer slowly and just took in the scenery when a polite, tattoo covered Polynesian man struck up a conversation with me. A nice change from the voices in my head! He spoke great English and was very interested in anything about the USA. He introduced himself as Pa'au. He explained to me that he went to college in Tahiti and lived in Papeete for several years but found the pace of life there "too crazy" as he said. He was about 30, leaner than most of the island men I had seen so far, but with very muscular arms. His jet black hair nearly reached his shoulders and he was bare-chested with a knee length sarong wrapped around his waist. I was surprised at how manly he still looked while wearing a skirt! He said he worked with his family in a business that supplies the resorts with a variety of items ranging from outboard gas to snorkeling masks.

I questioned why there are a number of empty moorings out front and he explained that after the three day limit here the cruisers move to a good, shallow and fully protected anchorage around the South end of the island. Pa'au said there were about ten boats down there at the time. I was anxious to get there and see who I would find; maybe *Cetus* or one of the other cruisers I'd like to meet back up with.

Pa'ua told me the passage to the anchorage is tricky to

navigate (very shallow and narrow with many coral heads) but he would be happy to guide me through when the time came. Seeing the momentary hesitation in my eyes at his generous offer, he quickly assured me that there wouldn't be a charge for his service as we were now friends. I finished my beer and signed the cruiser's Guest Log then rowed the short distance back out to *Rick's Place*. As soon as I got on board I was completely overcome with exhaustion and quickly fell into a deep sleep: the best sleep I'd had in 16 days.

The next few days were spent getting the boat cleaned up and trying to get rid of that funky locker room smell that develops during a long passage. I also had piles of laundry to do, too, since nearly everything I owned had gotten wet with salt water while passing through that nasty trough. I took opportunity to make a couple of international calls since I was once again in civilization. Mom was relived to hear my voice because it's been over a month since our last conversation. My next call was to Sheryl. She didn't answer on her boat, so I called the floral shop she owns.

"Hello, thanks for calling the Flower Pot."

"Yes, do you carry Ginger?"

Slight pause, then "No, sir, we don't" was her reply.

"Then how about Mary Ann?"

"Rick!! You butt! Where is my cat?"

Ah, ain't love grand.

"Nice to talk to you, too."

"I kinda expected to hear from you a week ago," softening a bit.

"Sorry, some nasty weather has Jack and me in Bora Bora instead of Tahiti."

"You both OK?"

"No problems," then I filled her in on the last month. The conversation was great. She's one of those people that are just extremely easy to talk to. So after about 10 minutes of non-stop gabbing on both our parts it is time to go. A phone call from French Polynesia was extremely expensive, just like everything here, and if I stayed on much longer I'd have to sell the boat to pay for the call.

Before she hung up she said, "Rick, I miss Jack…but I miss you more." That made my stomach light and I replied, "We need to get together. Come stay with us on the boat for a small vacation."
"I will, but right now the shop is just starting to take off and I just can't get away." So we said our goodbyes and promised to talk soon and then, with a solitary click, she was gone. I couldn't have been happier or more disappointed at the same time.

The next day Pa'au swam out to the boat and we powered the 3 miles to the entrance of the hidden lagoon. He was on the bow and signaled me to continue between two coral heads. From my position at the helm, I could see no possible way into the lagoon, so I powered back the engine and slowly followed the path Pa'au wanted me to take. Luckily the water was calm and clear. Several times the depth sounder read 6 feet, dangerously close to the absolute minimum water I needed to keep *Rick's Place* afloat, so I was getting pretty nervous. He then signaled me to make a hard right turn around another coral head. I really wanted to run up and ask him if he was sure, but I couldn't leave the tiller.

Suddenly, in front of us was a beautiful patch of sparkling blue water with a bright white sandy beach. Ten boats were anchored so close to the beach that it would only take a short swim to get to shore. The depth sounder was reading 20 feet as I found a spot safely away from the nearest anchored boat.

We set the anchor, turned off the motor and just bobbed under the tradewind sky. This lagoon seemed as protected as anywhere on earth. There were tall, lush, jungle covered mountains on three sides and the fourth side was a mile of barrier reef that held back the South Pacific. The mountains gave way to white sand beaches: a perfect place to land the dinghy for going to shore.

Using my binoculars, I searched for familiar boats. There was a French boat, a German boat and several American yachts, one of which I recognized from Hawaii. That was Serenity, skippered by Dick Ryan. Dick was 1/3 of the insanity that left Honolulu, along with Ron Gibbs and me. The ill-fated Boat-a-van, as it was called was in principle a good idea: three single handed boats traveling together, safety in numbers, yadda, yadda, yadda. I was anxious to see how it was going for Dick.

After a beer, some gabbing and a promise to take me on an Island bicycle tour, Pa'au dove gracefully over the side of my boat. It seemed like just a few strokes through the pristine liquid and he was standing in knee deep water. Wading to shore, he waved and disappeared into the heavy overgrowth beyond the white sand beach.

Jack and I spent a week in this wondrous southern anchorage. During that time, Dick and I shared several beers as we talked about our adventures since we'd last seen each other. It was interesting to learn about his trip to Palmyra. Apparently Ron, preferring to motor rather than using his sails effectively, ended up being left behind by Dick. It seems that he had gotten some bad fuel in Hawaii and he had trouble keeping the engine going. Dick stayed close until they got to Palmyra, but by then he'd had enough of Ron and Dick set off for Tahiti. Without his escort boat, Dick seemed to be living happily ever after. No word of Ron's whereabouts so far. The Cetus Crew had been in this anchorage until just a couple days before I arrived. I was really disappointed to have missed them! Word was they were heading to the Cook Islands, so maybe I could catch up to them yet.

My only history lesson concerning Bora Bora came from the old TV series "McHale's Navy". I remember that their shenanigans took place in the South Pacific and often times they'd make reference to going to Bora Bora. I was always intrigued by the name, it sounded so exotic, even though I had no idea where it was.

True to his word, Pa'au was back in a few days to act as my tour guide. He had what appeared to be a turn of the century bicycle while I rented a slightly newer model from a nearby resort. During our tour, Pa'au showed me old WW II bunkers and cannon emplacements. Several of these were only reached after leaving our bikes and taking what seemed like a death march through the jungle. The overgrowth was so thick in some places that a person could have walked right by the cannons and never see them if they didn't know their location. I was lucky to have Pa'au as my guide. He explained that in February 1942, the U.S. Navy showed up and began building airstrips, camps and bunkers. Bora Bora was a strategic point in the war of the Pacific. Location, location, location. When the war ended, the bunkers, cannons and airstrips were left behind, as well as more than a few blue eyed Polynesian babies.

More boats were showing up everyday as they picked their way up the Society Island chain from Tahiti. Most of these boats were coming from Mexico or had come through the Panama Canal. Since Hawaii had been our starting point, Jack and I were ahead of the mass of boats that was on its way. Some 300 boats were expected to leave the shores of the Americas and travel through the South Pacific this year. I planned to stay at the head of the pack so I could visit the islands before they were inundated with visitors this cruising season.

Beginning in April, after the last of the summer storms and continuing through October, the cruisers meander among the many islands of the South Pacific, trying to take in as much as possible before they have to flee to avoid the hurricane, or cyclone, season that would begin the following November. At that time you see a mass exodus as the boats head to safe waters out of the cyclone zones, either going to New Zealand or some small islands near the equator.

Five more boats had come in, and with 15 boats the anchorage was starting to get crowded. This was made very clear one morning around sunrise. With cocoa in hand, I stumbled up to the cockpit to greet the new day. What greeted me was a Frenchman hanging his derriere over the lifelines of his boat doing his morning business! No "Y" valves here! Apparently no toilet, either. My first thought was to row over and poop on their deck, but the last thing I needed was trouble that could involve the gendarme and my illegal cat. Unfortunately this wasn't the last time I would happen to see the occupants of this boat using this beautiful anchorage as their personal bidet.

Pa'au suggested a little, less crowded and less soiled anchorage several miles away. The snorkeling was supposed to be great there with an abundance of colorful fish and coral. We anchored off of a classic looking little white church with a tall red steeple. The main anchoring problem in Bora Bora is the deep,

deep bays. It was not uncommon to have 90 feet of water very close to shore. You had to pick your anchoring spots carefully so you weren't in deep water without enough chain out. Another peril was thinking you had a good bottom for anchoring, only to have the wind start to blow causing your anchor to drag into deep water. Having your anchor dangling by the chain and not touching the bottom is a real bad thing.

The snorkeling was great. Every morning after breakfast I was in the water. Up to this time, sharks were really the only sea creature that would get my undivided attention, but that soon changed. One morning while poking around a huge coral formation, I chased a small octopus into a dark recess near the bottom. I went up for a gulp of air then immediately went back down to the hole that the eight legged creature had hidden in. At least I thought it was the same hole. Just as I was about to stick my hand in the hole, the biggest set of jaws connected to the beadiest eyes I'd ever seen came shooting out at me. My underwater screams after seeing this strange snake like creature with a cavernous mouth did two things:

1. It encouraged the monster eel to retreat back into his hole.

2. It got rid of what little oxygen I had in my lungs.

Coughing as I broke the surface, I made a bee line to the safety of the dinghy making a mental note to add a pair of gloves to my snorkeling gear. Pa'au got a great laugh from my sea monster story, assuring me that the eel didn't like my looks any more than I liked his. But I've decided I dislike eels almost more than I dislike sharks.

Snorkeling, jungle hiking and bicycling were the order of the day, everyday. But there was a dark cloud hanging over Bora Bora. Food prices were crazy and beer prices were utterly insane. I still had plenty of canned food, so I just needed to supplement my stores with some fresh foods. Vegetables were especially overpriced, due to the lack of good gardening soil on this sand covered volcanic atoll. As an example, a medium sized tomato costs about $5 and a small watermelon is a $10 setback with lettuce coming in at around $7 a head.

Luckily, many foods are subsidized by the French government to make it possible for the local inhabitants to survive, so there are some reasonably priced goods to be found. I could actually buy a nice steak for about $4.00 (but not at a restaurant! When they get hold of anything the price goes through the roof and that $4.00 steak becomes a $40.00 steak). There are also inexpensive French wines (in boxes) and cheese is another subsidized commodity. But the main staple of my diet on Bora Bora became the Baguette. Those delicious crusty rolls of French Bread are 3 feet long, baked fresh daily and they only cost 35 cents a loaf! I would buy at least 3 every morning when they were hot out of the oven.

The high prices for food have hit some harder than others. One couple had to resort to breaking in to their emergency stores in their overboard bag after having entertained guests from home aboard their boat for ten days. Trying to show them a good time they went out to eat a lot and once the guests left they were broke and their cupboards were bare.

I decided I'd better be moving on before I too, was broke and out of food. I had been here nearly a month and that fulfilled my personal requirement to stay in a country at least as long as it took to get there.

The big question was where to? Fate may have answered that question when I met a boat couple that actually had a cat on board that was legal. They suggested that in American Samoa I could get the proper papers for Jack, thereby making an honest cat out of him. If we were going to continue our relationship, this seemed like a great idea because it was getting more difficult to keep him out of sight and down below. He was turning into a sun cat. As I plotted the course on my chart, I noticed that I could stop off at one of the Cook Islands on my way to Samoa.

Checking out elicited the same grunts and groans from the gendarme as when we checked in and that was followed by the usual round of goodbyes to the new friends I had met. Pa'au was especially hard to say goodbye to. As a present I gave him a spare dive mask he had been eyeing. He gave me a carved wooden bowl that I would always treasure. Pa'au also gave Jack a nice tuna fillet making him a friend forever. The next morning at sunrise, I pulled up the anchor and motored out of the pass. Once we were well out of the channel, up went the sails and away we went, off to a new adventure.

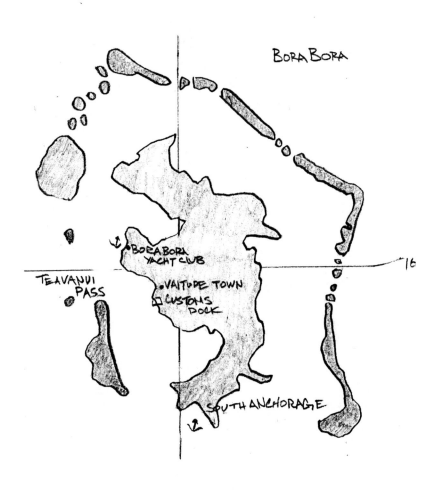

BORA BORA

BORA BORA
YACHT CLUB

VAITUPE TOWN

CUSTOMS
DOCK

TEAVANUI
PASS

SOUTH ANCHORAGE

16

CHAPTER 12

On the Road to Aitutaki

"Not all those who wander are lost..."

-J.R.R. Tolkien

With the peaks of Bora Bora quickly fading in the distance, I set a course for the Cook Islands roughly 600 miles to the west. As I'd noted earlier, the Cooks were a perfect midpoint between French Polynesia and American Samoa, where I needed to go to get papers for Jack. My interest in these islands was stirred while talking with other cruisers on Bora Bora and reading through a guide book that I was lucky to find in the book exchange at the Yacht Club. Another reason I set the Cook Islands as a destination is that this country, which is a small spattering of atolls, were trade partners with New Zealand, so reasonably priced food and supplies could be expected upon arrival.

Now the big decision I needed to make was which island in the group would I choose to make landfall? I'd learned that Raratonga was the capital of the archipelago, hence the largest city with of population of about 10,000 people. I battled with the voices in my head as they debated where we should go—it seemed Moe, Larry and Curly each had a different opinion. We could go to the population center which would have a bigger variety of supplies, or to one of the outer atolls where checking in would be less formal, as was the case in Bora Bora. Before too long it was decided that the remote check in would trump a large market place. I can't remember which side I took in that argument, but I agreed with the decree. I entered the coordinates in the GPS for a place called Aitutaki. According to my guidebook, it was populated, but not near so heavily as Raratonga. The book also said that on April 11, 1789, Captain Bligh from the famed *Bounty* was the first European to discover this remote island. So it was settled, good enough for Bligh, good enough for Rick.

For reasons I didn't understand, my body felt good right from the start of this trip. I suspect it's because I had plenty of rest and had added a few pounds to the bones along with having the best muscle tone since leaving the States. All the walking, bike riding and swimming had really paid off. Jack was also doing well and seemed delighted at the new companion I had inadvertently brought on board. A gecko had hitched a ride on a hand of bananas I'd purchased at the market on Bora Bora just before departure, so I now had a second stowaway. The cat was mesmerized by the small creature that could walk on the ceiling. I hoped this could keep him entertained for the duration of the passage.

I was also very happy about the number of new books I collected from the Bora Bora Yacht Club's book exchange. "Take one/Leave one" read the sign, so out with the old and in with the new—well, new to me at least. Reading on a passage had become almost an addiction, and nervousness would set in if I didn't have at least 2 unread books as back ups to the one I was currently reading. The Yacht Club was a gold mine. In addition to the cruising guide (that included not only the Cook Islands, but Samoa, Tonga and Fiji) I was able to score several spy novels and a book on tying knots. I gave up two sci-fi futuristic, on another world type books, a seafood cookbook and a romance novel that I didn't want to read because it would have made me start moping about Sheryl.

The weather information I received called for nothing out of the norm; but that of course immediately put me on edge. So it was with a fair bit of trepidation that I began my first night at sea in over a month.

The relatively short distances between ports, combined with the rich and bountiful fishing grounds resulted in many fishing boats in the area and lights from these boats were visible throughout the night. Fish trawlers with nets, long line boats, boats with mega bright lights and boats with no lights at all, seemed to surround *Rick's Place* in the first 36 hours. Luckily, staying alert was not a problem so early in the voyage.

Jack, who is normally very docile, almost to the point of appearing dead, was starting to show his frustration with the lizard that could walk on walls. Several times the cat managed to climb on to a cabinet to try and get a little closer to the green gecko, only to miss time his leap at the darting reptile and fall with a resounding thud to the floor. He would then resume his sitting and "looking at the ceiling" stare.

Three days out of Bora, *Rick's Place* suffered an outbreak of fruit flies, the result of an aging banana. Up until then, Godzilla (the name I'd given to our new lizard friend) had been staying pretty well hidden. But now with the big improvement in his food supply (Gecko's eat bugs) he was much more daring. One evening when I came down to make some cocoa, I turned on the red light and stopped dead in my tracks. There, on the ceiling was the once tiny Gecko, now twice his original size, surrounded by a group of fruit flies. The reptile was picking off the flying pests with his lightning fast tongue like there was no tomorrow. So having him join our crew had been very fortuitous for all of us. He had easy pickin's at every meal without the competition of other lizards, I had a great bug eradicator that didn't involve nasty chemicals and Jack had constant entertainment. It's what's called a win—win---win situation.

With Jack happily sitting on the chart table probably wishing he could do to the lizard what it was doing to the bugs, I slipped back outside with my cocoa and one of my new books. It was a spy novel by a well known author. He had obviously put in a lot of time and energy into writing this particular piece of fiction: to the tune of 824 pages!

When I'd picked it up at the book exchange from amongst the other discards, I realized that something this voluminous was a big commitment and not to be taken lightly. I generally stay with shorter stories so as not to get hooked into a long winded book that I don't like, because once I begin reading something, I very rarely will quit before the end, no matter how dull the story. I started reading the huge tome just before leaving Bora Bora and it turned out to be so captivating that I spent every spare minute I had glued to the book to find out what would happen next. As Mom would say, "I couldn't keep my nose out of it!"

Day or night, it didn't matter. Unwashed dishes, it didn't matter. Unchecked bilges, it didn't matter. I couldn't recall being so caught up in a fictional scenario in all my adult life. The book was cleverly written in such a way as to keep the reader guessing as to the ending from the very first page. In short, I loved reading it and the first four days of the passage passed in a blur.

On the morning of the fifth day, just as the sun was breaking the Eastern horizon, I was settling down in the cockpit, book in hand. I'd just placed a reef in the mainsail as the trade winds had freshened a bit, but things were still quite nice. That was my favorite reading time: a new dawn with the air just warming up having survived another night and a day closer to landfall. A loud whistle from the galley announced my tea kettle needed tending. So, setting my prized novel down on the cockpit seat, I went below to mix my early AM cocoa. Two minutes later I climbed the short ladder out of the salon to the cockpit and something floating in the water caught my eye. Leaning over the stern I puzzeled as to where the object had come from—it looked like paper. Then a gust of wind sent four more pieces of paper flying past my head. OH DAMN! BOOK PAGES! The wind was plucking pages from my well worn paperback and tossing them into the sea. My first inclination was to try and grab what was in the air and I began waving my arms around in a futile attempt to recover what I could. It proved impossible as more wind lifted more pages and carried them right past me. I kind of did a stumble dive onto the wind decimated novel As I rolled off of the precious book, nearly all the pages were now loose from the binding and further more they were no longer in any semblance of order. I was devastated. The next hour was spent trying to get the written story back in order, but after all the remaining pages had been reassembled, my worst fear was realized. The last quarter of the book was gone, kaput, bye bye. I just sat and stared at the book cover thinking how unbelievable this whole debacle was! I knew then that I would be on a quest to search for this title at every book exchange I encountered from here to New Zealand.

About 100 miles out of Aitutaki, the usually reliable trade

winds slowed down, then died completely. I knew from experience that a weather disturbance somewhere within 500 miles was to blame. The question was, is foul weather going to cross my path or will I just have the inconvenience of having to motor for a time?

With just a couple hours until sunset, I started the engine and settled into the drone of my one cylinder calliope. A short time later I caught a whiff of something that wasn't quite right. Rushing below, I opened the engine access door, but found, or rather smelled, nothing out of the ordinary there. The ice box was the next thing to investigate, and although there were some questionable items in it's confines, this wasn't the source of the funk.

Back outside the stench was even more pervasive. Jack took time out from searching for Godzilla to come out and sniff the air. I swear he wrinkled his nose as he dove back down below seeking olfactory relief.

The sun was just a half disk from being completely obscured by the horizon when a huge flock of birds caught my eye. They were a quarter of a mile away. Some were circling and some were standing on an object that was floating partially submerged in the gentle swell. Curiosity got the best of me so I altered course to rendezvous with the dark mass. I was quick to note that the closer I got to the squawking birds, the more pungent the mysterious odor became. One hundred feet was as near as my stomach would allow me to get to what I had discerned to be a whale carcass. The combination of seeing the birds feasting on entrails and a gentle puff of wind that sent the thick emanation directly at *Rick's Place*, caused me to get instantly sick over the rail and alter course.

I spent the rest of the night airing out the boat in an attempt to get that horrific smell out of my mind and the taste out of my mouth. Note to self: you don't always have to follow your nose.

The next morning's sunrise reveled Aitutaki five miles ahead! An easily identifiable channel entrance was a quarter mile from the basin where boats could be moored. There was room for about 4 boats to anchor according to some cruisers that I had met in Bora Bora. I could only count three sailboat masts, so I proceeded through the extremely narrow channel. As was the case at Fanning Island, this was a narrow pass and there would be no turning around mid channel.

When I got in to the anchorage, I discovered the boats already anchored had a line tied to shore. This would keep them from swinging and hitting each other in such a small space . A dinghy approached and a gentleman offered to take a stern line to shore once I dropped anchor. I motored past the bows of the anchored boats to the last open spot. Turning parallel with the others, bow pointing away from shore, I came to a stop, ran up front, dropped my anchor, let out some chain and tied it off. Hurrying back I handed the helpful cruiser a rope that I'd tied to the stern of *Rick's Place*. He took the line the 200 feet to shore and tied a loop around the trunk of a palm tree and then I pulled on the stern connection until my boat was about 30 feet from shore. I then went back up to the bow and pulled in enough chain to set the big anchor in the soft sand. I was anchored "Med style", as it is known since it is a common way to moor in the Mediterranean due to the crowded anchorages there. Another first for *Rick's Place*.

As I took a moment to relax, I marveled at a huge church that was on shore. Built of coral blocks, probably cut right out of the reef, it was a change from the small wood frame and red steeples of French Polynesia. A voice from shore brought me back to the present. A dark skinned local dressed in white shorts and a shirt with badges or patches was waving me to shore. Must be check in time. As the official waited for me, I launched my rubber dinghy. While messing with my oars and getting my papers together, I failed to notice Jack go out and hop up to his sun spot on the boom. As I came out from below, I could see the custom's guy intently staring at something on my boat. I turned to see what had his interest and there was Jack! "Damn it Jack! We're going to get in deep trouble," I hissed under my breath. He must not have liked my tone, as he responded with an open paw swipe at my face. That elicited a hearty laugh from the waiting official.

I hoped he'd still be laughing when he found out the cat didn't have any papers. No use putting Jack below now, so I jumped into the dinghy and rowed ashore.

The administer grabbed my hand as I nearly fell while

scrambling up the boulder strewn shoreline. "Welcome to Aitutaki," he said with a smile. His English was very easy to understand and held a bit of Australian or New Zealand accent. As we walked toward a cinder block building that had the Coat of Arms of the Cook Islands painted on it, I kept waiting for him to ask about Jack. After we went through all the check in forms, he stamped my passport and said, "You may take your friend off your yacht." I took a minute to answer, "No, that won't be necessary," because I was thinking he would want to quarantine Jack.

He continued, "You are allowed to stay 3 weeks on Aitutaki and you can bring your pet to shore as long as it is in your full control."

"Thank you," I said, slightly stunned, but not bloody likely I thought. I don't know how a person ever has full control of a cat. I shook hands with the official and left the building thinking Jack probably won't be so lucky next time he chooses to expose himself.

As I was walking the shoreline, I was taken aback when I noticed that three of the four boats anchored in this tiny basin were from Washington! I haven't been around this many fellow Washingtonians since leaving Gig Harbor many months ago.

Walking further I saw a small shack on the side of the road with six motor scooters lined up in front of it. These two wheelers were in differing conditions, one looked brand new, while the others appeared to have some serious mileage on them. A sign announced that I should "inquire within" to rent one of these beauties. Interesting. I would have to check this out.

I also saw a small grocery store and a post office, but both appeared to be closed at the moment.

"It's their lunch time," came a deep voice that startled me and I turned to see the guy that had helped me tie up in the anchorage. "I'm Vern," he continued while extending his hand.

"Hi, I'm Rick, hey, thanks for the help this morning!" was my response.

"No problem, always nice to have a hand when you gotta stern tie," he added.

"Which boat are you off of?" I inquired.

"The blue hull—*Money Pit*," as he pointed to a newer looking 40 footer that had lots of shiny chrome.

"So you're from Washington?" I asked, even though it was pretty obvious since that's what it said on the stern of his boat.

"Yeah, Seattle. Left about two years ago," Vern answered. Then I went on to explain to him that I was from Gig Harbor and about the route I took to get here. Vern had sailed down to Mexico from Seattle two years ago and then had crossed to the South Pacific from Mexico after that.

"How about the other boats? You all traveling together?" was my next query.

"No, not on purpose, but we've all bumped into each other many times this season. The second Washington boat over there is *Blind Faith*. A nice couple from Olympia," Vern informed me.

"Are you sailing alone?" I asked somewhat hopeful that I would find another solo sailor to commiserate with.

"No, I'm with my wife and our teenage son, Nels. They're out for a hike at the moment. At least that's what my wife calls it. I call 'em death marches," then he continued, "Plus, I had work to get done on the boat. That excuse gets me out of her torturous hikes every time."

"The third boat is called *R&R*, and it's from Australia. Home built—made of steel." Then he added, "Nice couple but I can't understand the guy when he talks. I guess because he's an Aussie, but he grew up in France, so his accent is really messed up." He went on to tell me, "his wife claims she can't even decipher what the hell he is saying when he gets excited."

I asked him what he knew about the scooter rental and he told me that they were only $15 a day US and they are the best way to get around the island. Then he told me the crews from the three boats were heading to the Blue Lagoon resort that night. "Rumor is that they have the best hamburgers this side of New Zealand. The restaurant is about 5 miles east on that road there," he stated as he pointed to the only road I could see. He said they'd already reserved some scooters to get there and then to use the next day for some sight seeing.

"Who do I talk to about getting one?" I asked, looking in

the direction of the cycles on display.

"The guys name is Paul, and he should be back from his lunch break pretty soon," he reassured me.

"Sounds great, Vern! Thanks for all the info. I'll see you guys tonight, if not sooner." Then I added, "Are there any book exchanges here?" but he replied that he hadn't come across any yet, but they'd only been here a few days. I thought it sounded like it would be a lot of fun to rent a scooter and join the group at the restaurant.

The sun was just starting to burn through the low overcast, causing the temperature to rise, and a wave of drowsiness came over me. Thinking I might have about an hour before Paul, the scooter guy, would return, I headed for a neatly maintained grassy area near where *Rick's Place* was moored. A perfect place to spend the time, I thought as I laid on my back in the course grass. The rocking feeling that I get after a passage actually helped me fall asleep.

As I came out of my short, but deep, slumber, I continued to lay there with my eyes closed and just took in the sounds around me. The wind blown palm trees were giving off a distinct rustling that blended nicely with the cooing of the island doves. Water lapping at the hulls of the nearby anchored boats added to the restful symphony. I could even hear Jack meowing from *Rick's*. Then I had a sensation of a small bug skittering across my forehead and I opened my eyes. There was a small child, perhaps 5 or 6 years old, staring back at me! She gasped and dropped the long grass stem she'd been holding in her hand and along with her three little friends, turned and ran away from where I was laying. They giggled loudly as they retreated. I guess they'd been having fun playing with the sleeping foreigner. I was happy that they weren't putting my hand in warm water--or maybe they don't know that old trick yet.

When I stood up I could see and hear Jack on the stern of the boat. He was getting louder, so he must have been pretty hungry, but, then again, he always seemed to think he was starving. He had to wait because I still needed to get to the cycle shack.

I walked over to the rental outfit and was met at the door by

Paul, who was a pleasant young fellow with dark hair and brown eyes and appeared to be in his late 20's. I was surprised to learn he was from the states! He was from the Oakland area and had been living on Aitutaki about a year. Then he explained how he ended up in this far off locale, "I finished college and went into construction management. I was miserable. A friend had just come back from his honeymoon here in the Cook Islands, and he raved about the people and the climate, so I took my next vacation here a year and a half ago. I stayed my 2 weeks, went home and sold my condo, then came here and bought this scooter shop. Couldn't be happier!"

"Wow! That's a great story. Didn't they have a problem with giving you a work permit?" I asked. Paul replied, "As long as I am contributing to the island's economy, the government is cool with what I do."

Paul handed me the keys to the small cycle and said, "don't miss riding the island's perimeter road—it's spectacular!"

"Thanks, Paul," I said, starting to push the cycle towards *Rick's Place*. Then I stopped and asked him what would become my standard line of questioning everywhere I went, "Hey Paul, are there any book exchanges around?"

"Yeah, at the resort," came his reply. Bingo! Everything was falling in to place for a great visit on Aitutaki.

I parked the scooter under the palm tree that Vern had tied my stern line to and went back out to my boat. After I fed the cat I did some dishes, aired the boat out and started reading. A couple hours later, I heard "Hey Rick! You home?" It was Vern calling to me from shore.

I popped my head out of the cockpit and gave a little wave and he asked, "We're heading off to dinner – you still comin'?"

"I'll be along shortly, but you don't have to wait for me," I offered.

"Just follow the road—you can't miss the resort. See ya later!" he yelled with another wave of his hand.

And with that, 4 underpowered motor scooters roared—no, whimpered—to life and headed out on the aforementioned dirt road. Each couple on a cycle with the teenager, Nels, on his own ride.

I had a good reason for not leaving at the same time as the Wild Bunch. Growing up I was a terrible bike rider suffering more spills and scrapes than could be counted. Not wanting to be left behind by my boyhood friends was the only reason I continued to get back on the damn things. What I didn't want now was to provide the awkward moment that came with an unintentional crash and burn. Once on shore, I sauntered over to the waiting machine. Inserting the key and turning it to the on position, I tried the kick starter. First try; nothing, second try; zilch. However I did manage to scrape my ankle on the exhaust pipe. Third time's a charm, as the saying goes, and the little engine yinged to life.

OK, I was ready. Using my right foot, I tapped the gear shift into low and applied some throttle. The engine revved slightly before the clutch grabbed and slowly the wheels started moving through the grass. My legs were then off the ground, but spread out like training wheels; just in case.

It's nearly impossible to balance one of those things while going so slow and my hands were fighting the handlebars back and forth in an attempt to keep the whole show upright. When I gave it a little more gas it was easier to go straight and keep my balance. As I headed up the gentle grass incline toward the road my confidence was building. I gave the throttle a little twist just as I turned on to the hard packed dirt road and my speed increased and I was feeling pretty smug.

The voices had been pretty worried about crashing, and a collective sigh in my head helped me to settle down.

As I traveled down the road with the warm air tickling my ears, I had to concentrate on avoiding the numerous potholes that obstructed my path. After a couple miles, the road turned away from the shoreline I'd been traveling along and I was surrounded by heavy jungle like growth. The late afternoon sun was now casting long shadows. The scooter head lights did nothing to help brighten things up. There was so much to see, but the voices were getting nervous again and asking me to keep my eyes on the road.

As I passed homes, some thatched and some of wood, more than one dog ran out to see me and run along side for a time. Kids and adults would wave, and I would brave taking one hand off the handlebars and return their greeting. There were flowers growing everywhere; brightly colored, some on bushes and others on long ropey vines. My mind was wandering, but then I saw a sign for the resort, though I couldn't see it yet, I knew it couldn't be far— maybe around the next turn?

Then, without warning, I caught movement right at my peripheral edge. My reaction, unfortunately, was to jerk the handles. This combined with a patch of loose gravel sent the bike skittering across the road. I crashed into waist high bushes that bordered the drive. Panicking, I squeezed too hard on the hand brake, which caused the front wheel to lock up. This, in turn, sent my body lunging forward as if I would fly over the handlebars. Maybe with more speed I would have, but since jogging speed was about how fast I'd been going, I simply smashed my groin on handlebars. Once at a complete stop, the final indignity came as I lost my balance and fell over, landing softly in the tall grass. That was exactly why I've always hated bikes.

Without hesitation, I exercised myself from under the fallen bike and quickly stood up. Glancing around, making sure no one had witnessed this debacle, I brushed myself off. I picked up the demon two wheeler and turned it around and pushed it out into the dirt road. There was a very large pig rooting around right where I'd gone off road and the voices were now howling with laughter. "A pig! That's what scared you?" It did seem pretty comical once I realized I wasn't permanently disabled.

Darkness was settling in fast. I got *Easy Rider* started again and continued up the road. Every bump I hit shot a bolt of pain through my beans and franks, but luckily I didn't have to suffer long before I reached my destination.

There was a clearing with a large thatched roof, open air restaurant built near the beach. On the other side of the road was a parking area that had a few newer small cars, that appeared to be rentals. Then I spotted the other four "Scooter Shack" scooters because they were parked side by side as if ridden in by the Hell's Angels. Pulling up next to them, I killed the engine, engaged the kick stand and strode toward the lights of the eatery.

I was really hoping to find a restroom mirror to check myself out before formally meeting the other boat people, so I poked my head in to look around. I saw about a dozen tables set up with silverware, napkins and a burning candle on each of them. "Rick, over here!" Vern yelled. Turning toward his voice, I saw that several tables had been pulled together off to the side. A quick mental count told me everyone I expected to see, was there. "Remember: first impressions..." The voices advised me.

Walking toward the group I could smell the fried food cooking and I was instantly hungry. Vern stood up to greet me as I neared his table, and reached out to shake my hand. I caught a flash of a questioning look from the guy, but before I had a chance to dwell on it, he introduced his wife. "Rick, this is the real captain of *Money Pit*, my wife, Alice.

"Glad to meet someone from close to home," I said shaking her hand. Alice was a pleasant looking brunette with well toned arms. She had a sprinkling of freckles across her cheeks and a smile that revealed a small gap between her front teeth, ala Loren Becall. Without letting go of my hand, she stood up and said "excuse me," as she reached for the top of my head with her other hand. "A little present," she added as she lifted a sprig of grass out of my hair.

Vern laughed, "doing a little off road riding on the way here?"

"Yeah, something like that," I stammered, knowing my face was getting red as I said it. And the voices in my head chimed in with "hey, nice first impression klutz."

"This is Nels, our son," Vern said as a rail thin, somewhat gawky 14-year old boy with a butch hair cut stood up and extended his hand.

"Nice to meet you Nels," I said shaking his hand.

Vern continued with the introductions, "Next to Nels are Roy and Rita from the boat *R&R*."

More handshaking and I stated, "You're from Australia," having remembered that from Vern's earlier dissertation. Rita answered in the affirmative with her lovely Australian accent that I always enjoy hearing. In appearance she reminded me a lot of my mom; late 50's, short in stature and a bit doughy.

"Did you have a good cruise so far?" was her first question.

"Yes, thanks," I replied, now looking at Roy who was ready to get glad handed. Roy was kind of stocky and seemed to have an inordinate amount of body hair—it was even sticking out of his shirt collar.

"Way wa ya list purt?" he said rather quickly, and in my head I was replaying his words trying to figure out what he said when Rita piped in with, "Where did you sail from last?"

"Uh, Bora Bora," I answered, feeling the red starting to return to my cheeks.

Rita, noticing this added, "Don't worry bout understanding Roy, no one, not even me can figure out what the bloke is saying half the time," and she went on to explain, about him growing up in France even though he was Australian. Everyone at the table laughed, followed by an awkward silence. Then I moved down the table to the last not introduced twosome for some more handshaking, and the husband offered, "Hi, I'm Mike and this is my wife Susanne."

"Nice to meet another boat from the South Sound," I responded, throwing in the nickname of our cruising grounds back home. Susanne asked, " How long have you been away from Washington?" and it took me a little while to come up with the answer, because even though it's only been a little over a year, in some ways it seems like forever.

Finally getting to sit down after all the introductions, I looked around the charming restaurant. The high thatched palm ceiling had lights hanging in old fashioned lobster traps. There was a long bar – probably about 20 feet-- made of bamboo with beautiful tapa cloth hanging behind it. And the view! The front of the building was open to the ocean and watching the waves breaking just offshore was magnificent in the moonlight.

The waitress came by to take our orders. She was one of the prettiest Polynesians I'd ever seen. Long silky black hair adorned her petite frame, and her sparkling hazel eyes and bright smile completed the perfect picture. Everyone asked for hamburgers and beer, and I was no exception. Only $5 for a large cheeseburger and $1 for a beer made dining out easy enjoyment. We weren't in French "break the bank" Polynesia anymore!

The evening was spent talking about storms, landfalls and people we had in common. After cruising solo for so long it took awhile for me to get into a conversation, but once I started, it was hard to shut up the beer induced blabber.

Vern seemed like the conversation starter, the story teller, the snoop of the group. "Rick, I see you have a cat on board," he prodded. I then spent the next half hour recounting how Jack had become my shipmate. Everyone was thoroughly amazed to learn he could use the toilet. Roy's reaction was to chime in with, "Ay ca rap un hed", which I could only guess had something to do with Jack using the head. A field trip to *Rick's Place* was planned so that Jack could perform, what my fellow cruisers considered a minor miracle. Again, many things are promised during these beer tasting events.

The rest of the evening went by without any further discomfort. Under the advice of the voices, I excused myself before the rest of the party. Not wanting to chance a major accident in front of my new friends, I bid goodnight and promised to see everyone the next day.

I was still a little sore from where the bike fell on my leg, but I managed to make it home without incident.

The next morning when I stepped out into the cockpit, I noticed two of the scooters were already gone. Someone got an early start. My plans for the day were to first of all go back to the resort and see about the book exchange – I'd forgotten to ask the night before. Then I wanted to tour the island's perimeter. I hoped to find some good snorkeling spots, too. Leaving Jack for the day was easier now that he was out of the closet, so to speak, as I didn't have to keep him hidden down below and out of sight.

So I hopped on my trusty steed, and with a belch of blue smoke from the exhaust pipe; off I went. As I neared the resort area, I saw the same pig that ran me off the road the night before. "Eat my dust!" I said under my breath as I gunned the throttle and increased my speed to a testosterone fueled 15 mph.

In the day light I could see the resort bungalows built over the water. With the limited lighting at night the huts were all but invisible, so it was a surprise to see them today. They were just a short walk from the restaurant and these little cottages retained the island motif being built of woven palm fronds and bamboo.

Walking toward the restaurant I passed the large swimming pool that was built near the beach, surrounded by palm trees. Upon entering the dining room, I again saw the waitress that served our party last night. She saw me and smiled as if she remembered who I was. "Hi there," I said, "I'm looking for the book exchange, do you have one here?"

"No, we sell no books here," she said looking very concerned.

"No, no, trade books – Take one Leave one," I said while making a back and forth gesture with my hands.

"Ahhhhhh, noooooo," she said, the smile now gone and she was looking as if she had lost her best friend. I'd seen this reaction from natives on other islands before – they want to be helpful and nice and it seems to pain them when they actually have to say the word no to anyone.

So I smiled to let her know all was well and said a light hearted, "OK, thanks!" as I turned to leave. Then a voice boomed from the back, "Try the store next to the post office." I saw an old man shrouded in the low light at the corner of the room. "Thanks," I called over my shoulder in the direction the voice had come from, as I walked outside.

I gave my two wheeled bomber a kick start and roared off following the road that I figured would take me around the island. Over on the west side of the island, I was surprised to see six other resorts in the span of about three miles. I stopped at each of them to have a quick look around and to find out if any of them had book exchanges. I was delighted to find modest trading libraries, but none had the novel I was searching for. I continued to the north along the road which hugged the beach. At the top of the atoll I discovered the small airstrip, complete with a fuel island and a cement block office with a bright orange windsock flying high above it. I stopped to check it out, but no one was around. There was a sign that read, "Cook Island Aero: We'll Get You There!" I found their slogan a little puzzling. Do they mean there is another airline that won't get you there? It's not like they were saying they'd be on time, or that they're happy you're flying with them, but instead they are saying that there is reasonable certainty that Cook Island Aero will not fall out of the sky before they get you "There." It almost felt like they were challenging you to fly with them. To much thinking started giving me a headache so I decided to move on.

Starting down the east side of the atoll, the road rose in elevation about 100 feet. This provided an unobstructed view of the Pacific Ocean, so I stopped to take it all in. As I looked out, I spotted a sail on the horizon and it was just a tiny speck. It brought home just how small and insignificant I am out there. When I continued on my journey the road turned inland after a couple miles leaving the beach behind and once again entering the jungle like growth. It was almost immediately dark, due to the heavy vegetation, and the ruts in the road were now filled with water attesting to the lack of sunlight reaching the ground. Once again I was in amongst a multitude of flowers and broad leaf plants that were forming an impenetrable wall just off the roads edge. After 15 minutes or so of dodging mud puddles and palm fronds that littered the road, I came to a clearing that was carved out of the dense foliage. There was a wall about eight feet high made of the trunks of palm trees bordering the property and a large double door gate that accessed the road.

The whole scene was reminiscent of the old *King Kong* movies, where the natives built the towering wall in the jungle to keep Kong out. A sign above the gates proclaimed this area "New Jerusalem". I stopped *Easy Rider* in front of the large doors and turned off the engine to get some silence. I thought I could hear soft chanting or singing from the other side of the wall.

I wonder what that is all about?" I whispered to myself. The chanting stopped and the only sound I heard then were the buzz of the bugs flying close by and an occasional bird in the overgrowth. Then a cloud passed over the sun and the whole scene sent a chill up my spine. It was way too much like an old movie— very creepy. Time to go.

The voices in my head were confirming what I had already determines, and I was going to listen to them for once. I pumped the kick starter and.... Nothing! Again I tried, this time with a bit more force, but still no belch of blue smoke. By then I could hear people on the other side of the gate and I was getting nervous.

"Damn motor bike," I said scolding the steel machine, as if it were a dog that had just peed on the rug.

I heard another voice, this one a clear oratory from inside my own head, saying, "the key stupid, turn the key!" I quickly fumbled with the key, as I saw the big gate begin to open, I switched it on, gave it a big kick and; NOTHING! By that time I was certain I would be grabbed by this cult and made into a zombie. My next attempt at starting the engine, this time with all my weight, and the tinny motor coughed to life. I inadvertently gave the bike full throttle and the front wheel lifted off the ground about 2 inches. I shot forward, down the road, more out of control than in. I looked back to make sure nobody was throwing spears and nearly lost control. An imagination can be a dangerous thing.

Half an hour later, I could tell that I was closing the loop, nearing my starting point on my round the island tour. Spotting the two cycles that had left earlier than me that morning parked to the side of the road near the beach, I slowed down. I could see Vern and his family snorkeling around a coral outcropping, and I was tempted to stop and join them, but I figured Jack had probably had enough alone time by now and I'd better just get back to *Rick's Place*. I putted back to home base, left the scooter resting on it's kickstand and decided to try to find a phone before heading out to the boat. But first I needed to walk around a bit to work the kinks out of my joints and to get some blood back to my posterior.

I strolled the short distance to the post office thinking it would be the most likely place to find service. I was anxious to call Sheryl.

As I walked into the older, but well kept building, I spotted 2 phone booths, each looked to be about 60 years old. A middle aged man greeted me near the door and explained that to place an international call, he would act as the operator. Then he took Sheryl's phone number from me and went back to a 1930's style switch board. Pulling plugs and pushing switches he spoke softly into a headset microphone that now adorned his bald head. I took a seat and waited for the operator to direct me to the phone booth. It was sort of like waiting for modern technology to connect to a tin can and string reality. Nearly 10 minutes had elapsed when suddenly the peace of the post office was shattered by a shrill sounding bell. The post master stuck his head out from behind the partition and pointed to the cubical in which I was to take the call. As I picked up the receiver I noted that it had been made before the use of plastic!

"Hello?" I said nervously, and a nano second later I heard my voice repeat lightly, "Hello?" Oh great! A time lag. Nothing says smooth, seemless conversation like a 3rd world telephone connection.

"Hello.......hello," came Sheryl's voice and echo.

"Hey, it's Rick..........rick."

"Is this the same Rick that kidnapped my cat?......my cat?

"If you remember...." Then before I can finish Sheryl said, "Cause if it is.....is", and then because we are both trying to talk at the same time the words start canceling each other out. Nothing but garble, then I waited for a break and yelled, "hold on! Hey the phone connection is goofy right now, I'll talk first and then you—just like on a VHF radio—it's the only way." I continued with, "Jack and I are in the Cook Islands. We'll leave in a couple days for Samoa. Things are going good. I think he misses you --- and I do too......do to." A bit of static on the line confirmed we were still connected then Sheryl said, "Rick, I am trying to figure a way to get some time off. Call me at a better time and we will get something planned out. In the mean time, don't let anything happen to Jack........to jack."

"I'll call you in about a week from Samoa.......samoa." I answered followed by a long silence, then, "Rick, you and Jack take care.......take care." Then an overly loud dial tone announced the connection had been broken. I hung up the handset and paid the postmaster/telephone operator twelve dollars for the privilege of hearing Sheryl's voice for less than 3 minutes. But it was worth it.

I walked outside and seeing my scooter I thought that I'd better get it returned to Paul before he closed for the day. Then my thoughts were broken with a loud, "Ain't you lookin' for a book exchange?" I immediately recognized the American sounding voice as the same I'd heard from the shadows at the restaurant this morning. I turned to see a guy who looked the spitting image of Moses after he returned from the Mount in the movie *The Ten Commandments*! He had the same long white flowing hair and beard, though Moses hadn't dressed in a t shirt and shorts as this guy did.

"Have you found the book you seek?" he queried.

"Ah, no, not yet," I responded staring in amazement because I couldn't believe how much he looked like Charleston Heston.

"Then come on in to my shop and look around," he said stepping aside and ushering me in the door.

It was a small establishment, much like a convienience store back home with just two aisles. Canned goods were the majority of the product on display and they were all unfamiliar brands to me since they get their goods from New Zealand. Then I spotted the bookcase which stood opposite of the door and looked like it held about 30 books. I stepped closer for a better look at the titles. Scanning each and every book, twice, with no luck at finding a replacement for the novel I'd lost at sea I muttered, "I can't believe it..."

All the while, Moses kept a close eye on me, so I asked, "Are you American?"

"Yes." was his short and to the point answer.

So I tried another angle with, "Been here long?"

"Awhile." Was all he offered.

The old man's attempts at being aloof drove the voices crazy. "Ask more, get nosey," they insisted.

Just as I was about to leave I spotted several cans of cat food on one of the shelves: Tuna Surprise, Salmon Banquet and Chicken with Gravy. I thought it would be fun to bring a treat home to Jack and let him try something that didn't come from the sea, so I bought the can of chicken cat food from the Chuck Heston look alike. His check out counter consisted of a calculator and a small gray cash box. It cost two dollars American for Jack to finally have a meal that didn't start with an F and end with an ish. But he deserved it, just like I'd deserved the phone call to Sheryl.

So I thanked the prophet look alike and as I reached the door I remembered one more item. It was a problem I hadn't had until arriving in Aitutaki, so I asked him, "Do you have mosquito coils? You know, to keep them away?" I added needlessly.

He looked at me and a thin smile came across his face. He reached down behind the counter to an unseen shelf and when his hand reappeared, he held a small green coil wrapped in plastic. The coil was tightly wound and about 6 inches in diameter made from a brown/green strand of something about the width of a pencil. "That will be $10," he said visibly warming up to me.
"Oh, I don't know if I brought that much money. I may need to go back and get more cash off the boat." I informed him as I fumbled with and tried to count what money I had left in my pocket.

"How much do you have?" He asked.

"Looks like about $8" I replied.

He then held out both his hands one with the coil and the other empty, palm up and said, "that will do," without any further explanation.

I placed the change in one hand and took the coil from the other and said, "Jeez, thanks, I'll bring the rest back later today or tomorrow morning."

"Don't worry." Were his only words.

"Thanks again," I said as I stepped out into the tropical sun.

I stuffed my cat food and flying bug killer coil into the backpack I was carrying and walked the short distance to Paul's Scooter Emporium. I saw Paul at his work bench and walked over and asked, "Hey Paul, what's with the guy in the store?"

"His name is Colby," was Paul's response not looking up from completing a tire repair. Then he added, "Doesn't get too involved with anybody here, I think he's a burned out hippie, probably trying to stay lost. Hey, how'd the scooter run?"

"It was great, no problems," I lied. "I'll bring it back tomorrow," I added.

"Take your time," he offered.

"Thanks," I was thinking how laid back everybody is here.

I pulled myself back out to *Rick's Place*, using the line that was tied to the palm tree on shore—it was even easier than rowing. Jack was meowing his displeasure at my tardiness in feeding him, so I announced, "Special treat Jackie!" As soon as I was standing on the boat, he was rubbing against my legs so hard he almost tripped me. I finally made it down stairs into the galley and opened the can. I put the precious contents into Jack's freshly washed bowl, placed the dish on the floor and stepped back expecting him to lunge at the *Chicken with Gravy Feast*. One sniff and he turned and walked away! What the hell? Then he sat down and looked up at me and gave me that "feed me now meow". "Forget it Jack—that's dinner," I informed him slightly annoyed that my special surprise wasn't the least bit appreciated.

Several hours later, it became quite evident that the only thing that was going to dine on the *Chicken with Gravy Feast*, was the swarm of Aitutaki flies that it had attracted. So, I threw the mistake over the side and washed out the bowl. The flies, unfortunately, decided to stick around, but I figured at least the gecko would eat well tonight.

The next two days were spent confined to the boat, as an extensive pattern of foul weather had parked itself over the Cook Islands. Another lovely trough, but this time I was at least in a very protected anchorage and all I had to deal with was the thunder, lightening and a lot of heavy rain. I enjoyed the extra reading time and even got a couple projects done that I'd been putting off.

One of those projects, that was particularly frustrating, was to find a leak that would cause a drip off the ceiling in the V-berth. Anytime I'd try to sleep up there, a droplet would form and no matter where in the bed I positioned myself, the water would be drawn to my head like a magnet to iron. That, in turn, would wake me from the deepest slumber. Very unpleasant.

Several times since leaving Hawaii, I made what I thought to be successful fixes, only to find myself a victim of the Chinese water torture the next time it rained. I never could figure out why it only seemed to drip at night, as I never saw any evidence of it during the day. I would place sealant around the areas that I guessed were allowing the water's egress, then watch the area for droplets when it rained during the day, and no drips developed. Success! Then around midnight, a passing cloudburst had water running down my cheeks. I believe there were tears mixing with the leaking rainwater. I pulled the soon to be damp covers over my head and tried to get some meaningful sleep. Sometime before daybreak the voices in my head woke me up. After talking amongst themselves for most of the night, the popular leak theory was as follows: the reason the leak only seemed to happen at night had to do with the weight of my body in the Vberth. My weight up front was enough to lower the bow slightly into the water which made it the lowest point on the boat. Following this hypothesis, meant that the water could be coming from any where along the 30 feet of exposed deck! Good thinking guys. Armed with this new insight, I now had a better idea of where to look. There was a loose fitting about 10 feet away, near the mast, which was a prime suspect. At first light I applied sealant around the offending fastener and waited for the next deluge.

The next day an afternoon squall provided the perfect opportunity. As soon as I heard the rain start to drum on the deck, I grabbed a book and headed to my cozy sleeping area. I read a couple sentences and immediately fell asleep. I awoke naturally a couple hours later, felt around for wet spots but found none! Let the pigeons fly!

Free of that pesky problem I then filled my few remaining days on Aitutaki with snorkeling and short hikes. The snorkeling was somewhat disappointing because the otherwise crystal clear water was quite clouded from all the runoff due to the heavy rains we'd experienced.

On "Leave Eve" I rowed myself to shore to say my goodbyes to Paul at the scooter rental outfit. There was a sign hanging askew on the front door of his shop that indicated he would be back shortly. So I walked up to the small store where I'd wasted my money on the special cat food. When I walked in, I didn't see Moses around, and I headed back to the book shelf to look one final time for the lost spy novel that had been buried at sea.

"How'd the coil work out?" he said startling me as he'd come up behind me suddenly and silently.

"Haven't tried it yet," I responded. In truth, I had totally forgotten about it because the rains had kept me inside so the mosquitoes hadn't been a problem.

Not finding anything that I needed, I thanked him, and just before leaving I remembered I still owed him some money. Digging two dollars out of my pocket, I handed it to the white haired, white bearded expatriate and left.

I saw Paul just coming out of the post office and called out to him, "Hey, I'm leaving early so I wanted to thank you for everything."

"Where are you going?" he inquired.

"American Samoa's the plan, unless the weather gets crappy."

"Have a safe one and come back for another visit one day."

"Take care Paul," I said shaking his hand.

Having said my goodbyes to my new cruising acquaintances, I rowed back to *Rick's Place* and began preparing for the next day's early morning departure. Just as the sun began to set, I fired up the mosquito coil to keep the bugs away while I settled in to enjoy my last evening here with my Mac & Cheese dinner and a nice cold beer. Jack joined me in the cockpit and the heavy smoke from the smoldering bug deterrent had his curiosity up and he was drawn to the burning object. One sniff was enough and he scampered back down below as if he'd been slapped on the nose. I just hoped it worked as well on mosquitoes as it did on cats.

I sat for another hour watching the faintest of the stars finally popping out of the darkness. The coil was nearly used up and I tried to will my body to go below to bed. Finding it hard to move, I realized that the coil probably didn't do a thing to drive bugs away, but it put me into a state that I didn't mind being eaten alive. I wonder what was in that coil? I pondered as I absently scratched a fresh bite on my arm.

The next morning as I motored out of the pass at Aitutaki, I noted that the sky was a brilliant red color. The old saying came to mind, "Red sky at morning, sailors take warning." Hmmmmmmmmm.............

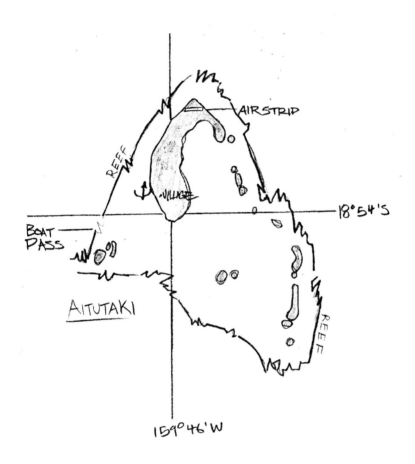

CHAPTER 13

By the Numbers

"That which we call a rose by any other name would smell as sweet."

-Shakespeare, *Romeo and Juliet*

Sheryl and I walked hand in hand along the beach, the waves lapping at our feet. We spotted an ice cream vendor and raced each other through the warm white sand to the old fashioned looking cart. We each ordered a cone, Sheryl chose strawberry and mine was dark chocolate covered with sprinkles. Feasting on our delicious treasures we continued walking on in silence. Suddenly, my double scoop started melting at an alarming rate! The faster I licked, the quicker it seemed to melt. What was even worse was that every time I tried to get it close to my lips there was a sensation of hair or fur on my tongue, like it was embedded in the frozen treat. Turning to Sheryl, I was about to ask about her cone, when a garbage truck started backing down the beach, which struck me as rather strange. It's back up alarm blaring BEEP – BEEP - BEEP - BEEP – BEEP.....

As the slumber fog cleared from my head, I reached for my alarm clock that was on my nightstand. Oh, yeah, no nightstand! I'm on the boat in the middle of the South Pacific. BEEP - BEEP – BEEP. As I was trying to get out of the pilot berth, I realized that my shipboard cat buddy, Jack, was lying close to my head. While dragging myself out of the confined space, my hand brushed over Jack's tail which seemed suspiciously wet. "Oh #*%! I think I found what I'd been licking in my dream!"

BEEP – BEEP – BEEP. Back to the problem at hand because the beeping is my radar detector warning me that *Rick's Place* was being scanned by another vessel, one that is probably very close by. I rushed up to the cockpit and was surprised to see that the sun had already set, but I could still see a fishing boat about a mile away. It was about 90 feet long and was slowing to bring in his long line. I'd spotted 3 such vessels during the last couple of nights all brightly lit with lights and I tried to contact each of them. They either would not, or could not reply to my radio calls, but several times I picked up what sounded like Japanese voices on the VHF.

With VHF reception limited to line of sight, or horizon to horizon, making contact with another boat that you can't see is a rarity. Luckily I was able to keep track of many cruisers using my short wave receiver. An organization calling themselves the Pacific Seafarer's Net orchestrates daily check-ins via radio to those who where equipped with Ham radios and the proper license. Latitude, longitude, wind and wave heights are reported to a net control person. The coverage area is nearly all of the north and South Pacific. So, every night at a pre-set time I would turn my receiver on and eavesdrop on the roll call to find out where people were and what kind of weather cruisers ahead of me were encountering. Listening to the net three days out of Aitutaki, I was delighted to hear *Cetus* check in! Quickly plotting their position I realized that my friends were only about 25 miles away from *Rick's Place* and we were both headed in the same general direction. With no way to transmit on the short wave, I decided to try calling on the VHF about once an hour hoping to make contact.

"*Cetus, Cetus, Cetus*. This is *Rick's Place*. Do you copy?"

Knowing someone on *Cetus* was on watch 24 hours a day, I continued trying even though it was past midnight. After about 4 attempts to reach them with no response I decided to survey the horizon one last time before joining Jack for a much needed nap. This time I made sure Jack wasn't sleeping anywhere near my head!

I was just closing my eyes when suddenly a voice cut through the static of the radio.

"*Rick's Place, Rick's Place, Rick's Place*, this is *Cetus*. You there Rick"?

I lunged for the microphone and had a huge grin on my face as I replied, "Gotcha *Cetus*, go ahead"

"Hey Rick, we heard you calling a couple of times but couldn't raise you. We finally switched to a spare mic. The old one must be shorted out." Terry said.

"It's been a while since Honolulu," I replied, "How's the

Cetus Crew?"

"Everyone is great. Heidi's catching a nap until her next watch."

I could hear talking in the background, but I couldn't make it out. Terry continued, "Carly and I are standing watch right now, counting shooting stars" I could hear more background talking. "Rick, Carly wants to know how Jack is doing. Is he still using the head?"

"Jack is doing great. He's still the same old rat cat." I replied.

"So Rick, where are you headed?"

"I'm going to American Samoa. How about you?"

"We are headed for Tonga," he said firmly.

I was disappointed at the prospect of not meeting up with my friends.

"You know, Rick, Tonga is a lot closer, an easier sail and it would be great to rendezvous and swap stories."

I thought about it for about 10 seconds and replied, "You tell Carly she better get to bed and get some rest, because she is going to have her hands full taking care of Jack when we see you in Tonga!" So much for making Jack legal!

There was no reply, so I thought I had lost the signal which wasn't that strong to begin with.

"*Cetus*, you still there?"

Minutes go by then a slightly husky, sleepy sounding female voice came through the speaker.

"Now we're all here Rick. Carly just woke me up with the news we're meeting Jack in Tonga. I guess that includes you as well?"

I was laughing now. That 6-year-old was in love with my cat.

"Sorry about all the commotion Heidi, yeah, I think we'll see ya there!"

"We should be checking into Neafu in about 5 days if the weather holds."

"Roger that. I will continue to try and keep in touch on the VHF, but for sure I will keep track of *Cetus* on the Ham net."

"OK Rick, it was great hearing from you. Stay safe; give a radio call at noon local boat time. This is *Cetus* out."

"Thanks, looking forward to it, *Rick's Place* clear."

Turning to my crew I advised him on my new course. "Well Jack," I said, "I guess the world really does revolve around you!"

Sensing I was talking about him, he rolled on his back knowing I would rub his stomach. Then he gave me a playful bite on the hand.

The following noon I attempted to contact *Cetus* as planned but immediately I noticed more static on the radio than the previous night. When *Cetus* attempted to call me, Terry's voice was just barely audible over the heavy disturbance. Even without making direct contact, it was somehow comforting to know another boat was relatively close by.

As the sun was completing its daily march across the South Pacific sky heading toward twilight, I performed my customary check up on deck. I was looking for chaffed lines, loose nuts or bolts and any unusual wear on the sails that would require an ill-advised trip to the deck at night for repair. It is simply bad form to try and make emergency repairs at night on a pitching deck trying to hold on with one hand, so catching potential problems before they happen and in the daylight can be a real life saver.

Another aspect of my daily routine was scanning the horizon before the sun set. The funny thing about checking the horizon for things like ships, land or upcoming weather is that a person (at least me) tends to look forward and side to side, but not often behind. This changed when I heard the radar detector give off a single beep. At first I didn't think too much about it, but the voices in my head did. I had discovered after installing the device that the lighter I used to fire up the stove would cause it to emit a single "beep". The action of pushing the lighter trigger produced a charge of static electricity, thus setting off a false alarm. So the question that formed in my head was "Is Jack down below lighting a cigarette?" I didn't think so, so when the unit beeped again about 5 minutes later I started to go below to have a look, but something caught my eye.

Behind me, about 5 to 10 miles away, was a very nasty

looking black cloud. Now I've seen my share of black, ugly, nasty looking clouds, but what made this so scary was the bolt of lightning that exploded from its base. It didn't take a big debate with the voices to put 2 and 2 together. The bad radio reception and the radar unit going off were all caused by one of God's giant Bic lighters and it was creating a lot of anxiety in my stomach.

The next hour was spent willing the Black Menace to move in some other direction. I actually talked myself into believing that it was moving away from *Rick's Place*. All the while the crazy zig zag bolts would fire down, followed by a thunder clap sometime later. It became clear that I really hadn't put any distance on this monster, so I altered course hoping that it would pass by at a safe distance (all the time asking why this stuff always happens at night?). As if the cloud was being drawn to me like a magnet, it altered coarse and now was most definitely catching up to us. The lightning was now coming out of its base with more frequency and it was taking the thunder less time to rattle my fillings after each flash, so I instigated Plan B.

Here's a brief history of Plan B: While sitting at the transient dock in Honolulu some months back, a boat came in that had been struck by lightening the night before. A prominent black streak was evident on the mast just above the spreaders. While talking with the skipper he kept telling me how lucky he was so I asked him how he could consider himself lucky when he just lost about $10,000 in electronics. His reply was that he still had the boat and his life. He went on to explain to me that many times the lightening will travel down the mast and blow a hole through the boat in it's attempt to connect to the water. A hole in a boat is not a good thing, to say the least.

I was determined not to let that happen to *Rick's Place*, so I started asking around on how to avoid this terrible fate. Unfortunately, after talking to six different people about what preventative measures to take to keep a vessel safe during a lightning storm, I got the customary six different opinions. However, there was one common theme on keeping oneself and their boat from getting fried, and that was having a direct route for the lightening to travel to the water; a route that doesn't go through the interior of the boat.

So, off to the nearest auto parts store where I purchased the biggest, gnarliest set of jumper cables I could find. The idea was that if you connected one of the clamps to your mast rigging then threw the other end in the water, this would create a path from the mast to the water that didn't involve blowing out the through hull fittings. It looked good on paper, besides you always used Plan A first, which was to avoid the lightening in the first place.

After I clipped the jumper cables on the rigging of *Rick's Place* I watched in horror as the ends that are supposed to be in the water were actually skipping along beside the boat on top of the water! They were unable to sink as they had at the dock because of the boat's speed. I hadn't thought of that.

The outer edge of the squall was now starting to dump rain on my little boat. Every time I am in a storm my boat seems to become much smaller than it is on a calm and sunny day. Within seconds the rain replaced the wind and proceeded to flatten out the seas. I had seen this once before: the rain coming down so hard and intense that it rounded off the waves and made the water look flat as far as you could see, which was only about 50 feet at that moment. Lightening seemed to be coming non stop now so I thought my number was up. I looked below for Jack and the cat was nowhere to be seen. I needed to locate him in case a hasty departure was in the cards for us.

There was no chance to leave the tiller. The thunder was so loud and there seemed to be more light than dark with the constant lightening flashes. And best of all, the jumper cables, my Plan B, ace in the hole, were gone! Washed overboard. Then, suddenly everything went dark. The lightening had stopped! Instantly the rain stopped, too, the winds returned and the seas jumped back up. It was like breaking through a wall. Then I was headed in the opposite direction of the storm cell. I could clearly see the edge of its influence and the lightening still belching out of its center. It took no time to put a couple miles between the storm and *Rick's Place*. Exhausted I dropped in the cockpit and quickly fell asleep. The whole thing took less than an hour to come and go, but it felt like an eternity.

Two days later the inactive volcano peaks showed themselves on the horizon, right where the GPS said they would be. What a relief! Ain't science great? My cruising guide told me that a town called Neafu is the official check in point for this part of Tonga called the Va'vau Group. As I entered into the group of islands, my first impression of Tonga was that it reminded me of the San Juan Islands back home in Washington. Except in this archipelago, the islands have palm trees instead of fir trees. But, just like in the San Juans there are lots of small islands and rock out croppings to explore.

I started hearing radio traffic on the VHF, but it was somewhat confusing. I'd hear people talk between boats, but everyone's using numbers to describe where they are instead of location names which I found very strange. For example, "boat A" will call "boat B" and talk about the snorkeling or whales at #10 or that they plan on moving over to #16 tomorrow. What the hell? What was this weird code they were using and why is it so secret? I tried to call my friends on *Cetus* to see if they were in yet, but so far I'd gotten no response.

Once again *Rick's Place* was tied up to a pier that must usually be used for supply ships, as there were the familiar large tires hanging down to protect the ships from the dock and the tires left long black steaks on my boat's beige colored hull. There were a dozen shipping containers strewn around the dock area and it made me think of Hilo, which seemed so very long ago. I had my yellow quarantine flag flying to let the officials know I was ready to be checked in. I waited about two hours and finally I saw an important looking guy in pressed shorts and white shirt approaching. Jack, of course, was hidden away and luckily being very quiet.

I was sitting in the cockpit as the official came on board. He was very polite as he checked my passport and asked about any guns on board. "None," I replied. Then a second gentleman came aboard and he was from agriculture and his job was to check my fresh foods. Luckily I didn't have much left because they did confiscate it: a lime and half a head of cabbage. They do this to keep unwanted bugs and vermin from hitchhiking from island to island and potentially destroying their crops.

The snag came when Mr. Agriculture announced that he must set off an aerosol bug bomb inside of *Rick's Place* to further ensure no unwanted creatures would enter the Kingdom of Tonga. Fearing a cat discovery and not knowing if that is one of the creatures they don't want entering their country, I didn't dare resist. Before I could come up with a plan, the officer slid open the hatch and activated the canister on the top step! The deadly cloud of hissing gas started to dispense and he slid the hatch shut. "Best leave for one hour," he says in somewhat broken English. We shook hands and he disappeared behind some containers on the dock.

Nervously, I looked to see if there were any more government people lurking about. Seeing none, I grabbed my snorkeling mask that was laying in the cockpit. I took 3 deep breaths, put the mask on and charged down below. Holding my breath in the fog, I grabbed the bag that contained Jack. Cautiously I peeked out of the hatch and saw that the coast was clear and jumped into the cockpit, keeping the bag low. I slammed the hatch shut, and, with my heart racing, I partially unzipped the canvas cat carrier. Jack immediately poked his head out and bit my hand HARD! None the worse for wear, I guess. At least Jack won't have to worry about fleas for a while. For the next hour we just sat in the cockpit together.

Once everything was aired out, I motored away from the dock and dropped my anchor off the town square. I started eavesdropping on the radio and continued to puzzle over everyone's anchor locations just being numbers. How do they all know the right numbers? I drifted off to sleep completely baffled by this strange new world.

Jack woke me just as *Cetus* was calling *Rick's Place*.

"Rick, how soon can you be at #11? We're going to have a pig roast over here tomorrow night." Terry asked.

"Terry, I don't know where the heck number 11 is!!" was my reply.

"Look, its right near number 10, and just south of number 8," He informs me.

"He's lost his mind," I say to Jack. Now there's calling the kettle black!

"Rick, have you been to town yet?" Terry inquired.

"Just to check in, then I came out and anchored to catch some sleep," I answer.

Terry told me, "Go into town and find the boat charter office. It's right by the post office and I promise everything will become clear to you."

"You're not making any sense," I said.

Terry's only reply was "Just go!"

So I rowed to the public dock and tied up the dinghy. I immediately saw that this tropical paradise was different from my previous encounters. As I walked to what looked like the main street, I had to navigate around a huge pig that was lying in the dirt road. Chickens were nervously running everywhere with more than one rooster crowing his displeasure. I was surprised to see the main street was just another dirt road with mud filled ruts and not paved as all of the roads had been on Bora Bora. The small stores or buildings along the road were neat and tidy, but lacking the fresh paint I'd seen in French Polynesia and Aitutaki. Once again I was struck with the vast differences in all of the islands I've been to since leaving home. I'd always thought that one tropical paradise would look like the next, but each is so unique in every way it's astounding.

I found someone to give me directions to the post office (thank goodness they aren't using numbers here!). A short walk later I was standing in front of Oceanic Sail Charters of Tonga. Upon entering the office my questions were quickly answered. Covering one wall was a huge chart of the area. On it are the numerous bays and anchorages, each with a number right next to its hard to read and harder to pronounce native name.

"Can I help you?" came a female Aussie accented voice breaking me out of my gaze. Looking behind me I saw a rather tall, shapely green eyed strawberry blonde and she was smiling at my obvious bewilderment. She went on to explain that when the charter company started several years ago it was very confusing for the patrons to identify where they were because most couldn't learn how to read or pronounce the names of the locations. So the company assigned numbers to all of the anchorages and printed up charts with the numbers on them to simplify matters for everybody.

"Now all the cruisers that come here pick up the charts to use, too. So there you go, Bob's your uncle," she stated. What the hell does that mean? I pondered.

Anyway, I bought a chart and hurried back to *Rick's Place* and called *Cetus* to let them know I now had the secret code, too and that I would be on my way as soon as day broke.

In the morning, Jack and I sailed into a small lagoon where the turquoise water was wrapped with a necklace of white sand beach. Palm trees provided shade from the tropical sun and a small waterfall near where we were dropping the hook added to the near perfect beauty. Sitting on the bow with Jack on his back and me rubbing his belly, I watched some local kids playing in the waterfall as brightly colored birds squawked from the palms.

"You know Jack, this place is so much more than a number," I said and Jack's reply was to bite my hand.

Our entire time in Tonga was magical. Jack and I spent most of our time buddy boating with *Cetus*. Carly devoted endless hours playing with and keeping Jack company. She'd dress him up in some of her doll clothes, which was a pretty funny sight and Jack patiently put up with it. Jack was spending more time up on the deck since we were in such peaceful anchorages. And, just like Aitutaki, the price of food was reasonable! I could actually afford groceries and had even been to a couple restaurants. The supplies came mainly from New Zealand and there was a great public market with cheap locally grown vegetables so I was in hog heaven. I got my fill of lamb and pork, and was able to gather all the ingredients for salads at a fraction of the price in Bora Bora. I was delighted to find green apples for a tasty dessert treat. The weeks flew by as I spent my time snorkeling, hiking, eating and relaxing.

Since the anchorages were so calm, I had started leaving the port holes open for fresh air at night but they have screens on to keep out unwanted bug guests and to keep Jack in. One night, about 2:00 in the morning, I was startled awake by a thoroughly ocean soaked Jack. He was sitting right next to my head washing himself. It took me a bit to figure out how he'd gotten so wet, but it became apparent he had somehow fallen off the boat and then gotten back aboard. Further investigation showed he had pushed out one of the window screens to get outside and then once outside he was probably goofing around and fell off the boat! Luckily the dinghy was in the water, so he was able to climb into that and from there back up into *Rick's Place*. Probably won't have that problem again. I think he learned his lesson.

The seasonal migration that, as Alien Allen had told me, is called "The Coconut Milk Run" was in full swing. Tonga seemed to be the crossroads where cruisers are forced to make the decision of where to go before the upcoming cyclone season hits. The majority of the boats will go south to New Zealand and a few will head north to the equator, two places you can go to get out of the cyclone belt. Since I was ahead of the vast number of boats and cyclone season was still a couple months away I would have time to move on to Fiji, which is the next logical stop on the Milk Run (an easy 6 day sail away). Once in Fiji I could decide whether to head north or south. My friends on *Cetus* were staying longer in Tonga, but our plan was to meet up again later in Fiji.

Jack and I sailed back to Neafu to check out of Tonga, which was much easier than checking in because they didn't have to board the boat. I took the opportunity to call Sheryl, since it had been a month since we had talked to each other. I always have high anxiety dialing her number. Although I hadn't seen her in over a year, I held out hope that she still missed her cat and hopefully I could tag along on that sentiment.

In Tonga the public telephones are in the post office, so there was a good deal of commotion going on. After several unsuccessful attempts to get through I finally heard the required beeps, clicks and switching noises that let me know the signal at least got to the other side of the world. I was all set with some clever lines for when she answered the phone. After several rings I was about ready to hang up when a male voice answered, "Hello."

Knowing I must have been somehow switched to a wrong number I replied," I'm sorry, I was trying to call Sheryl Jones, but I must have gotten the wrong number."

"Hold on a minute, I'll get her," came his reply.

"A male voice answering Sheryl's phone?" How could that be? A hundred things ran through my mind all at once. A brother, a neighbor, a lover? I was just sick. One of the guys in my brain was saying "Don't worry, it's nothing." But the rest were saying "You blew it pal." After all I had been gone a long time. Out of sight out of mind.

I was just about ready to hang up when Sheryl's familiar voice brought me back to reality, "Hello?" I didn't answer and again she said, "Hello?"

"Hi Sheryl, its Rick." I finally got out.

"Rick!!" I thought she sounded excited! "Put Jack on the phone," she said.

"Very funny. How are you?" I asked. What I really wanted to know was who had answered the phone.

Her response was, "Rick, I'm just great! I finally turned the corner at the flower shop. It's doing fantastic and I've even hired an assistant. How are you and Jack doing? And where are you?"

Wait a minute. I get the same billing as Jack, her cat. That can't be a good sign.

"Oh, we're both doing good and we're in Tonga. We spent the last few weeks here with *Cetus.* You know the friends I want you to meet."

"Maybe now with some help at the shop I can get away," she said. Maybe, what's with maybe? I wondered. It was always a lot more for sure back before what's his name came into the picture.

"Jack and I are off to Fiji now. It will take about 6 days to get there and then I will call you. I really miss you Sheryl, please come down." I blurted out. Kinda whiny, kind of desperate, but hey…. "So what do you think?"

The only reply I heard was a dial tone piercing my eardrum when our connection was suddenly broken. Damn it.

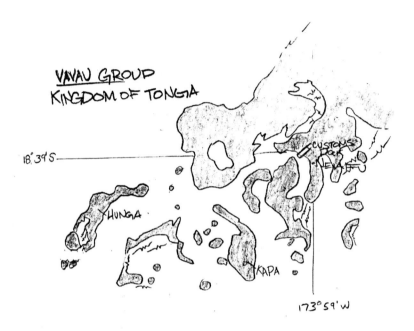

CHAPTER 14

Cannibal Café

*"Cannibals aren't vegetarians,
they are humanitarians..."*

-Unknown

Sometimes the shortest passages seem like the longest and this was definitely one of those times. It was taking far too much time to get my sea legs back. I felt cranky and uncomfortable and the weather was poop. Most every day of this crossing brought some nasty squalls. The usually very consistent trade winds had given way to some confused, trough like patterns that kept me busy changing and adjusting sails and simply having to work way too hard. With these contrary winds, came short choppy seas that made for an uncomfortable and wet ride. Even Jack seemed more lethargic than usual due to the rough conditions. I'd also seen fishing boats on the horizon nearly every night, which put me on edge and kept me from getting much sleep. With the lack of sleep I had way too much time to think. And I mostly thought about Sheryl.

In retrospect I should have called Sheryl back after we were disconnected but I wasn't sure what to say. Besides, we had crossed the International Date Line, so I didn't know what day it was at home, let alone what hour of the day. I really didn't want to call back and find out it was 11 o'clock at night on a Saturday and the plumber was answering the phone.

I continued to mentally beat myself up for not telling Sheryl my feelings, but an approaching squall quickly snapped me back to the tasks at hand. Note to self: There are no easy 6 day sails. And as if Mother Nature had to reinforce this, I spotted Suva, Fiji 7 days 12 hours and 23 minutes after leaving Tonga, about a day and a half later than I had planned.

From what I've read, Fiji is dark and mysterious and different than anywhere Jack and I have been. In high school, Mutiny on the Bounty was my favorite read. Captain Bligh purposely avoided these islands because of the savage cannibals. Missionaries, "the other white meat", came to mind. I was looking forward to meeting descendants of the early people eaters.

My guidebook cautioned that although the entrance to Suva looked to be a mile wide, most of that water was only about 3 feet deep. The entrance was dredged through the shallows but it wasn't as apparent as other passes I had seen because there were no breaking waves to mark the channel boundaries. I strained to see the markers which would guide me into the pass. I was reminded to stay vigilant as I passed a large hulk of what was left of a freighter that had missed the channel and was driven up on to the coral some years before. The overcast, grey skies were adding to the difficulty of finding the entrance as colors both in the water and on shore were muted. Luckily, another cruising boat had entered just ahead of me, and I carefully followed behind making my entrance uneventful for a change.

I tied up to the customs dock and quickly cleared through. The routine of hiding Jack was now so well practiced that there was very little howling and almost no biting and it all went very smoothly. Plus, they didn't need to bug bomb the boat here, so I guessed they didn't care what critters we brought with us.

After finishing with the officials I was able to take a bit of a look at the city of Suva before moving away from the customs dock. What I saw appeared to be a cross between New Delhi and my old stomping grounds, Tacoma, which was the "big" city across the Narrow's Bridge from Gig Harbor. Suva is crowded and bustling with a strong East Indian flavor and I was having a problem with the pace of life there. Four lane streets, busses, too many people, too many cars and way too much horn honking going on around me. Add to that the thick blanket of humidity that kept me in a constant state of sweat, my senses were overloaded. I went back down to take refuge in *Rick's Place*.

I moved the boat out into the harbor and dropped the hook off of the Royal Suva Yacht Club, just in time for an afternoon squall. The intense rain shower was welcome and I took the opportunity to wash down the boat, as well as collect some water for clothes washing. Using my binoculars, I checked out the boats that were already anchored. I figured that there were about 8 beers that were owed to me from the surrounding cruisers. But on the other hand I probably owed about 6 to some of the others; it was almost a wash.

I took the dinghy, rowed into the Yacht Club and met up with some cruisers I hadn't seen for months. We sat and swapped stories about everything from snorkeling to storms to where to find the best buys on supplies. Everyone had a storm story and each story told was bigger than the one before. In the end it sounded like the last six months were basically non stop hurricane force winds. Each day sounded more death defying than the day before. Cruisers have the best imaginations and gossip is huge at these informal get-togethers. Finding out who was jumping ship, whose marriage is on the rocks, whose boat's been on the rocks; I always felt it would make a great soap opera, "As the Rudder Turns."

After collecting a little more than half the beers that were owed me, I excused myself to walk the town. The East Indian influence was really quite a shock to me. It was everywhere, from food to dress to the high pitched music blasting from the stores. Oh, that music! Obviously the music came after the cannibals or I wouldn't still be suffering it. There doesn't seem to be any trace of paradise in this city. I found the local market and was surprised at how big it was. It was a two story building filled with everything from brightly colored cloth to butchered pigs, vegetables and carved wooden swords.

I spotted a vendor selling lemonade, I made my way to his stand only to find he had 2 drinking cups, so a person needs to drink the concoction right there, and then he washes out the cup and serves the next victim. He sure kept his overhead low, but I opted not to partake after all. Back out on the streets of the city I felt like I could have been in any industrial city back in the states, in an older, dirty part of town, anyway. There are lots of low rise buildings that aren't new, but built about a decade ago. One thing that I was happy to be finding there is something I hadn't seen since Hawaii: Marine stores! Well, actually they were hardware stores that had marine products. I would finally be able to buy those odds and ends that I didn't bring along as spares, or have since used up, and that would make life aboard a bit easier.

One important thing I did learn at the Yacht Club gathering

was the rules concerning Savu Savu. This is the custom in Fiji where a visitor to a village must present the chief of that village with the root of the Kava plant. That root would then be ceremoniously crushed into a powder and mixed with water and then with great fanfare the drink would be passed around the room. When the visitors and the chief drank this concoction it signified that the visitor was accepted into the village and was therefore protected by the village. I assume this will also mean a person would be invited for dinner rather than being dinner.

So the next day I found myself at the local market looking for Kava root. The first thing I noticed was that Kava root is fairly expensive. So how much do I need to buy? How many chiefs will I have to please? This was going to be tough. Adding to my dilemma was that there were several stalls selling Kava and different prices being asked. Would the chief know if I bought the cheaper Kava? Were there different grades of the stuff? This was all very confusing.

After several hours of contemplation, I came to the conclusion that this was quite a racket. There were probably kickbacks involved, somehow. Anyway, I bought enough to fill a brown paper grocery bag and was assured by the vendor I would be met with open arms at any village.

The second day of our stay in Suva concluded with a visit to Fiji's Museum of History. One item I found most interesting was the rudder from the HMS Bounty. It gave me chills knowing the history behind this simple wood and iron display. I also was fascinated by the cannibalism memorabilia. It was amazing to see the variety of tools that were used to eat unfortunate dinner guests. There were clubs and several types of axes, but the most surprising were the specialized forks, spoons and paring knives apparently designed especially for eating human flesh.

On the wall were pictures of the missionaries that came to Fiji to save the savage's souls but became their dinner instead. It was pretty eerie seeing the faces of those that met such a demise. Someone should have warned them that when they were told "We'd love to have you for dinner" that they should decline the invitation.

It seems the phrase "to the victor goes the spoils" originated with the island's cannibals. After a victorious battle, the wives of the winners didn't need to go shopping to prepare the celebratory dinner. I kinda thought that had I been a savage tribesman back in the days of cannibalism and I was facing the prospect of maybe losing a battle, I would eat something beforehand that was sure to send the guy who dined on me running for the biggest banana leaves he could find.

Rowing back to *Rick's Place*, I was greeted by Jack mewing loudly at the door. He knew good and well my habit of bringing fresh fish back from the market for him and he was hungry and impatient. While he ate, we discussed where to go next. My first mistake was to discuss travel plans with a stowaway cat, but that wouldn't be the worst mistake I would make.

Terry J. Kotas

CHAPTER 15

Ruku Ruku

"A chain is only as strong as its weakest link."

-Proverb

After only six days in Suva, Jack and I set a course that would take us around the large island of Vitu Levu into Bligh Waters. Bligh Waters looked interesting on the charts because it is a vast expanse of coral studded shallow water, not unlike the entrance to Suva. A person has to pick their way through the maze of coral heads, but the reward of visiting places not often braved by other cruisers would be well worth it. Motoring along I thought of the irony of Jack and I traveling the road less taken and how comfortable I was with the risks involved. I finally understood what Capt'n Joe had been advocating back in Honolulu. "A lot has changed in the last year. " I said to Jack. But I think he already knew that.

After the first day of travel I was beat. Constantly looking for coral heads and the steady drone of the engine hour after hour was very wearing. The channel was so narrow with many sudden turns that sailing was out of the question. Finally we tucked into a quiet little cove to anchor for the night. What a relief to turn the engine off and enjoy the silence. After the sun went down, Mother Nature put on a galactic display that was unmatched. The Milky Way was spread out like I had never seen before, even on those long nights at sea. Jack came up for a belly rub, so I engaged him in a little one sided conversation. "So, Jack, do you think there's any hope for Sheryl and me?" I took his bite on my hand as a yes.

"Who was that that answered the phone that day? Plumber, brother, landlord?" No bite, so I don't know what he was thinking. I guess I should really stick with yes or no questions with Jack.

"I should probably just call her and quit turning to a stupid cat for my answers," I said out loud, at which time Jack clamped down hard with his mouth and thumped my arm with his back feet. I wasn't sure if Jack was agreeing with my decision or felt insulted.

By the third day we had cleared the shallow depths of Bligh Waters and I hadn't seen one other cruising boat. According to the chart, several islands lay ahead of us. We were anchored behind a sand spit in water that was crystal clear. The sound of an outboard engine broke the silence of the morning so I poked my head outside and watched as a 15 foot runabout was deftly brought alongside *Rick's Place*.

I was getting ready to use my best sign language and my few Fijian words when it hit me that the guy driving the boat didn't look at all Fijian or East Indian. Instead I was looking at a 40ish, stocky guy with a dark full beard and brown hair parted to the side. He was wearing a brightly colored Hawaiian print shirt and as he got closer his shorts even look like they'd been pressed; sort of the opposite of my crumpled, tattered and stained shorts and tee shirt. His boat also gave the impression of being very well maintained and expensive with a large 50 horse power engine on the scratch free, highly polished, Boston Whaler. This was certainly no work boat.

"Good morning! I see from your flag you're from the US," he said with an American accent that I would guess to be from Chicago. I was speechless. Where had this American appeared from? There were no other cruising boats to be seen.

"Yeah, I'm from Washington State," came my stumbling reply.

"Welcome! My name's John, John Marth, and I live on this island," he informed me.

"Nice to meet you. My name's Rick," I babbled as I tried to understand this new situation.

John asked me how long I'd been out and said he didn't get many cruisers up here, but was always happy to see them when they did appear. I related some of my adventures between Washington and here and he invited me to join his family for a lava lava that evening. When I failed to reply right away (not knowing what he was inviting me to) he added, "It's a pig roast. A lava lava is just a BBQ Fijian style. Don't worry about bringing anything, just take your dinghy to shore over there," as he gestured to the beach, "and follow the trail for about ½ a kilometer. You can't miss it. Our house is the only one on the island."

"What time?" I queried.

"We'll start cooking about 3," he said with a wave as he started off in a cloud of smoke from his outboard engine.

I called after him, "thanks John! I'll see you then!"

I watched where John took his boat to shore, still puzzled over his sudden appearance out in the middle of nowhere. Hmmmmm, this could prove to be very interesting. Jack had no comment.

I set about getting ready for my excursion to shore. I showered; I shaved and took out a clean, stain free T shirt I had been saving for just such an occasion. I felt I needed to put some extra effort into my appearance, because judging by the unspoken impression John gave, this would be a bit more formal than the usual cruiser's potluck. Just before leaving the boat, I took a look at myself in my hand held mirror, and I was struck by two things: A. I don't look in the mirror very often. B. I was beginning to take on the same weathered look I'd seen on so many other people I've met on my journey.

I pulled the dinghy up on the beach and started walking along the trail to John's house. As I walked, I wondered what I would find; a thatched hut or tree house? What a surprise when I broke through the thick jungle trail onto a point of land that was over looking an endless expanse of azure water. On the precipice was a house that looked as though it could have been right from main street USA. It was a standard rambler with a two car attached garage. I didn't see any cars, but that wasn't too surprising because there weren't any roads, either. The house was painted yellow, with white trim and white shutters. A small, closely cut lawn out front was in the shape of a putting green which even had a flag and cup! Seeing a brick chimney, I wondered if the attached fireplace got any use in this tropical climate.

I could see a thin veil of smoke rising from behind the house. My knock on the door drew no response, but I noticed what must be a doorbell so I gave that a try, even though I thought it must be some kind of joke. As I pushed its lighted button, I heard a faint rendition of "As Time Goes By" announcing my arrival.

What a bizarre coincidence that I was named after a character from the same movie that song came from. I was starting to feel rather surreal about this whole situation, rather Twilight Zonish.

Then the door flew open and standing before me was a very attractive 30 something woman wearing a sundress that didn't leave much to the imagination.

"Hi, I'm Rick," I managed.

"Of course you are! I'm Kathy. John said you'd be by for dinner. He's out in back with the pig."

Walking through the house I was stunned at how nicely the place was decorated. There was what looked like expensive art hanging on the walls with display lights focused on them. The floors were beautiful hardwood and the air conditioning made for extremely comfortable living.

Following Kathy through the back sliding door, we came to a swimming pool with a waterfall cascading into it. It was all designed to fit in with the natural surroundings . My senses were on overload. John had himself a little Eden going in his back yard with huge plants, coconut palms and brightly colored flowers growing all around the pool and waterfall. It was all so incredible! Mrs. John chose this exact moment to come between the rays of sunlight streaming through the palm fronds and my field of vision. I needed to start breathing again and I broke my trance just as John came at me with a beer in each hand. This truly was paradise!

"Rick, great you could come. You met my wife, Kathy? Good." He said as he handed me one of the ice cold brews. Two things were processing in the area of my brain I call the confuser. One was what was this guy with the Chicago accent doing here and the other one was what was Kathy doing here with him? She was obviously much younger..

"John, you've got a great place here. Thanks so much for inviting me." I extended.

"We don't get many visitors up this way, so when a boat does show up; especially if they're from the US, we invite them in. Cocktail hour, ya know."

So we drank beers, roasted pig and talked in detail about what Jack and I had been up to for the past year.

John wasn't as forthcoming with information on himself. When I asked how he ended up with such a beautiful place in paradise he replied that he was a retired school principal. He added that he was indeed from Chicago, and had come here to get away from the rat race. I don't know many school principals that can afford this kind of luxury anywhere and there are a lot of places in the U.S. to get away from the rat race, so I began to suspect Witness Protection Program.

"So, the house," I asked, "did the locals build it for you?"

"Heavens no," he laughed. "I got it sent over piece by piece in 20' container boxes like the ones you see on freighters. It took me a year to put it all together. There's a landing craft that comes up from Suva that carries two Connex boxes and a winch system to unload them. We get supplies delivered that way a couple times a year."

"The detail is amazing, right down to the doorbell." I stated.

"Yeah, the doorbell was a little whim. Living out here we knew it might never get used, but it finally did!" he chuckled.

With the sun going down and things cooling off just a bit, Kathy announced that the pig was ready. During my talk with John, Kathy had been going in and out of the kitchen bringing out delicious looking side dishes. She also changed into something a little less revealing, which would make dinner a bit more comfortable for me, too.

After we ate, we moved inside where John showed me his rec room with a huge TV, a desk with a computer, a pool table and a full bar. One wall was a huge bookshelf and I noted that he had every Stephen King novel ever published. I made a poor career decision when I didn't become a high school principal, I thought sarcastically.

"The tube is hooked to a satellite and gets stuff from all over the world" he said. Somehow that didn't surprise me. "Helps me keep in touch with what's going on else where." Family business? I pondered to myself.

"Anyone you'd like to contact? We can arrange it," he offered.

I half thought of calling Sheryl, but I didn't want to start blubbering in front of John and Kathy in case the plumber or whoever he is answers the phone again, so I declined his generous offer.

After a game of pool and a night cap, it was clear I needed to get moving or else I would be spending the night in the jungle. I asked John if there was a good protected anchorage nearby where I could ready the boat for the trip to New Zealand. He replied without hesitation that I should go to the island of Ovalou where I would find a great little bay called Ruku Ruku. The name itself means safe and it's protected in all weather. "You might have problems if an East wind comes up, but that's a rarity this time of year," he advised. John went on to tell me that there was an old Plantation there and a village where you could catch the school bus to Lavuka, one of Fiji's oldest cities.

With that information in hand we said our goodbyes and I started up the trail with a borrowed flashlight. I heard John call after me, "Be sure to take some Kava. I hear the chief is a stickler for tradition."

Two days later I was sitting at anchor in Ruku Ruku Bay. Right after I arrived the local kids swam out and played around *Rick's Place*. They were hanging on the anchor chain and climbing on the wind vane jabbering away. There was a whistle from shore and the kids beat a hasty retreat to the beach near the village.

"Well, I guess it's time for my audience with the chief. Wish me luck," I said to Jack. Jack had no comment. He was however very interested in the Kava I had in the bag. I think he thought it was a special cat nip treat for him. Sorry to disappoint you Jack. There were a few other pieces of "going to meet the chief" protocol I'd learned at the Royal Suva Yacht Club. I had to abide by some dress codes for the visit. No flip flops, no bathing suits, no sunglasses. Just dress up a little; island style. Stepping into the dinghy wearing my cleanest, dirty shirt, slip-on boat shoes and some khaki shorts I felt overdressed and hot. And of course I had my bag of Kava. I was ready.

Some of the same kids that were on *Rick's Place* earlier now swam out to help pull me to shore. As I climbed out of the dinghy, they all tried to hold my hand. That was the royal welcome I'd always dreamed about! They led me along the beach to a thatched hut that was somewhat bigger than the rest and there was a middle aged man standing at the entrance. Was this the chief?

"Bulla Bulla," he greeted me.

"Bulla Bulla," I said in kind as I tried to hand him my bag of Kava. He just held up his hand refusing to take it. Now what do I do? What did I do wrong?

Then the mahogany colored man said, "I am Kawana, second elder to Chief Vatua."

I was stunned. His English was better than mine!

"Hello," was all I could muster in reply.

"Do you wish to anchor your yacht in the chief's protection?" he asked me.

"Yes, I do. I'd like to stay here for a week or two."

Kawana said I was to wait where I was and he would go speak to the chief.

So I stood there drawing stares from all of the villagers who were streaming by checking me out. I could hear Kawana inside pitching my story to the chief. There was an awful lot of discussion going on considering no one here had met me before. Boy I hope I brought enough Kava and that it was the chief's favorite kind; if there is such a thing. Finally Kawana came out and motioned me in. It took a minute for my eyes to adjust to the dim light in the hut. "Bulla Bulla," came a voice strong and clear. Coming into focus I could see a rather frail looking, heavily tattooed gnome like male, sitting on a woven mat on the floor. He looked to be about as old as the earth itself and I had a hard time believing the powerful voice I had heard could come from such a tiny person.

Then he started talking to me rather rapidly, but not in English so I didn't understand a word of what he said. I hope it didn't mean I'd done something wrong and I would end up as the main course at dinner tonight. But when he stopped talking, Kawana said, "By presenting a gift to Chief Vatua you become part of our village and you will be protected into eternity." That gave me a shiver up my spine. I had only asked for a week or two.

At this point I opened the brown bag and removed a

handful of root and placed it in a woven basket that Kawana had picked up and was holding towards me.

The Chief looked at the roots and a thin smile came across his weathered face and he said something to Kawana, then Kawana repeated to me, "The Chief said you are most generous, please sit down."

For the next hour the Chief asked questions through Kawana, and I did my best to answer. He was very interested in all aspects of life and politics in the USA. I learned that Kawana had studied at the University of Washington. Talk about your small world! This certainly helped to keep the conversation going between us with our newly found shared history. Then a group of elders came into the dimly lit room. Sitting, they formed a circle when they joined the three of us already on the woven mat. They were an odd looking group: one was shaped like a bowling ball weighing probably 400 pounds. He had a baritone bellow that rattled my teeth when he laughed. Next to him sat a rail thin fellow whose eyes were as big as dinner plates with snow white hair and no teeth. A short man was sitting to his right. He was only about five feet tall and he had a slight hunch. He reminded me of Yoda from *Star Wars*. His smile was infectious and when he looked at me I began to smile. The last of the elders sat directly across from me and he had a tattoo on his face. The design made half of his mouth look like it was in a permanent frown so I found myself staring at him more than I should.

There was quite a bit of jabbering going on that I couldn't understand in the least. The men seemed almost giddy with anticipation and by their demeanor I got the impression this was Happy Hour, Fiji style. The short man had brought with him a large shallow bowl that was about 16 inches wide but only 8 inches deep. It was carved out of wood and had 3 legs. It was truly a piece of art. He placed the bowl in the middle of the circle and I saw that in the bowl was a brownish liquid that looked like dirty dish water. Kawana explained that this was the kava I had presented earlier and had been prepared it for this ceremony.

The Chief took a cup made from half of a coconut shell and scooped some of the liquid up. They all clapped 3 times and the

Chief took a long swig. Then the room went silent and I could feel their penetrating stares as Vatua passed the cup my way. I clapped and scooped and drank, then I had to well up all my strength not to throw up! The murky liquid tasted exactly how it looked: like used wash water. I imagined this was what dirty socks tasted like. Yuck! Skinny, Yoda, and Tattoo, as the voices in my head had christened them, continued their silent appraisal of my reaction, but Bellows let out such a deep laugh that dust came off the ceiling.

I happily passed the cup to my right, relieved to be getting rid of it and out of the lime light, but I unfortunately saw there would be plenty for a second round. I also knew I couldn't blow this ceremony, or cannibalism could return to Ruku Ruku.

The cup was two elders away from me and I was trying to psych up and steal my stomach for the next onslaught when something strange started to happen. My tongue and lips started to tingle. It was much the same feeling that my arms or legs feel when they fall asleep after I lay on them wrong. This is what the group was waiting for. They saw that the Kava was taking effect on the white guy. There is now non stop yapping amongst them and somehow I almost thought I could understand what they were saying. By the time the second round got to me I hardly noticed the taste, and by my 3rd serving I knew it was time for me to go; in more ways than one. The voice in my head told me that Kava could be a gateway drug and soon I would want to move on to licking toads.

I asked the Chief, through Kawana if I could be excused, and that was just fine with him. Possibly he remembered what it was like the first time he drank Kava, or maybe he just wanted more for himself. With some difficulty I picked myself up off the floor and headed for the door with Kawana following me. He showed me through the village and all the while the kids were circling around and again trying to hold my hand. I was shown a new generator that was hooked up to serve the village, but unfortunately they could not get it to run. I told Kawana that I would be happy to take a look. After all, I have had some success fixing something I know nothing about.

"How long will the Kava ceremony go on?" I asked.

He replied with a smile on his face," Well, seeing how you gave the Chief about 3 times what you needed to, they will be drinking the Kava for hours. Maybe all night." Better them than me!

The rest of the day was spent going from hut to hut meeting families, eating foods I didn't recognize and drinking things I probably shouldn't have. They even took me on a walking tour of the hill behind the village where there were culinary delights at every turn. One young man scampered up a coconut tree and picked a green coconut, sliced the top off with a machete and gave it to me to drink. They picked peppers and even sugar cane for me to take back to the boat. Simply delightful.

Ruku Ruku was spotless. There was no garbage, no piles of leaves or downed branches lying around. The whole community was always picking up around the village and the dirt streets were constantly being swept. Young and old alike took part in this sweeping chore with their brooms fashioned from palm fronds. I noticed that their neat, little huts were built several feet above ground and it was explained to me that it's a form of flood protection as well as helping to keep the multitudes of bugs roaming the ground from coming into their homes.

Some of the villagers make a meager income through their weaving. They use the long, slender, fibrous leaves of the Pandanus tree to create beautiful baskets and mats. What they don't use themselves they send to the market in nearby Lavuka. There are a few older men that are excellent wood carvers and they fashion turtles, dolphin and swords from local wood and those are also sold in the tourist markets. Almost everything that is grown in the village stays in the village and they don't have much need to buy food from elsewhere. They are content with their diet of bananas, coconuts, fish and taro, a starchy fibrous tuber that is a main stay here just as I've seen everywhere in the South Pacific.

That night when I got back to *Rick's Place*, I could see why they wanted a generator. There was almost no light coming from the village save for a couple lanterns and candles that were still burning and it was only about 6:30 pm! Nighttime comes early in the tropics. Maybe that wasn't really so bad, though, "What do you think, Jack?" As usual, no response came from my boat buddy.

During my stay I was able to observe that when Sundays rolled around nearly all of the 100 or so villagers would go to church. For several hours the most beautiful singing would drift through the anchorage. After the service they would all gather in the churchyard for a quiet afternoon brunch. I learned early on that it is bad form to swim, do laundry or any other activity on the Sabbath. Even the children were quiet and well behaved this one day of the week, everything was very low key.

It soon became a habit for the kids to swim out to the boat before they went to school. They'd wake me up, give Jack a fresh fish for breakfast and then be gone until they returned home about 4:00. I'd spend my days doing the usual boat projects aboard *Rick's Place*, but I also helped out in the village. Mostly I provided muscle for the things they were building. I'm good at holding a board here or digging a hole there. I didn't need to know the language to help out, but I found I was actually learning a bit more of it everyday. Once I saw a small group of women weaving some palm branches together for a new roof. After watching their nimble fingers at work for some time, they invited me to sit and give it a try. I fumbled through my first lesson, drawing giggles from the ladies. After a couple of days of practice I became a welcome participant.

Many of the younger men of Ruku Ruku would fish, using nets from the shore or spears out on the reef, and I would also lend a hand here, again drawing belly laughs at my ineptitude. The locals were very grateful for my help, but I was never sure if it was for the work I did or the comic relief I provided. The one thing I was good at, was working on their outboard motors, I seemed to have a natural talent there. I also managed to get the town generator working. There was a fuel metering problem, so it was a pretty simple fix since I'd dealt with a similar problem on my own engine. When the generator fired up, there was a celebration throughout the village. It was not unlike the joyous occasion on Fanning Island when I was able to fix their VCR. Only here the festivities involved Kava drinking. Luckily I'd become skilled at taking small sips of the distasteful liquid and none of the natives seemed the wiser. That night, sitting on the boat with the moon and the stars shinning so brightly, the hum of the generator seemed out of place. It made me wonder if all of our technology is really a blessing or a curse.

Out of habit I continued to listen to the short wave radio to check on my cruising friends and see where they were going. It was really interesting keeping track of everyone. I found out *Cetus* had ended up in Samoa instead of Fiji, the victims of a refrigeration break down. American Samoa is the best place in the South Pacific to have parts shipped in. Since it is an American territory, FedEx, DSL and even the US Postal service deliver in a timely manner.

I'd also use these sessions to check on the weather in the area. That night I heard there was a general warning to mariners traveling between Fiji and New Zealand. Apparently two low pressure systems were about to merge making what one prognosticator describe as "a bomb", a monster low with high winds and very extreme seas. I knew how bad a trough could be, I couldn't even imagine how bad a bomb would be. I was relieved Jack and I were up here out of harms way. How terrifying it would be to hear a weather report like that when you were out to sea! As I turned off the radio the voices in my head started talking amongst themselves, but, once again, I wasn't listening.

The next morning dawned differently than had the previous ones in Ruku Ruku. I'd been anchored here for two weeks and the change was quite dramatic. The usual trade winds were non-existent and the air was heavy and humid. There was a light overcast that I found very eerie.

Today's plan was to hitch a ride into Lavuka aboard the truck that traveled daily taking kids to school and other villagers to town for work or shopping. They called it a bus, but it was really an old military vehicle with a full canvas cover and long bench seats on either side. The kids loved having me along and during the long ride they tried to teach me the songs they sang to pass the time. They were absolutely delighted when I would learn some words and actually sing along. Once in Lavuka I shopped for some rice and various staples. The best deal was the fish packing plant where I could buy tuna by the case (sans labels) it was a great price and the best canned tuna I'd ever had.

I was really having a hard time with the mugginess while shopping in town. The air just wasn't moving and neither was I. The sky was becoming more overcast by the minute. This weather pattern was really putting me on edge, so I found a taxi that could take me back to Ruku Ruku instead of waiting for the school bus/truck to return. It was late afternoon by the time I'd rowed back out to *Rick's Place*. Even Jack seemed out of sorts and hadn't eaten his daily amount of grub, which he usually gobbles right down.

I turned on the short wave right away to hopefully find out what was going on with this weather and I was greeted with horrible reception. There would be no weather report tonight. Darkness was coming fast due to the heavy overcast which was blocking out the usually beautiful South Pacific sunset. Nervously, I walked around and did the daily check that I always performed at sea, but don't usually bother with in such a calm anchorage. I paid extra attention to the anchor line and snubber where it connected to the deck cleat.

Just before total darkness set in I took one last look around. Satisfied that *Rick's Place* would be safe in any wind direction except an Easterly (which according to John, would never happen here) I settled in down below. Jack curled up in his usual position by my head and we both nodded off.

A short time later I was jolted awake by some dishes that hadn't been stowed away crashing to the floor. Jack was up in an instant with all claws fully extended. As I tried to get out of my bunk a second big gust hit. This time it spread knives and forks among the dishes that were already on the cabin sole. The boat was now starting to pitch up and down like a hobby horse. Looking through the ports I couldn't make out the familiar land marks that I used for reference points. Suddenly, lightening lit up the sky, blinding me for several seconds.

Covering the distance from my bunk, in the front of the boat, to the hatch was proving very dangerous tonight because my feet were being cut up by the errant knives and forks. I was finally able to turn on an overhead light and see the mess that was about. The motion of the boat was causing the silverware to march first toward the bow and then reverse and come shooting back to the stern, with my feet in the middle.

I threw open the companion way hatch just as another blast of lightening illuminated the sky and once again destroyed my night vision. It didn't take long to ascertain that *Rick's Place* was in dire straights. The wind was gusting from the east! That's the direction it "never comes from" and the one direction not protected here in Ruku Ruku. This put the boat dangerously close to some prominent coral heads because the change in wind direction had repositioned us into some very shallow water. The dinghy tied to the stern of the boat was actually bumping into those razor sharp coral heads.

I looked down at the wind speed indicator and was horrified to see the needle jump to 45 knots when the wind would gust. But it wasn't the wind speed that was really worrying me, it was the building seas. This Easterly wind was sending the waves uninterrupted from the Pacific Ocean. With such a long fetch they continued to build in height right through the entrance to Ruku Ruku where they would make a direct hit on my boat. As the boat continued to hobby horse, I could hear the anchor chain sawing on some coral with an unnerving sound as it reverberated through the hull. Another gust and another blast of lightening hit. Now Jack was howling. "Sorry about this buddy, I'm scared, too."

The generator in the village had been turned on and it was helping me keep track of where I was because the lights on shore were a good point of reference. The rain was now coming down in sheets and it was an unusually cold rain; a very cold rain. I sat in the cockpit not knowing what to do. The waves were washing over the bow as it dipped down then when it would raise back up, the water would rush over the sides and back to the cockpit.

The water seemed to be boiling around me and the coral heads were closer than ever. The dinghy was completely filled with water and it looked like one side was nearly flat, probably torn on the coral it was beating against. There was another gust, but this time from a slightly different direction and the boat swung with it.

A moment later the anchor chain went from being bar tight to slack and then back to bar tight. The motion of the boat had changed dramatically and was jerking up and down in very short stabs. I realized the chain must have wrapped around a coral head!! This was keeping the bow of the boat in a kind of nose down position with the waves pounding the front unmercifully.

Just as I started to get up to let out more chain the boat shook with a resounding BANG followed by momentary silence. The bow popped up, but instead of being pointed into the waves we had moved sideways to them. I realized something must have broken so I desperately tried to start the engine. NO LUCK. Seconds later the next big wave swamped the cockpit and water was pouring in down below. I heard a terrified Jack whining.

As I tried to make my way below to deal with the engine problem, the first coral head ripped through the hull of *Rick's Place*. I was thrown headfirst down into the cabin into several feet of water. Books, cushions and food were all floating in a crazy spasmodic dance around me. I couldn't find Jack!! "God damn it Jack, we've got to get out of here!" I screamed. Not finding Jack was scaring me more than anything else that was going on right now. We hit bottom again and the boat leaned to one side at an angle it wasn't recovering from this time.

"Jack!"

Then I heard a faint meow! I threw some cushions aside and found Jack huddled in a cabinet, soaked, scared and covered with cracker crumbs. At least he chose this time to finally answer me after all these months of no response to my ramblings at him.

Just as I grabbed him another wave broke over the stern and spilled through the companion way making the water level about waist high down below. Jack had a death grip on my head and neck as I struggled up the stairs for the last time. I turned to take one last look below before we abandoned ship, and ironically the flyer describing the "Semi-completed yacht" washed by us as we prepared to plunge into the turbulent waters. The boat had hit hard against the bottom once again and I could tell we were being blown to shore. The dinghy was useless, so I would just time our jump for when the boat quit moving and hopefully the coral cuts wouldn't be too bad.

When the lightening flashed again I could see we were much closer to shore than I'd realized and the waves were now completely crashing over *Rick's Place*. It was getting really tough to hang on.

"Jack, here's the plan, you're going to let loose of your grip and I'm going to hold you tight and we're swimming to shore."
He growled in response and with great difficulty I peeled him off my head, but I was able to get a good grab on him and hold him tight to my body.

"OK buddy, three, two, one…"

We were then washed into the water and I struggled to keep Jack above the turbulence as I gasped for air. He was clawing, biting and spitting and then a huge wave picked us up and slammed us down hard. I was struggling to get Jack above the waves but he was suddenly gone! In a panic I began thrashing around trying to find the cat when I suddenly felt several pairs of hands grabbing me by the shoulders and pulling me up to shore. I collapsed on the beach, exhausted and thankful that all of the terrible motion had stopped, but then I realized I had left poor Jack in the water! I tried to get up but the villagers held me down. I saw blood pouring out of a leg wound and I yelled, "My cat! He's out in the water!" I tried once again to get up and I stumbled onto my face. After the pain from my leg subsided I opened my eyes and staring back at me was Jack. One of the girls from the village had wrapped him in a blanket and was comforting him.

With the lights of the village on I could just make out the outline of *Rick's Place* in the surf. I was sitting on the beach with Jack nestled in my lap. He was still shaking from time to time. My leg hurt, but my heart hurt more.

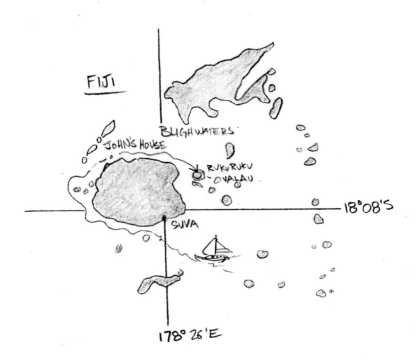

CHAPTER 16

Rick's Place

"When one door closes, another door opens."

-Alexander Graham Bell

"Mom, we've been over this more than a few times. I'm not ready to come home yet," I said slightly annoyed.

"But you're living in a grass house aren't you? Aren't there bugs?"

"Mom, the phone is going bad again. What did you say about rugs?"

"Bugs honey, bugs. Are there big bugs?" she said sounding very agitated.

I guess it should be noted here that my mom's hearing is terrible and pride keeps her from getting a hearing aid. That combined with the less than perfect phone connections in Fiji made for some pretty confusing conversations between the two of us.

"I'm looking forward to meeting your friend Zak." She stated further confusing things. "And by the way, have you talked to Sheryl?"

That's one thing about Mom. When she's not confused she's really nosy.

"Yeah, we've talked a few times, we're trying to set up a visit, but her mom's been sick for a while." It seems like it's always something that gets in the way.

"Mom, I'd better get going, but I will write soon. Remember to send letters to General Delivery S/V Rick's Place."

"Goodbye Ricky. And please think about coming home. I love you…" and then the line went dead.

That was about the sixth time we've had that same conversation with her wanting me to come home. I know she worries, but I'm just not ready to leave my little piece of paradise.

It had been 4 months since *Rick's Place* broke loose from its anchor in Ruku Ruku. The out of season cyclone was dubbed

"The Queen's Day Storm" since it occurred on Queen Elizabeth's Birthday. Happy stinking birthday, Queenie. The village adopted Jack and me with open arms. I guess the days preceding the accident were well spent helping the villagers with the construction of new housing and hooking up the new, town generator. It proved to be a real P.R. coup, as we now have a two room hut not far from the beach. It's complete with traditional thatched roof and sleeping mats, and it was all donated by Chief Vatua.

It was painfully evident shortly after the boat came to shore that it wasn't going to be sailing again other than in my dreams. Needless to say I was an emotional wreck during the following few weeks. I managed to salvage many items from the boat, and what I couldn't use I sold to cruisers that would anchor in the bay. The local charter boat company bought the anchor chain and hundreds of feet of rope. So I had some cash in my pocket. With the prospect of a little insurance money and my low cost of living here, my finances weren't an immediate concern. After all, I was living in a grass hut.

The problem was I just wasn't ready to go home. After spending more than a year single handing a boat across the Pacific, going to different countries, experiencing their diverse cultures and learning to be self sufficient, I couldn't bear the thought of going back to the daily grind. Since cruisers seem to have a short and selective memory, the storms, the bouts of mal de mar, the fear, the heat and the cold are all but forgotten once you get to a new place. And so it was with me. I only remembered the good times and the bad times were merely exciting adventures that I enjoyed talking about. How could I give this up? So, instead of flying home, as Mom had hoped I would do, I decided to stay on in the village. Jack and I shared the bungalow on the beach and *Rick's Place* lay on the sand like a beached whale, less than 100 yards away.

The Plantation was a popular side trip for the tourists coming to Fiji. Many cruisers congregate there, as well. After the tours of the Plantation, the locals put on a Lava-Lava. As I'd seen at John's house, that's a festivity where an unlucky pig is roasted under ground all day: the South Pacific version of a BBQ. Then, with great flourish, the porker is carved up and served with taro, coconut and many other tasty fruits and vegetables; a fantastic feast! When the meal is done, the local women would dance, outfitted in traditional attire. After all the feasting and dancing, they'd put out the tapa cloth, woven mats, shells and coconut bras for the visitors to purchase. It was quite an event, but something was missing. The little voices in my head caught on to this and actually discussed it amongst themselves. It took a while for me to tune in, but when I finally started to listen, it seemed like a great idea.

The first step was to talk to Chief Vatua and get him to buy into my little scheme. The chief had his hand in everything that went on in the village and surrounding area. He reminded me of Louie, the character from the movie *Casablanca*. With the right amount of economic persuasion he could move mountains, or more importantly, get things built. During one of the frequent Kava drinking sessions, I put forth my idea. Naturally the benefits to the village and more specifically the chief were discussed at length. After several minutes of silence, a grin slowly spread across his weathered face.

It was time for step two. A small patch of land was selected that I would lease from the chief. The Plantation had the necessary equipment, and the villagers would supply the muscle. The hull, which was now minus the mast and boom, was dragged and placed in a 5' deep hole that was dug in the sand. This hole accommodated the keel, and kept the interior floor close to the outside ground level. After the hull was leveled up, the pit was filled with sand, securing *Rick's Place* in position.

I spent the next couple of days gathering the tools I needed for phase two of my project. There was a method to the madness! Arrangements were made for a small generator to supply temporary power. In Suva, I managed to rent a Saws-All electric saw, and purchased a dozen blades to go with it. Meanwhile, the locals were getting curious. Every day the men of Ruku Ruku would come by to see what was going on and my boat in the sand became quite the gathering place. The kids were constantly being shooed off their newly adopted monkey bars, which was once a world cruising yacht.

When all tools were gathered and all the measurements taken, it was time to get serious. I drew a line down the center of the boat, from bow to stern. When the generator fired up it was the signal that everyone had been waiting for. I took the power saw, walked to the bow of the boat, and began to cut. I cut through the bow pulpit, I cut through the teak, I cut through the deck. I cut and cut and cut. Then I cut some more. For most of the week, during the daylight hours I cut cabinets, settees and bulkheads. There was always a crowd on hand. Watching me cut my boat down the middle was festive, a real happening. It was a crazy American cutting his boat in half.

A dozen blades didn't come close to cutting it, as it were. It took twice that. To make the project successful, I was careful not to cut electrical wires and some plumbing hoses that were in the cabinets. I stopped making vertical cuts at floor level, and started cutting horizontally along the floor. The plan was to keep the floor intact. The 6' gash in the hull was on the port side. This was the half that was being discarded. The only lucky aspect of the grounding was that the reef ripped the hole on the side where none of the essential systems were located. The battery boxes, electrical panels, most of the pumps and tanks were all in tact after the beaching. With the final cut, near the stern, the left side of the hull dropped and rolled unceremoniously on its side.

This brought cheers from the by standers who faithfully came to watch my antics, everyday. With the aid of several of the men, and the village horse, the discarded piece of fiberglass was dragged off to be put to some use somewhere in the village. No need for garbage dumps here. They're the world's greatest recyclers. I would have to wait until morning to see my handiwork, however, as the short South Pacific twilight ushered in total darkness.

The light of the new morning revealed a sight that was as comical as it was sad. Here were the remains of a project that I had poured my heart into for several years. The open boat surgery, as I was fond of calling it, turned out better than expected. Standing back, looking at *Rick's Place* on the half shell, a smile came to my face as I thought about the adventures we had together.

It was necessary to remove a few more cabinets, as well as the toilet. The interior floor was 6" above the ground level, making for a nice step and would help keep out the outside elements. The vision that I had in my head was now sitting before me. When I removed the toilet, I just set it to the side as I continued my work. Shortly there after, I looked up when I heard peals of laughter from the village children. What they were finding so amusing was watching Jack sitting on the toilet taking care of business. Their laughter buoyed my spirits, so I decided to leave the head right where it was. I filled the bowl with sand and Jack now had a custom made litter box.

To protect the interior from rain showers and beating sun, I enlisted the aid of the villagers once again. Together we built a thatched roof the length of the boat. The roof was supported with poles at both ends, made from coconut tree trunks. A beautiful piece of mahogany about 2'x15' was donated to be used as the bar. It was rumored that this piece was from a turn of the century schooner that had shipwrecked nearby. Its usage seemed rather apropos. Four foot lengths of tree trunks, half buried vertically would serve as bar stools. I made another trip to Suva where I managed to scrounge a couple of tables and chairs for additional seating.

I still had my oil lamp and several working 12 volt electric lights. These were powered by the battery bank that was still in good working order, which in turn were kept charged by the solar panels which were hung off the stern just as they had been while we were cruising. It took several more trips to Suva for supplies before *Rick's Place*, now a "barefoot bar" was ready to open.

There was never really a grand opening. It started out one beer at a time. Then the word started to spread amongst the cruising fleet. The charter company started to refer to the bar in their local cruising guide. With the tours of the Plantation and a wonderful beach, a bar for a cold beer was a natural. Location, location, location.

CHAPTER 17

Island Life

"Here's looking at you kid."

-Humphrey Bogart in *Casablanca*

It was on a Saturday late in August. I'd lost track of the exact date, but it was a typical South Pacific morning. Warm trade winds were blowing white puffy clouds across the cobalt sky. Vacationers and cruisers had been coming by to look at and take pictures of the boat that is cut in half. It had become a very popular barefoot bar and tourist attraction. Some came hoping to catch a glimpse of the cat that was rumored to sit on a toilet to answer natures call.

I was sitting at one of the tables with Jack lying on a chair next to me, seemingly exhausted after his big performance for a few lucky onlookers. I was just putting the finishing touches on a newspaper article I was writing for my old hometown paper. It turned out that my misadventures made good reading back home and the paper was actually paying me a meager sum for putting the last two years down in words.

Jack suddenly looked up and then got into a sitting position. In the next instant he was off the table and running after something! That was the fastest I'd seen him move since we'd been in the tropics. I turned in my seat to see what had agitated my normally docile feline. Coming down the path that lead from the village was a female with blonde hair and features that looked vaguely familiar. Jack practically leapt into her arms.

"SHERYL?" I said, not believing my eyes.

I was up in a flash and covered the distance between us in just a few strides. We embraced and the cat struggled to get free, fearful of being squashed between us.

"What on earth are you doing here? Why didn't you let me know you were coming?" My questions were asked rapid fire.

"Rick, every time we made plans to get together, hurricanes or broken planes, my mom's health or something would manage to mess it up. So I thought I would keep it a spur of the moment thing. I just didn't want to jinx it again."

We held each other in a long tight hug, with Jack rubbing against our ankles and purring the whole time. We finally broke our hold on each other and began walking in the direction of *Rick's Place*. Sheryl's eyes flew wide open as she took in the sight of the beached boat turned barefoot bar.

"It's so different from the last time I saw it," she said with a sad smile on her face.

We took a seat at one of the tables and Jack immediately jumped up onto Sheryl's lap and she reached across the table and took my hand in hers.

"Rick, how did all this happen?"

"Well," I began, "it was a dark and stormy night......."

EPILOG

It's been a year since I reunited with Sheryl on that beach in Fiji and 6 months since I left the island and returned to the United States. Sheryl stayed with me in Ruku Ruku for two weeks, but she had to get back to her blossoming flower business. She was able to take Jack with her since she brought all of the proper paper work with her and an official cat carrier instead of the canvas bag I had been using.

I stayed on to figure out what I would do with my life, but I suddenly needed to return to Gig Harbor because Mom had a bit of a heart problem. I ended up selling my one time home turned barefoot bar to an Aussie that had come through and fell in love with it. That was a difficult decision, but the political climate in Fiji was becoming a little tenuous with words of another coup in the near future, so I felt it was time to get out of Dodge, so to speak. At first the Chief wasn't in favor of my selling *Rick's Place*, but when I assured him it would make more money than ever, thus increasing his take, he was all for it.

After Mom had fully recovered and was back to her feisty old self, I headed south to the bay area to check up on Jack and see where things stood between me and Sheryl. I also went in search of a new boat, because I knew I had to continue cruising.

One day while I was on my quest for my new cruising boat, I found myself standing in front of the building that had been home to Coast Boat Building where I had purchased the deck and hull that eventually became *Rick's Place*. A flood of memories washed into my head: the crazy trip up I-5 pulling the empty hull with my small Toyota, the years building the boat (those are a little fuzzy, probably due to the fiberglass fumes), launch day, my first sail, working at the marine store, meeting Sparky, Hawaii and on and on. A honking horn snapped me back to the present and I realized

I'd been standing in the middle of the street.

All the nostalgia strengthened my desire to get out cruising again as soon as possible, so a week later I purchased a nice used boat that I'd been looking at. It was in good shape and the previous owner had it offshore before, so it was already well outfitted. But I would like to change the name.

While I was busy getting the boat and me ready to go cruising, I was also busy trying to convince Sheryl that she should come along with me this time. But with her business doing so well she just didn't want to sell it at this time, and I couldn't blame her. We'd talked about my waiting another year before heading off, but I knew that I couldn't possibly do that either. I'd gotten a taste of the cruising lifestyle and I had to return to it or I would go nuts in the rat race.

There were two bits of good fortune that had made it possible for me to afford to buy this new boat and set out cruising again. The first was being able to sell *Rick's Place* and the second was selling my book. All those months in Ruku Ruku when I had been writing articles for the local paper back home, I'd started compiling them together and going over my log books and writing some more and before I knew it I became a published author.

I'm not sure where I'm headed this time, except that I'm going to start by going down the coast to Mexico and look up Sparky, who's taken up working at a surf camp in a small town called Troncones. Mom had heard from Sparky that he was getting married down there to a girl named Tami, and I definitely had to see how that would play out. I still needed to thank Sparky, too, because if it hadn't been for him I would never have met Sheryl. I'd also like to cross the South Pacific again and hopefully catch back up with the *Cetus* crew who are currently living in Australia.

I passed under the Golden Gate Bridge three weeks ago to begin my journey south. There'd been a tearful goodbye with Sheryl the night before my departure, but the next day, just an hour before I was going to cast off the dock lines, Sheryl came running down the dock with a duffle bag in one hand and a cat carrier in the other and announced she was going with me! Her sister who had been helping with the shop, had insisted she go after seeing how hard it was for her to watch me leave. She assured Sheryl the shop would keep running strong.

So, now Sheryl and I are sitting in the cockpit of *Casablanca*, Jack sprawled out between us as we watch another beautiful sunset in San Diego bay. We're just waiting for the end of hurricane season (November 1st) to sail into Mexican waters and see what this new adventure will bring.

Special thanks:

I would like to thank Monica and Doug Edwards for always keeping us connected and taking care of things back home while we were out cruising.

Thank you to Mike Fak, a talented editor, for his help and words of encouragement as I was completing this book.

Many thanks to Travis Johnston for his outstanding artwork.

Finally, a heartfelt thank you to the real "Sparky", Spark Johnston (who is nothing like his namesake in *Rick's Place*). Without his help our adventures would have never gone to sea.

Author photo courtesy of Tom Isralian.

About the Author

Terry J. Kotas lives aboard his Fantasia 35' Sailboat, *Cetus*, with his wife, Heidi.

They have logged 20,000 miles in blue water cruising along with their daughter, Carly.

The first cruise, aboard their boat *Cassiopeia*, which they built from a bare hull, took them to Hawaii, Fanning Island, Bora Bora, Aitutaki, Fiji and American Samoa.

The next adventure was aboard their current boat, *Cetus*, and this had the family exploring Mexico, The Marquesas, Tuamotus, Tahiti and again to Hawaii.

Terry and Heidi are currently living in Gig Harbor, Washington and are readying *Cetus* for their third offshore cruise, with plans to depart in 2009.

Printed in the United States
133467LV00005B/1-63/P